Family

Catastrophe

Fiction from Modern China

This series is intended to showcase new and exciting works by China's finest contemporary novelists in fresh, authoritative translations. It represents innovative recent fiction by some of the boldest new voices in China today as well as classic works of this century by internationally acclaimed novelists. Bringing together writers from several geographical areas and from a range of cultural and political milieus, the series opens new doors to twentieth-century China.

HOWARD GOLDBLATT

General Editor

Wang Wen-hsing

Translated from the Chinese

by Susan Wan Dolling

General Editor, Howard Goldblatt

University of Hawai'i Press   *Honolulu*

Family

Catastrophe

Originally published in Chinese in 1972.
Taiwan edition published in 1973 by
Huan-yu Publishing Company, Taipei.

oo 99 98 97 96 95   5 4 3 2 1

Library of Congress Cataloging-in-Publication Data
Wang, Wen-hsing, 1939–

    [Chia pien. English]

    Family catastrophe / by Wang Wen-Hsing ; English translation by
    Susan Wan Dolling.

        p.   cm. —— (Fiction from modern China)

    ISBN 0–8248–1618–8 —— ISBN 0–8248–1710–9 (pbk.)

    I. Dolling, Susan Wan, 1950– .   II. Title.   III. Series.

    PL2919.W37C513   1995

    895.1'352—dc20   94–33940
                        CIP

Excerpts from *Family Catastrophe* have appeared in the spring 1993 issue of
Renditions in slightly different form.

English translation sponsored by the Council for Cultural Planning and
Development, Executive Yuan, of the Republic of China.

University of Hawai'i Press books are printed on acid-free
paper and meet the guidelines for permanence and durability
of the Council on Library Resources

Designed by Richard Hendel

Family

Catastrophe

Part One

A

One windy afternoon, an old man with a face filled with misery quietly closed a bamboo gate, tossed a final glance at the house fenced in behind it, turned . . . and, in brisk strides, left. He walked straight ahead without looking back, all the way to the end of the alley, and disappeared.

The fence was made of thin stalks of bamboo spaced far apart. A front yard, overgrown with weeds and wild grass, lay on the inside. Beyond it was a row of glass sliding doors, the front of a Japanese-style wooden house. The house appeared old and dirty; its owners had evidently not refurbished it in a long while, and the wooden slats had turned a dingy gray. To the right of the house stood an empty cement trough, once used for storing sand in case of fire. Three steps, much worn and indented, extended from the middle sliding door. An assortment of wooden clogs, slippers, and old shoes littered the steps. This middle glass panel was the only one with a screen door in front of it. The panes had not been washed in a long time, and a few of them had in fact been replaced by wooden panels. From long neglect, myriad spider webs woven under the eaves and over the lintels were left unswept.

B

"Have you seen your father?"

No answer.

"Have you seen your father?" she asked again, fixing him with eyes full of hurt and anxiety, peering at him from behind wispy, white hair.

He looked up, putting down his book as he did so. "You've come in here to ask me the same question three times already. Who cares where he's gone to? *Who* has seen him? I am I, and he is he; it's not as if we have anything whatsoever to do with each other, you know. I haven't eaten more than my share of rice, so why am I responsible for his whereabouts? He's not here. All right? To hell with him!"

He looked sallow and wasted, but his delicate features lent an air of refinement to his face, an effect that was heightened by a small black mole to the left of the bridge of his nose; his pale forehead was half covered by a shock of thick black hair. At the moment, his eyes exuded glints of hatred. He picked up his glasses and put them on.

"He's been gone for almost two whole hours," she said. "Strange that he should've gone out without a word, and he doesn't even have his shoes on; he went out in his slippers. I heard someone opening the front door, but I thought it was you. It wasn't until I called and called to him to fetch me some water, and no one replied, that I realized he wasn't in the house at all. I went out to the water pump to look for him, but he wasn't there; then I went next door and climbed upstairs, but he wasn't there either. So I thought he must've gone out, but his shoes were still there on the steps. I even went to the corner store to see if he was there, and looked all over the neighborhood, but he's nowhere to be found. Isn't that strange? Where could he have gone?" She kept her gaze on him. "He's only got his slippers on, which means he ought to be in the neighborhood . . . but he's not. Besides, it's not like him to stay out for two hours and not come back. And if he's gone farther . . . but how far can he go in his slippers? But he's nowhere to be found, not anywhere around here anyway. He should've said something before going out; he usually tells me when he leaves the house."

He took off his glasses but started to pick up his book again. "I heard you. Now get out!"

Hurt feelings and rising anger combined to inform her next expression. "You are speaking to your mother!"

He stood up, put on his glasses, then flung them onto the desk, threw his arms in the air, and at the top of his voice hollered, "Okay, okay, all right already!" He tapped his temples to punctuate his words. "Do-not while-I-am-reading come-in-here to-disturb-me. I've told you a hundred times. But you just barge in here whenever you feel like it. You – and him too – you people take no damn notice of anything I say; when I open my mouth, you think I'm farting. God, what sort of life is this? Who can even imagine the sort of life I have to live! You want to read? Right, we'll let you read three sentences before, wham, somebody comes in to get something, or sweep the floor, or ask you some nonsense just for the hell of it. You two simply can't leave a person alone, can't give him a little space to do something on his own. This is an invasion of my privacy. Do you understand? What is it with you people? What have I ever done to you to deserve this?

"God, this house is simply hell. Not one day goes by without someone shouting at someone else; not a single day can I escape that deep, dark, sorrowful face of his. He's a great tragic actor, that one; he puts on a free show for anyone to see. And don't you stand there looking as if you're about to be hanged; you don't deserve to wear that look. That look belongs to *me*. Do you hear? *I'm* the one with the noose around my neck! And you tell me I should be more respectful when I speak to you. Well, my beloved mother, don't you see, respect or no respect, I simply don't want to be bothered! I have nothing to say to you, not one word! I can keep my mouth shut like a clam from dawn to dusk, for twenty-four hours, for forty-eight hours, and not suffer for it. Not suffer? Did I say not suffer? If only I were so lucky!

But I know it's no use dreaming such dreams. What's the point? I may as well forget it."

His mother had backed off some time ago. He went to the door and slammed it shut.

It was getting dark outside, and in the room it was darker still. He went back to his seat. Tired out, he decided not to read any more. He just sat there in the silence of the darkness.

Little by little, he became unsettled by what his mother told him. His father had indeed been gone for a long time. In his slippers, he couldn't have gone far and certainly should've been home by now. Night was closing in. He reached to turn on his desk lamp.

He picked up his book, read a couple of lines, then put the book down again.

Heading for the kitchen, he called out, "Get dinner on the table! Time to eat! I'm hungry. You can leave him something and heat it up later when he comes in. It's way past dinnertime. Don't wait anymore. Let's eat."

His mother turned to him and asked, "What time is it already?"

"Seven o'clock."

"I'll go get it for you."

She set out bowls and chopsticks. At the center of the table she placed two dishes to go with the rice; one was four-season beans cooked in soy sauce, the other steamed pork and pickled cabbage. She had brought out only two pairs of chopsticks. She picked up a small plate and started putting a little dinner aside.

Under the glare of the naked lightbulb he began to eat in silence. The beans soaked in soy sauce looked a sullen black; the pickled meat and cabbage was submerged in a layer of grayish-white grease. He put his bowl down and asked, "Why aren't you eating?"

"I'll eat later."

"It's just like you to worry about the sky falling down.

What kind of perverse pleasure do you get from scaring yourself half to death? So what if he comes back a little early or a little late? So he didn't tell you where he was going. Why should he? He's a grown man, you know. Let him do what he wants. Don't treat him like a child." From beyond the fence came the sound of someone tapping at the bamboo gate. "See, he's home! What did I tell you? You've been scared over nothing!"

He got up right away to let him in. It turned out to be Mrs. Yang.

"Oh, is the old missus home? I came to ask if she can spare some leftover cinders. Do you happen to have any left over tonight?"

"Please, come in and see for yourself."

Mrs. Yang went into the kitchen and came out carrying a piece of burned charcoal in a pair of tongs. "Thank you very much. Had dinner yet?"

She left, going out the bamboo gate. He, too, stepped out to look down the alley, but there was no sign of anyone coming or going, only the night mist clinging to the light of the streetlamps. He left the gate open and went back into the house. On entering, he said, "It was just Mrs. Yang."

"I heard."

He didn't feel like eating any more. She cleared the table. He started pacing about, stopped by his parents' bedroom, looked in, and saw that his father's trousers were still there on the hanger, proving that he had indeed gone out in his pajama pants, which were nowhere to be found. He started looking for the shirt that was usually hung next to the trousers; it was not there.

He returned to his room, closed the door, and sat in the shadow of the desk lamp. He had no idea where his father might have gone. Where could he have gone, dressed as he was, in his pajama pants? It was completely dark out by now, and he had still not come home. He sat quietly, listening. Several times he heard footsteps in the hallway – footsteps that sounded tantalizingly like his father's – but soon realized it was just his mother milling about. He strode into his parents' room again. His mother sat miserably on the bed, following him with her eyes. To avoid meeting those eyes, he went back to his own room.

His father's absence continued to haunt him. He couldn't just have gone out for fresh air; he had been gone too long. He must have had a destination; perhaps he was visiting friends. Since his retirement several years ago, his father had become a homebody; maybe he felt stifled and bored and had gone to find someone to talk to, someone to pass the time of day with. So it followed that he must have gone to a friend's house. The friend, not having seen him for such a long time, asked him to stay for dinner, and at dinner they probably had a few drinks; chatting and drinking, they didn't even notice it was getting late. Father had a few too many, so his friend persuaded him to stay on and have a rest, which was why he didn't come home. What a simple answer. Such obvious reasons. How stupid of him not to have thought of them sooner! In that case, there was no need to wait up for him tonight. With this in mind, he went to his mother.

"There's nothing to worry about. I'm going to bed now," he said to her, bringing his own thoughts to a conclusion out loud.

He climbed into bed.

For a long time, however, his eyes remained wide open. No, what he had just imagined couldn't have happened. Father had no friends, not for the last few years. And even if he had gone visiting he wouldn't have stayed overnight. He had never done such a thing before. He wouldn't have gone out without saying a word. That was totally out of character. Besides, how could he have gone visiting in those clothes?

He saw that he had left the bamboo gate unlatched. The wind blew it open and closed and open again. Every time it pulled to, the catch clattered against its frame. The bamboo gate was his bedroom door. He was sleeping in the dark, but outside his room everything was lit up. The door was blown closed and open and closed again. A shadow slipped in, hesitated a moment, then proceeded to come toward his bed and peer at him. He recognized his father.

"Papa! You're home!" He sat up in bed.

"Yes, Sonny, Papa's back." His father's face glowed with happiness; he looked young and vigorous, not much over thirty. He was wearing a newly pressed suit. "I'm back, Sonny! I am home, home, home. . . ."

"Where are your pajama pants and slippers, Pa?"

"They're inside the desk-lamp shade."

"Oh. Inside the desk-lamp shade." He nodded vigorously, as if he found this answer very satisfying indeed.

His father seemed thrilled to be back; he was looking around the room in high spirits. He remembered that his father had been away going on six years now.

"Where have you been all this time?" Mother asked, beaming at him. She was also very young, no more than twenty, or maybe thirty at most; she was even wearing a jasmine flower in her hair.

He could see Father's mouth opening and closing in reply to her question, but he couldn't make out what he was saying to her.

"It's great to have Papa home again," his extremely young mother murmured, beaming.

"Sonny, I'm home. . . ."

"Papa's home! Papa's home!" he chimed in gleefully.

"Wake up, wake up, Sonny." He opened his eyes to see Mother standing by his bed. "It's 1:30 in the morning, and your papa's still not home!"

Mother was a white-haired, worn-out old woman.

"Where could he have gone, Sonny? It's so late already."

It hit him in an instant, the reason for Father's departure: He couldn't take it anymore; he was running away from abuse.

"Strange. Gone for so long," he muttered.

A spasm of weeping broke the stillness. His mother had suddenly started to sob uncontrollably.

"Stop. You stop it this minute!" he roared. "You're driving me crazy with your shrieking!"

Such a rare and immense disaster had befallen him, he thought, an item of news that had the potential to shake up the whole province, a family matter so shameful and yet so impossible to hide from the public eye.

"It's too dark out. There's not much we can do now. We'll just have to sit and wait till daybreak," he said in a whisper.

Dawn came at five o'clock. The morning light shone into the hallway, illuminating clothes left lying helter-skelter. On the table by the hallway were scattered a disorderly array of drinking glasses, a copper teaspoon, and a crumpled handkerchief. He walked past his parents' room, stole a glance inside, and took in the fact that the bedsheets were still folded up, indicating that they had not been slept in. He went about his business stealthily, as if any noise at all would alert the neighbors to their secret.

He decided to search for his father. He figured the best thing to do would be to start with his father's acquaintances. He would have to be careful, however, so that they would not suspect that he himself had no idea where his father was. Therefore he came up with a story: His father had sent him to find an old friend's address. Uncle Chang could be the one – he had left Taipei for Kaohsiung a few years ago. He would use this excuse if Father were not at a particular house and the people there did not volunteer the information that he had been there.

He then went rummaging through his father's trouser pockets, hoping to find a slip of paper or something with a message on it; but he found nothing of the sort – just a one-dollar bill. His father had left home without a cent, he thought. Father always carried one dollar in his pocket, no more, no less. He went to ask his mother if she thought he could have taken any other money with him. Mother said no, the money she kept in her pocketbook was all there. According to the clues uncovered so far, his father should still be somewhere in the vicinity. But since his shirt was missing, it was obvious he had planned to go somewhere.

In any case, he was completely baffled by Father's sudden departure. Yesterday, before Father left home, there had been no quarrel whatsoever between them. As for the day before – he thought long and hard – he could think of no quarrels either (even though he knew that the daily cold-shoulder treatments were enough to drive him away). But what was it recently that had led to this sudden action? What was the immediate cause?

He lowered his head to brush his teeth. Before Father took off yesterday, the circumstances were exactly the same as they had ever been. He looked back over the period, searching for clues, but could find nothing unusual. Since it was spring break, he had been at home all day yesterday. Father got up at five in the morning, just as he was wont to do. (And, just as always, his father's noises intruded into his dreams and woke him.) At six, as usual, Father helped Mother start the fire. In the morning, Father swept the floor for a while, then he dusted the tables and chairs for a while, and after that, still in his pajamas, he went puttering about the house, making the rounds. After lunch, Father did not deviate from his usual habit of taking a lengthy afternoon nap and didn't get up till almost four o'clock. Then he brought in the clothes that were left out to dry in the sun, folding each item and putting them all in a pile. Thereafter, he lost track. As far as he could recall, his father had given no hint that he was about to run away. He couldn't think of anything that might have prompted him to take off like that. He brought in the clothes – then what? Why did he go? Was it possible that Father was schizophrenic? Not a chance. There were no symptoms whatsoever. He was simply always in a muddle, confused and confusing, that was all.

He was now dressed, but he wasn't ready to go, not yet. Instead, he planted himself by the screen door, sitting on the steps, impatiently waiting for the morning paper to arrive. An animal adroitness compelled him first to pore over the paper for reports of accidents and deaths. He waited, watching for the paper's arrival at the bamboo gate.

A screech of tires outside the fence — a rectangular object flew in from the outside and fell on the ground. His heart thumped wildly against his chest as he leaped toward the object; he bent over and picked it up. Just as impulsively, he straightened up and covered his face in silent prayer. Then he picked up the paper and flipped it open. He strained his eyes, scanning the pages.

A murder case; a pedicab driver axed his boss; a young man committed suicide for no apparent reason; a car accident, driver and passenger both killed.

He tore through the paper from beginning to end, twice. Nothing to warrant speculation. He heaved a sigh of relief.

He pushed his bicycle out to the gate, got on, rode through the narrow alley, turned right, and headed up a slope.

Meandering alongside him, remaining all the while within his vision, was a wide river, shallow and gray. Dawn and the early morning mist intermingled, shimmering on the body of water. Two green peninsulas of bamboo groves jutted out from the river's bank, and little island clusters appeared on the water looking like schools of fish. Oh, the river spring of childhood! For the past eighteen years, whenever he saw this body of water, his spirit soared, and even today he was refreshed by the sight of it. But in the twinkling of an eye fear reasserted itself and shook him. In the past, every year without fail, there had been three or more suicides here; people drowned where the water was deep. Could it be possible that Father's body too lay here in the riverbed? It usually took three days before a body resurfaced. From today on, he must keep a close eye on this river.

He rode out onto the main street. His mission, thus, was to search for, to go after, a father who had abandoned his family, had run away from home. He couldn't believe that this disaster was his reality. In its manifest cruelty it was like the time when the neighbor's house caught fire and he refused to believe that his would be the next to burn. It was the *immense* proportion of the disaster that made him think it couldn't possibly happen – perhaps it was the immensity of this disaster that he found incomprehensible. He rode on, heading into the search.

His search took him to eight houses. Father was not at any of them.

The last two families he visited didn't even recognize Father's name; it had simply been too long since they last saw him.

Although he had not found his father, he felt, contrary to expectations, rather exhilarated. He had the notion that by this time Father was already sitting in the house. Yes! It was midday already. Having been out all night, his father had come home that morning. He must have come in immediately after he himself had left to look for him. He sped home.

His grief-stricken mother rose up to greet him. "Have you found him?"

Lunch was perfunctory. She bought two pineapple-shaped buns so they could fill their stomachs, but neither of them could swallow more than a couple of bites.

At half past one he decided that it wouldn't hurt any to give his brother a call, though he knew full well there was not even a remote possibility of his father going there.

Nonetheless, he went out to the public phone.

His brother lived in Hsinchu and worked for a life insurance company. It had been two years since they had last seen each other. That was when his brother gave him his telephone number.

Before heading for the phone booth, he stopped off at the store across the way to get change and came out with a batch of dollar coins.

He entered the booth, dropped in the coins, and dialed.

"Hello? Telegraph Company."

"I'd like to make a long-distance call to Hsinchu."

"What's the number?"

"698."

"Who are you calling?"

He gave her the name.

"Twenty-four dollars."

"I'm putting it in now. . . . Okay?"

"Hello?" A mere whisper.

"Long distance," she said. "What is your number?"

"Oh – who are you looking for?"

She gave the name.

"4612," he said.

"Please wait a minute. . . . Long-distance call! Long-distance call!"

"Please wait a minute."

He waited, holding the receiver close to his ear.

". . . is he there? . . ."

". . . yes, he's upstairs. . . ."

Voices came on and off from the other end of the line.

"Hello?" A middle-aged voice, stern and cool, spoke into the receiver.

"Erh-ko . . . it's me!"

"Hello?"

"It's me . . . Erh-ko."

"Ah. Oh! What's up?"

"Papa's nowhere to be found – gone all of a sudden."

"Huh? Where has he gone to?"

"I have no idea!"

A short pause. "Oh."

"I don't suppose he's been to your place?"

"Nope."

"If he should come to you, tell him to come home soon; tell him we're waiting for him."

"All right. When was it he left?"

"Yesterday. At four in the afternoon."

"Mm."

"I don't know why he ran off."

Silence.

"There's nothing else; that's all I have to tell you."

"I'll help you find him. I'll take a look around here first; you take a look over there in Taipei. I can't see that it can be anything too serious. I'm sure we'll be able to find him."

"Mm."

"How's Auntie?"

"Very well." How strange that he should say she was well at such a time as this. His brother had never been able to bring himself to call his mama "Mother," he thought to himself.

("Put it on top of the cabinet over there.")

"There's nothing else I have to say. I'll be seeing you, Erh-ko."

"Good-bye then. Remember to call me if there's any news."

A click at the other end of the line.

"Is that it?" the telephone operator asked. "Two and a half minutes. You didn't go over."

Too agitated to wait indoors, he wandered up and down the alley outside the bamboo fence on the lookout for his father. Several times he stopped in his tracks, hoping to find that this was a dream, hoping that if he blinked hard enough he would be able to shake off this dream and make everything in it go away.

He circled the block several dozen times before retracing his steps back to the house.

He stretched out on the bed, looking up at the ceiling, his eyeglasses dangling from his hand, his mouth wide open, breathing hard, trying to rest.

At three o'clock, it suddenly occurred to him that his father had been gone a whole night plus another whole morning and an entire afternoon. Father's running away had become an undeniable fact: it was no longer possible to think that he had simply stayed somewhere overnight. This afternoon was soon coming to an end. Father had *clearly* run away.

He imagined how happy they would be if Father were to return home now. "Ah. . . ." The sound of a familiar sigh. "Ch'iu-fang, Sonny, you've been waiting for me a long time, eh? I wanted to come home much sooner, but I just couldn't get away. What with this and that, the time just slipped by. Where do you think I've been? Have a guess, go on, *see* if you can guess." He was playing that game of his again.

"So where have you been?" Mother asked him playfully.

"Well, I'm back now. All's well now. You two won't have to worry about me anymore. Boy, I haven't cleaned these shoes for only one day, and look at the dust on them." He bent down, took off his shoes, and, as was his habit, began tidying up the other pairs at the entrance, arranging them neatly in a row. "I shall have to give these shoes a good shine."

A smile spread across his face. Intoxicating, that smile. The smiling face was suddenly snuffed out. He loathed himself for succumbing to such an absurd fantasy.

In swift succession, he recognized to his horror his negligence: he had let a whole day pass without taking positive action. Why didn't he even now go to the police station to ask for an investigation? But no, he still couldn't be absolutely certain that Father had truly disappeared.

He couldn't yet accept the idea of going to the police station to make a report. Even the thought of it was so brutal that he had not been able to bring himself to confront it. He had been hoping for a way out. And though by now it seemed inevitable that they would have to resort to a police investigation, he was still looking into the darkness before him for some miracle, some transformation of the situation. He was holding onto this last hope, his head barely above the torrent.

"Huh?" he asked.

"Come with me. Come to my room for a bit." His mother was standing at his door, beckoning him.

He followed her into her room.

Great piles of photos and certificates were strewn about the bed.

"I was looking for his certificate of identity," she said. "And it's here. But look what I discovered. Two pictures are missing – one of your eldest brother, the other the picture of that mother of your two older brothers."

"Then that means he's really gone!" he exclaimed.

"That's what I think."

He looked straight at her and said, "We must go to the police, then."

"Is that so?" the policeman asked as he leaned back in his chair.

"Yes."

"You can't find him, and you want us to help."

"Yes."

"Let's get this on paper." He flipped open a registration booklet and dipped his pen into the inkwell. "What's his name?"

"Fan Min-hsien."

"Fan? . . ."

He told him which characters they were.

"Age?"

"Sixty-seven."

"Origin?"

"Fuchou region, Fuchien Province."

"Occupation?"

"He's been retired for some time."

"What does he look like? Any distinctive features?"

"He's short, quite skinny, and he has a slight limp in his left leg."

"What did he have on when he left?"

"A white shirt on top of a pair of striped pajama pants and slippers on his feet."

"What is your name?"

"Fan Yeh."

"Uh . . . how?"

"Sun radical by the side of the character for *China*."

"Ah."

He dipped his pen in the inkwell and continued. "How old are you?"

"Twenty-seven."

"Occupation."

"Teaching assistant in the History Department at C University."

"Okay. Now, please go back to the beginning, and give me a detailed account of events."

C

SEARCH
For Father

Father, since you left on April 14th, Mother and I have been worried sick. Hurry home please when you see this. Everything will be resolved according to your wishes.

Your son,
Yeh

He folded the newspaper and inserted it into his suitcase pocket.

"Have you got his photo in your suitcase?"

"I've got it."

Fan Yeh had decided to go south in search of his father. Two days, and the police had come up with nothing. Nothing had turned up from other quarters either. In the end, he had decided to take up the search himself. He went to school yesterday to ask for a leave of absence and an advance of one month's pay. He was careful not to let his colleagues know the reason for his request. He had also taken extreme precautions to hide the facts from his neighbors; as a cover, he had told them that his father had gone to his *erh-ko*'s home in Hsinchu for a short visit. Despite these measures, it was impossible to prevent the truth from leaking out. Was that not so? Why else had there been people straining their necks to look in through the bamboo fence over the last two days? It was as if their house had been the site of a recent murder. One person had even asked him to his face where his father was. At the time, he had replied, "He's gone to Hsinchu to my *erh-ko*'s home."

Fan Yeh planned to stop over at T'aoyuan, Hsinchu, Chunan, Miaoli, T'aichung, Changhua, Chiayi, T'ainan, and Kaohsiung. This search would take him half a month. He would concentrate on the Buddhist temples because his father had intimated on various occasions after their family brawls that he would like to give himself up to the monastic life. Then he would seek out the various local police stations, churches, and welfare centers. Since his father had no money on him, churches and welfare centers might very well be the places he would go.

"And his certificate of identity, do you have that?" she asked.

He felt that she had aged a lot and seemed much weaker than before. Was this proof of their common crime?

"I've got it."

"Your umbrella."

He took it from her.

"Write home."

He picked up the suitcase, threw the travel bag over his shoulder, and tucked the umbrella under his arm. He stepped out of the house and walked deliberately through the alley toward the main street.

I

A youngish looking father and a small child were walking slowly down the street, hand in hand.

"Great, great, door, man, man," the child called out, pointing to the words he recognized on the storefronts along the way.

"Man, Every-*man* Department Store. Hsia-*men.* *Great* Tea Company — Hsia-*men* is where our family comes from in China, and *men* is the same character as *door* — see? And what about that word, Sonny?"

"Grand. And there's the word for *door* again, Pa! Pa, look! Many *door*s, Pa."

"Yes indeed, many. The *door*s or *men* in Hsia-*men* Company *Grand* Opening, and Hsia-*men* Department Store, and Hsia-*men* Ice Drinks."

Father gently explained to him in his kindly, loving voice. His little hand rested comfortably in Father's large, warm hand.

"We've walked very far; we should be going back now," this father said.

They turned round and walked back the way they had come. A rickshaw pulled alongside them, overtook them, went pattering by.

"Walk faster. Ma's waiting for us at home."

So saying, this father picked up his child, wrapped one arm round his little body, set him on the other arm, and proceeded on down the road.

2

The wind had toppled the tree. He was looking out the window from his room; all the windows were tightly shut against the storm. Behind him, he could hear his father and mother moving about. Inside the house, it turned alternately light and dark as the cassia that was shielding the window tossed back and forth. Dried leaves were blown about wildly by the typhoon. On a branch, deep within the cassia's canopy, sat a magpie, holding itself in resolute stillness.

3

Above the transom in Mother's bedroom was a pane of stained glass.

4

"Pa will go out and get you one tonight, a yellow one for you."

"What, did you burst another one? And you want more?" Mother said.

"Yes," he said.

"Rascal. Come! Come to Mama. How old is Sonny this year? Tell Mama."

"Five."

"What's your sign?"

"I'm a Dragon."

"He remembers. Where do you live? If you were taken away by a stranger and you saw a policeman, what would you say to the policeman? Where would you say you live?"

"At Hsiamen Embankment, Alley 5, Number 6."

"You hear that! What is Papa's name? What would you say to the policeman if he asks you what your papa's name is?"

He forgot. His father laughed and told him.

"And Mama?" Mother asked.

He forgot that too.

"Ma's name is Yeh Ch'iu-fang," his mother said. "You've forgotten?"

He went back over to Father's side.

"Let Pa have a little kiss." Father bent down and gave him a peck on the cheek.

"Let Mama have a kiss too," Mother said.

"Go, go over to Mama now."

"You have to be told? Come, you little rascal. Do you love Papa or Mama best?"

He did not reply.

"Who do you love best? Hurry up, say who!"

He couldn't decide. In the end, he turned toward Father.

She reached out and grabbed him. "No, no way. You can't love Papa."

5

One night he saw a huge monster, like a bull, trudging slowly past the second floor window where he lay. It was going up toward the third floor. He was not dreaming.

6

One buck was a dull red color, the other black. They were part of the design on the gold glazed teapot. The picture was done in relief. The red buck's head was tilted back, and hanging down beside it was a grapevine covered with purple fruit and green leaves. You couldn't see the bucks' eyes or their snouts and mouths, just the shapes of their bodies. He stared at this pot's belly for half an hour at a time.

Then there was Mother's makeup case. On the lid was a lake scene. A little boat with a white sail shaped like a seagull's wing floated on the lake; the boat was moored by the shore. In this scene, too, he had spent many hours, wandering in daydreams.

7

He got sick. Yesterday afternoon he felt a little burning sensation under his nose. Last night, Father had made a hot mulberry drink for him. He said, "This will help you sweat it out. You'll feel better in the morning." He sweated all night long, but that burning sensation under his nose was still there when he woke up in the morning.

"The clinic Mrs. Chung goes to is not bad – should we go there?" Mama asked Papa.

Mama hurried out and then back into the room again. "It's at Hou-san Road. Mrs. Chung gave me the address. She says they're open every morning."

They got ready to go. Father took a bedsheet and bundled him up from head to toe. He struggled and yanked it off. He didn't want to be seen going out in such a strange getup.

"You can't go out with nothing over you – you'll catch cold!" Mama kept saying.

He adamantly refused. His father tried again to pull the sheet around him. He started to cry.

"Don't cry when you're sick! You won't get better if you cry."

"No crying," Father said. "Put it on now, and Papa will get you some bananas tonight. Would Sonny like some bananas?"

He stopped crying – he liked bananas. So he let Father cover him up with the bedsheet; he was thinking of the bananas he would soon see.

"Ah – open wide, that's right." The doctor was a kind man. He was clean shaven, but you could see the shadow of a beard on his fair skin. Papa and Mama were very respectful toward him.

"Pull up his clothes, and let me listen to his chest," the doctor said. He could feel the doctor's cold fingertips on his ribs and the icy stethoscope pressing on his chest.

"Tonsillitis," the doctor pronounced. "Your tonsils are sick; they're near your Adam's apple," he added kindly.

". . . tonsillitis . . . tonsillitis . . . tonsil . . . Adam's apple . . . ," he said to himself, taking in the new terms he had just heard. He thought of the apple he had eaten not too long ago; tonight he'd be getting bananas.

They came home. "First, take your medicine, the powder then the syrup. Then go off to bed and close your eyes for a rest, and you'll be all better in a few days," his mother said. She kept the windows in the bedroom tightly shut and drew the dark blue curtains over them. He could feel the thermometer in his armpit, cold and tingly.

That night, his fever seemed to have risen even higher. Everything in the house looked dull and somber. Both his cheeks were hot with fever; he could hardly hear. He asked for the bananas.

"Uh . . . bananas." Father looked over at Mother and said to her in a whisper, ". . . very expensive, not in season."

"We'll wait a few days, okay? Sonny, wait till you get better, and Papa will go and get you some," Father said.

So they tricked him. They lied to him so they could trick him into letting them put that bedsheet over him. He opened his mouth wide and bawled.

"Don't cry, don't cry," Mama said. "The doctor said you shouldn't have any. He said you have to wait till you get better before you can have any. Aren't you going to listen to the doctor?"

He howled with all his might. His grief over the loss of those bananas was not to be appeased.

That night, he went to sleep earlier than usual. He had a lot of fast-moving, prickly, jumpy dreams. He felt his body burning up, as if it were pressed up against a tub of hot coals. He came to a few times. He couldn't understand why his parents were both standing by his bed, looking at him so anxiously. He got out of bed once to go pee; his urine was not the same as usual; it was an orangy-red color. The insides of his thighs were on fire, and he saw that his little birdie had shrunk; it was bright red, hanging there in front of two hard marbles. He went back to bed and once again entered those darting, fitful dreams.

The next day he was allowed to have only soupy rice and pickles at mealtimes. His fever had gone down a little from the night before. From time to time, Mama came in under his mosquito tent to put her hands over the soles of his feet to feel his temperature. Whenever she left his bedside, he would think about those bananas. By four or five in the afternoon, his temperature had risen again.

He was sick for over ten days. He was confined to bed, and his days were tiresome and boring. He spent large chunks of the daylight hours staring at the water stains left by the rain on the mosquito tent where it hung from the ceiling. Sometimes, a tiny mosquito would find its way into the tent. At such times he would call out to his mother to come and chase it out. The most depressing time of day was when the sky grew dim and the lights came on. At such times he would stretch out his arms and play catch with his hands' shadows on the mosquito netting. Or else he would turn his face to the wall and dream of his bananas.

Ever since he had been taken ill, he was allowed only to overhear the sounds of the streets outside the curtained windows; he wanted badly to see the sights.

During this period, his father asked for leave from work to come home in the afternoon. He helped Mother look after him and sometimes went to the hospital to fill his prescriptions. On those nights when his fever suddenly sneaked up on them, it was Father who stayed up with him all through the night. One night, he woke up to see Father dozing off in a chair by his bed, his hair sticking out like a wild nest.

Gradually, he recovered. On one of those afternoons during his convalescence, he was standing by the window, watching the street scene that he had long yearned for, staring at the cars going by, when his concentration was broken by a voice from behind.

"Sonny, do you see what I see?"

In Father's hand, held high up in the air, was a great big bunch of bananas.

8

"Sonny, come, come inside, don't go playing with those kids." She stood in the door, inhibiting his play.

She forbade her son to play with the neighborhood kids. They were not good enough for him. She liked to remind her son that theirs was a family of substance, going back generations; that his grandfather had been governor of the province during the Ch'ing dynasty; that his granduncle was a district intendant of Fuchien Province; that his grandfather on his mother's side was also once a district magistrate in Kuangtung; that it was not until this generation that the family had moved out of Fuchou to this foreign land. Theirs used to be a house of gentility, and he mustn't forget it, no matter what.

9

"Spinach by the dung heap – grown again!" She laughed, teasing him. "'Spinach by the dung heap,' who rained pee on you to make you grow this tall?"

"Ma!" He pounded his mother with his fists.

"Not grown in pee? Okay, then you must have been

sprinkled by manure to have grown so fast." She was shaking and laughing.

"Ma!"

"He's really gotten quite a bit taller recently, eh?" Father said as he took another sip of tea.

"Even his arms have grown. See how his wrists stick out of his sleeves," she chimed.

"Children go through these growth spurts. He's about that age when they suddenly shoot up," his father said.

Mother heaved a sigh and said, "Still, this son's far too young for us. We're almost old people now. Where can we find a pipe and blow him up big right away?"

"Ai. . . . I wonder how long it will be before I can sit back and let my son take care of me." His father drank another mouthful of tea.

"Him take care of *you*? You might as well stop dreaming. How many sons have really taken care of their parents in their old age?"

"Too true, too true." Father shook his head despondently. "They're all the same. This child will no doubt turn rebellious like the rest of them."

He was grieved and deeply hurt. He argued in his own defense, "No, I won't. I won't be like that!"

"It's easy to say that now. We'll have to wait and see how you turn out. When the time comes, you'll probably think your parents are too old and ugly for you. You'd rather not have to look at them. They'll be a burden to you, and you'll throw them out of the house. This son of ours is no filial son. There's no denying it. Just look at his features, and you can see that he has the look of an ingrate. He'll abandon his own father and mother. He's a rebel, this one – likes to go against the grain. He's the sort who's liable to turn his back on his own parents."

As he listened to his father's predictions, his eyes, which were at first cast to the ground, gradually filled with hate and resentment. He turned to glower at his parents.

10

Father's body was covered with lots of little black moles. Mother's body was full of red moles. On his body were black moles and some red moles.

11

After each meal, be it lunch or dinner, his father made his way toward the washbasin on the round stool, calling, "Hey Son, come clean up. Come wash your face."

A face towel was hung on the wall above the stool, and on its footrest was a white metal soap dish. By the side of the stool stood a coal-black thermos flask. Father poured hot water into the basin from the thermos, reached for the towel, took it down, and spread it out on the water. Thus engulfed in hot, steamy vapors, he bent down to rinse out the towel in the basin, making splashing noises.

Fan Yeh went over then, and Father placed the hot, steamy towel on his face, covering it up completely. He remained covered in this way for a full half minute. After that, Father rinsed out the towel and covered up his own face. Father said that this covering up of the face was very good for one's health.

12

He sat hunched up like a snail on the rattan stool. His father sat across from him, cutting his fingernails for him. He could cut the nails of his left hand with his right hand, but he couldn't cut those on his right hand with his left. He could never get the scissors to work properly that way.

13

His father let the narrow fingernails on his baby fingers grow long.

14

If he sat for a long time in his chair, he would feel a tingly, stinging sensation from his knees down to his toes, until he could hardly move his legs at all.

15

His sister was born half a year before he started school. He used to sleep in Mother's bed; after that, he slept with Father.

16

Before he came into bed, Father first switched off the light, then turned on the night-light by the bed, and then, with a rhythmic motion, wound up his watch. After that, he would let out a long sigh of contentment, dim the night-light, and lie down to sleep. He slept on the inside, against the wall, while Father slept on the outside. His corner of the bed was a sweet haven of peace. He felt that this was the safest place on earth. Father's body was like a fortress, protecting him from all manner of danger and invasion. It was not the same sleeping with Father as it was with Mother. Father's body was warmer, and his breathing was heavier and more even. Also, he hardly tossed about at all through the night. Soon, the sound of his own breathing would follow the rise and fall of his father's rhythmic snore.

17

His sister contracted pneumonia at three months and died. Mother beat her chest and wailed in grief.

18

His mother came in, shouting, "Eat, eat, eat up! Hurry, or you won't make it on time!"

Golden sunshine flooded every corner of every room; a shimmery reflection swam across the ceiling. Father, with a towel slapped across his shoulder, was washing up and combing his hair. Mother came tearing back into the room, rushing Fan Yeh, yelling at him to finish up at the table, clearing away all the bits of fried dough sticks that he had already dipped in soy sauce and that were his favorite part of breakfast. He was so sorry to see them go.

"Look at him taking his time. What a slowpoke. Go on, drink it up!"

"Sonny is going to school today, his first day of school," Father sang.

"Going to school, *he* thinks! It's ten past nine already."

"It's all right. It's all right to be a little late for the first day," Father said.

"Says who?" Mother said.

"He's already late to begin with. We were late registering him. Classes started a week ago."

Father took off for work soon after that, telling Mother to take him to school.

Mother went about the house, locking up, and came out holding a brand new schoolbag. It looked like a woman's handbag. It was made of a white silky material, with two straps for handles, and it had two red roses embroidered on it. He didn't like this schoolbag one bit. But his mother was behind him, hurrying him on and making him pick it up. He had no choice but to take the thing along.

On the way to school, a kid standing by the roadside stared at him. The kid made a nasty face and raised his fist menacingly in the air. He quickly looked the other way. All the while he was acutely embarrassed by the schoolbag he was carrying. He kept the side with the roses against his leg, making the bag swing back and forth with his calf, hoping no one would notice those silly ornaments.

They arrived at the school. It was ever so quiet, ever so awesome. The green school buildings were cast in the light and shadows of their surroundings. Just a little beyond was a seesaw and a swing set with two swings on it. An old man with white hair came toward them; Mother spoke to him. He led them into the main building. They walked in toward a huge, rectangular mirror. The old man held a bucket and a scrubbing cloth in his hand. Mother stood waiting while the old man walked down the corridor. As they stood there, he watched the shadows of leaves and flowers sketching themselves on the wall. In a little while, a lady wearing a green cheongsam approached them; the old man stood back and fell behind. The lady and Mother immediately started talking to each other like old friends. The lady was full of smiles and occasionally turned toward Fan Yeh, giving him gentle, reassuring pats on the head. They went on talking and talking, and the lady kept on casting him kindly glances and friendly smiles. He liked this new auntie.

Then Mother said to him, "All right, I'll be going then. I'll come for you after school. Go along with Miss Mei; she's your new teacher. Don't make a fuss now."

He let out a faint cry of alarm: "Ma. . . ." He clutched at his mother's dress and held on tight.

"Aw, okay, it's okay. Look here, all right, Mama won't leave. Mama's staying. But look, Mama has to go to the toilet right now. Mama's not leaving, just going to the toilet. You can't come to the toilet with her, right?"

"Mama's not going home. She *will* come back. We'll wait here for her, and she'll come in a while. She'll be right back." Even as she was saying this, the lady took his hand and led him on.

"Ma," he called.

But Mother was already walking away. He followed her with his eyes.

"Okay, let's go to the classroom now," the lady was saying.

He glared back at her. "No."

"Don't worry, Mama *will* come to look for us in the classroom in a minute."

"I'm not going."

"Come, come. Come along."

"No!"

"Over here!" she snapped, her face darkening instantly. "Over here and follow me!"

He flinched. His mouth dropped open till his chin almost fell from his face. "No!" he screeched, all of a sudden realizing what had happened.

"Come!" she said, digging her nails into his flesh where she grasped him; the pain was comparable to being squeezed by iron pincers. "Follow me, you nasty little devil!"

These last few minutes of agitation finally brought him to the fullness of expression; he broke into a thunderous wail. He would never have guessed in a million years that she'd turn out to be . . . and he thought she was. . . . He was stunned into silence, his voice trapped by the horror of his situation. She applied brute force then, hauling him all the way to the classroom. He bellowed at the top of his lungs, "Ma, quick! Ma, hurry, help . . . ," just like the time when he was beaten up by those bullies. He was dragged into the classroom.

"Sit down." She pointed to a seat by the wall. "And no crying! Stay here, and don't you move."

She turned around and walked to the front of the class. He sat where she put him, but he didn't stop crying at the top of his voice. The other children all turned their big, round faces to look, laughing at him. The teacher resumed the lesson but had to stop and once again came toward him. He held his breath, his voice choked back in fright. She suppressed a smile of victory and turned back in mid-course. He sobbed quietly to himself.

Oh, but the Bodhisattva had come from heaven to save him! Mama was standing there at the window. She was wearing an apologetic expression and was smiling sheepishly at the teacher. He was mad with joy. Unfortunately he didn't dare proclaim his happiness, so he had to make do by calling out to her with his eyes: "Ma, I'm here. Here I am, Ma." It was then that his teacher spotted Mother at the window. She frowned at her in disapproval. Mother immediately retreated, contrite. O what a pity! Mama was once again lost to him. He waited for her to reappear. He strained his eyes, willing her presence at the window. But Mama did not appear again.

He surveyed his surroundings and saw that all the children were looking straight in front of them. He, too, looked in front of him. What was there to see? Not much. Just the teacher standing there. Then the children broke into a chorus, shouting something, staring straight ahead, shouting and stopping, shouting and stopping. He looked out of the corners of his big, round eyes at the shaved-head kid seated next to him. He was sitting bolt upright and looked happy. The chorus turned into a commotion.

After a while, he became aware that the teacher was speaking to him and appeared to have repeated herself several times already: "Take out your pencil and paper, and put them on your desk." In a daze he reached into his schoolbag and took out pencil and paper, but he was at a loss as to what he should do with them. Like a good buddy, the shaved-head kid sitting next to him showed him what was on his piece of paper. He saw that it was full of characters. He picked out the one for *great* and wrote it on his page.

Later on, he picked out the word *cow* and copied it onto the corner of the page.

A loud ringing pealed through the air, startling him; he listened, awestruck. In the classroom, the other children stirred, some getting out of their seats, some chatting together. Mama suddenly reappeared at the window. This time he tossed caution to the wind and fled the classroom without a backward glance, calling as he went, "Ma! Ma!"

He ran into Mama's arms, crying so hard he could hardly open his eyes. The teacher was coming at them, but now she was full of smiles again.

"I'm so very sorry. He can't be left, not for a minute. Teacher must have been exasperated just now. He was a lot of trouble, wasn't he?"

"No, no, not at all," the teacher said.

When the bell rang for the next class, he categorically refused to go back into the classroom. His mother had no choice but to apologize to the teacher for taking him home early on his first day of school. And it was Mother who had to go retrieve his schoolbag, because when he dashed out he had left everything behind, and nothing could entice him back into that classroom now.

D

SEARCH
For Father

Father, since you left on April 14th, Mother and I have been worried sick. Hurry home please when you see this. Everything will be resolved according to your wishes.

Your son,
Yeh

Fan Yeh folded the paper up into a small square and put it in the back pocket of his trousers. It had been four days since he had left Taipei. He had yet to come up with a single lead. He was just now emerging from the District Police Office.

Here in T'aichung the heat had overtaken itself and approached midsummer in April. To protect themselves from the fiery sun, pedestrians wore all manner of straw hats, looking as if they had on African headgear. He was not properly equipped for this kind of weather; sweat poured down his cheeks. It was now nearly midday, but before going back to the hostel for a rest he wanted to give this area another try. So, continuing in his search, he made his way toward the shrine ahead, joining the tidal wave of worshipers. He took off his glasses and put on his sunglasses to search the faces passing in front of him.

19

He walked all the way to school by himself, dangling that schoolbag with the roses embroidered on it at his side as he shuffled along.

Since he was one of the shorter kids in his class, he sat in the front row. He did pretty well at school. He picked things up effortlessly even though his heart was not in it. He was always thinking of home – he had never gotten used to school.

The lesson began, and the teacher was at the board, explaining something. Though he was sitting in the classroom, he was thinking of home. He was thinking of the long period of time he had to endure before he got to go home. It was only the second class of the day; there would be a third session, and then a fourth, before Mama Ch'en came with his lunch; then he still had to wait all afternoon before he could go home to see Papa and Mama again. The teacher had started to lead the class in recitation. He glanced up at the board and read:

O how I love my family,
O how I love my home.
Papa goes to work in the factory,
Mama makes my clothes at home.
I do my best and study my books,
And everyone is happy as can be.

He conjured up Mama's gentle smiling face and Papa's warm and kindly features. He felt a tingling sensation at the tip of his nose; a surge of tears almost made him sob out loud. All through the rest of the class he kept his head down, weeping quietly to himself. He was extremely homesick. For the next few sessions, he was simply overwhelmed by his longing to go home.

He was finally on his way home. As he was nearing his destination, he had a sudden anxiety attack. What if, during the hours he had been away, there had been a great fire, and now his home was burned to the ground? He ran with all his might; he wanted to find out immediately what had happened. In his dash for home he tripped and fell down twice. His heart was beating so fast it felt as if it were about to jump up into and out of his throat. He could almost see it! The house was still standing. All was well; everything was as it should be. He breathed a great sigh of relief. He closed his eyes and thought that he could lose anything in this world and it wouldn't matter so long as this home remained intact.

20

"Truth be told, he's poor because he's an honest man, your Uncle Chang, running out of rice for the family like that," Mama said.

"What did he come to us for yesterday?"

"He came to borrow rice from us. Actually we're not that much better off than he is. Papa finally lent him half a catty."

"Will I be like Uncle Chang when I grow up?"

"No," Mama said after a deliberate pause, "but it'll be up to you. If you work hard, it won't happen. First comes the bitter, then comes the sweet: olive fate."

"First comes the bitter, then comes the sweet . . . ," he repeated after her.

"First comes the bitter, then comes the sweet: olive fate."

"What does that mean, 'olive fate'? Why is it first bitter, then sweet?"

"Haven't you ever tasted an olive before? First it tastes bitter, and then when you've chewed on it a while it tastes sweet. A person's life can be like that."

"Ma, what did you say this morning?"

"What did I say?"

"You know, when Mama Ch'en came."

"What did I say?"

"Mama Ch'en had on leather shoes, and you said . . ."

"Oh! Yes, yes. She was wearing new leather shoes with an old dress, and I said she's 'heaping cheap potatoes on good chicken.' "

"Heaping cheap potatoes on good chicken," he repeated.

21

The dense fog fell thick on the narrow alleyway. He watched the water drops gather and drip down the window-pane like sweat. The muffled singsong of the woman selling tofu at the street corner came to him in fits and starts: "Tofu-aiy, tofu-oiy. . . ." She sang through the fresh morning every day.

22

Frenzied gusts howled through the air; window frames shook all by themselves; a red leaf as big as a man's palm flew by the window.

"It's a typhoon! No school today," he heard Mother say as he roused himself from sleep. It was then that he realized the reason for that vague feeling of lateness he had felt but hadn't bothered to identify.

The wind had sliced open a passage between the trees, and the church's bell tower now stood right before their window. He luxuriated in the feel of quiet warmth around him. Pa had already gone to the office and had told them that because of the typhoon he would probably not be able to come home for lunch, and that he'd most likely be late coming home in the evening as well. Mama was not going out to the market that morning; she was going to stay home with him. Mama brought out two low stools and placed them by the bed. All the windows and doors in the house were bolted shut. She told him old stories, and then she taught him to sing every song she knew.

"This howling wind will have blown itself out by the time the sun comes up in the morning," Ma said.

23

Fan Yeh ended his ringing recitation.

His father was sprawled out on the cool rattan recliner, a cup of strong, newly brewed tea by his side; he was in his undershirt and underpants. Mother was lounging on the other rattan recliner, fanning herself with a rush-leaf fan.

"Excellent," Father said.

"First rate! Tip-top!" Mama held out her hand and gave him a thumbs up.

He felt a little embarrassed by their applause.

"There's no telling what the future may bring. He might even turn out to be a real scholar, this one," Mama remarked gleefully.

"O yes! A bookman he is, a learned man, a scholar," Father chimed in.

24

He came in fourth in his class. When he brought home the news, his mama was beside herself with joy.

"Wow! Can it really be? Can this sort of thing really happen to us?"

"Woah! Such a thing!" Father exclaimed.

"I'm going to be first in my class next time." He was aglow with pride.

"Mm, yes you will," Mother replied.

"This is truly, truly, once in a million years, unexpected . . . not in a million years would I have thought. . . ." Father was shaking and nodding his head at the same time. "I am more than satisfied; one son like this is more than enough to make me happy. Other people may have gold bullion and silver dollars. I don't envy them. I have a son worth tens of thousands of times more than their gold. This son of mine is beyond compare. No rich man is better off than me!"

25

One morning, there was a funeral down their alley. The shrill and somber sounds of brass and drums burst in through the rear window.

Looking out from this window down to the house where death was, he saw that the doors and shutters were all closed up. The brass and drum players of the funeral band were seated on a bench outside that door. Once in a while people went inside, and occasionally people came out as well. The sky above was gray and cold and cast in melancholy.

"It's gone inside; the coffin has gone inside," Mama said.

He felt the room go cold and solemn, as if a shadow had come over it.

"It's the owner of the little store who died," Mama was telling him.

He recalled the image of this store owner: a pair of tortoise-shell reading glasses hung low on his nose; most days he wore a black padded vest. It seemed impossible he could be dead.

"'Man's life is like a candle flame in the wind' – give it an extra blow and it's gone," Mama proclaimed.

"What happened, Ma, what made him die?" he asked her.

"Hard to tell. I only heard that the night before he died he was fine; he even drank half a bottle of white liquor. Then the next morning he stopped breathing, just like that."

"Where do people go after they die?"

"When people die, they go under the ground and become ghosts," she told him.

"Grandpa and Grandma have become ghosts, then?" he asked her thoughtfully, remembering how she had once told him that her father and mother had passed away a long time ago. "Is that right, Ma?"

"Hm."

"How did they die?"

"When people grow old, they die."

"We will die too, right? When we grow old. . . ."

"Don't say any more – don't talk about such unlucky things!" she said.

The drumbeats became louder and more insistent, and wailing could be heard coming out of that house.

He crouched behind the window and kept his eye on it from this safe distance.

His mother left the window often to go to the kitchen, and, because he was afraid, he followed her. But soon his curiosity would get the better of him, and he would venture back to his post by the window to listen to the ringing music and to look up at the vast, gray sky above: several times he was scared into running for cover. The blare of brass and drums lasted long into the afternoon. Intermittently, wailing could also be heard.

Near evening, a bier was carried out into the street. Mother said, "Quick, don't look! Put your head down, now!"

He bowed his head in compliance, but not for long. Soon, he was looking up again to steal a glance at the coffin and thinking to himself how, if the coffin was closed so tightly, the store owner managed to breathe – when suddenly his mother yelled.

"Here comes the ghost! Run for your life!"

He swung round and ran.

Mama came in to open the window. The funeral proceedings had come to an end. The musicians had disbanded, and all the people in front of the house had left.

"Whew. Let's let some air in here. We've been shut up all day. There's no more water in the tank. I'll have to go downstairs to fetch some from the well. Don't you follow me now. Wait here, and I'll be back in a minute," she said to him.

After Mama had gone downstairs, he kept a respectful distance from the window; he sat on the wooden clothes trunk against the wall by the window. This was the very first time ever, ever since the beginning of time for him, that he had contemplated the fact of death. He wondered whether his own papa and mama would also be taken away one day. Papa was now forty-six, and Mama was just two years younger than him. When people turned fifty, they died easily. That meant his papa would have only another four years to spend with him, or at most five or six. And Ma wouldn't have that many more either; a mere four years! He was shattered. He shuddered as cold blasts came through the window. Outside the window everything was now plunged in darkness; the wooden trunk he was sitting on felt especially hard.

Oh, please, please don't let Papa and Mama die so soon, oh merciful Bodhisattva. If Papa and Mama died and left him right now, he'd only be ten years old. What could he do? Who would look after him and come to him when he needed help? He'd probably end up on the streets, begging for a living. The thought horrified him. They simply mustn't be allowed to die, oh Papa and Mama. He still needed them very much; he needed them to look after him and to bring him up, to cherish and sustain him. . . . Why, oh why did he have to have such old parents, and he himself still a mere child? He envied his school friends; they all had very young papas and mamas. They were all either the eldest child or the second eldest in their families. He was the only one among them to be the last child. Why was he born to be the littlest in the family? They had lots of time, countless days to be with their parents, while he would lose his parents soon. Oh heaven above, Bodhisattva. Oh Goddess of Mercy, listen to me. Please don't let my beloved Pa and Ma die so soon. Let me have them for a long, long time to come. Oh, how I love them, love them so very much. Tears blurred his vision. . . .

"What's up? Why are you crying like that?" Mama stepped in just then . . . (still) young and hale and hearty.

"Ma!" He rushed into his ma's bosom and erupted in an explosion of tears.

E

SEARCH
For Father

Father, since you left on April 14th, Mother and I have been worried sick. Hurry home please when you see this. Everything will be resolved according to your wishes.

> Your son,
> Yeh

He was walking along the road under the ruthless blaze of the noonday sun. There was not even the ghost of another's shadow in the empty streets. On either side of the road were rectangular concrete buildings; the lower stories were sunk in the shade. He walked straight ahead, a rolled up newspaper held tight in his hand – he had just visited a church and had come away with nothing. He forged ahead; behind him fell his short shadow. In the sky, at his back, hung a cross.

26

His *erh-ko* had come home. He wore a navy blue student's uniform. Mama said he had been at the boarding school and was now going to be home for a few days. He was always hunched up in his room; every time he passed through, skirting past his brother's doorway, he could see him inside, brows knit above eyes of fury. Mama explained to him that this *erh-ko* was not her own; only he himself was a child of her womb. She also told him that their eldest brother was not hers either. Those two were borne by a different mother, who was now dead. His own mother was this eldest brother's and Erh-ko's stepmother. His eldest brother – where, he asked, was he now? He had long ago been sent to a boarding school far, far away, she said. He could count on not seeing him much at all, this big brother. Would he be coming back soon? he asked. His boarding school was too far away, Mama said. He would not be coming back any time soon.

27

He had caught a cold, and his coughing made *k'e k'e* noises long into the night. They sounded funny, like the echoes of bronze bells. He was given malt sugar to eat for his hacking cough, a great big hunk of it, twirled round a chopstick, gummy and transparent and sweet. He held it in his mouth and savored it.

28

His mother taught him to recite "Mu Lan T'zu," the song of the woman warrior:

> Sick-sick goes the shuttle,
> Mu Lan weaving at her window.
> You can't hear the sick-sick sounds,
> For the sighs of the girl at the shuttle. . . .

He repeated it over and over to get it down by heart, but no matter what, he couldn't get the whole thing down.

> Sick-sick goes the shuttle,
> Mu Lan weaving at her window.
> You can't hear the sick-sick sounds,
> For the sighs of the girl at the shuttle.

> Her Pa has no grown son,
> Mu Lan has no big brother. . . .

He had been reciting this poem for several days now. He was aware that the neighborhood children who had, like him, been on winter break were already back at school; they had been passing by on their way to classes for quite a few days now. Mama told him he wouldn't be going to school for now, not for a little while, not until Papa found a new job; then he could go to school again.

29

He sat glowering at the kitchen table. The tabletop was grimy with dirt and grease. The sky was heavy with clouds. Indoors, too, it was gloomy and humid, stuffy and gray. On the table were displayed a whole lot of origami creatures.

Mama was trying to sound entertaining, but the unhappiness in her voice came through anyway. "What a whole lot of monkeys. Look, monkey sons and monkey babies all lined up in a row. Look." She was calling those pointy-headed, stiff-bodied things "monkeys" and "sons." They looked exactly like those filial sons in funeral processions with mourning sackcloth caps on their heads. Mother was staring sightlessly in front of her, mouthing the words: "Look at all those monkeys . . . Which one is your favorite? Go on, take one, take him to your side and play with him." But he just sat there, refusing to lift a finger, glaring. She kept up the flow of words. "Ma will fold you a great big monkey, the biggest one of them all. He can be the Monkey King." She took another piece of old newspaper and folded it into a big paper monkey, as big as a clay pot. It was a gigantic, dumb, ugly monstrosity. The whole tribe of strangely shaped, weird-looking monkeys great and small stood together facing him, looking straight at him. He swallowed hard but kept his ground, unyielding. Her hands moved automatically and started to fold another monkey as she cast a glance at him and said with a sigh, "What a pity you're such a small boy still. If only we could take a blowpipe and blow you up right away into a big person." She took another look at him and then continued, staring into space. "These are real hard times for us. You don't know how much trouble we're in. Ever since your papa got laid off he's been looking for work, but it's been nearly two months now, and he hasn't been able to find anything. I don't know what we'll do if this lasts much longer. That's why you've had to give up school. Oh, and you're such a good boy." Her eyes softened and the rims turned red. "And just when you were doing so well at school, we had to take you out. At first, I tried to talk your father into letting you go on so we wouldn't interrupt your progress, but he wouldn't agree to it. Now, don't feel bad. Ma will do whatever she can to let you go back to school. You must be allowed to go back to school! Ma's willing to scrub floors if she has to so you can go on with your studies. Ma wanted to take the plunge a long time ago, go work somewhere, go off to an office like others." (She squeezed out the words through clenched teeth.) "A pity Ma has had so little education. It's all your grandmother's fault. Your grandfather enrolled me in one of those modern schools, but your grandmother had to go and take me home again, claiming that girls have no business reading books. Learning to recognize a few words was more than adequate for girls, she said. They were so rigid in their thinking in the old days! And because of that Mama has never learned how to speak Mandarin. All those places where the jobs are require that you speak Mandarin. There are some pretty cushy jobs at those offices. All those girls working in those offices – if they can do it, I don't see how hard it can be. Things like filing documents, registering this and that, putting stuff away – these are things Mama can do. It's just that Mandarin, that's the hitch." She paused. "Several times I asked your papa to teach me, but he wouldn't. Your papa, he's not a good man. He's always looked down on me. He's a very hard-hearted man, and don't you ever forget that. Don't ever oppose him; he's truly capable of throwing you out of the house! Your little sister's life was finished off by that man. If only he had been willing to go borrow money at the time, but he was afraid he couldn't pay it back. Who can think of money at a time like that? If only he had rushed your sister to the hospital right away, she'd still be alive today. She'd be with us now, and what a very pretty little girl she'd be. She had such beautiful eyes. It still makes me . . ." Tears welled up again, filling her eyes as she started to sob. "Ah, what a bitter fate Mama's been dealt . . . just take a look at Mama's hands. All swollen and puffy like soap left to soak in water. We even had to let Mama Ch'en go. A few lousy dollars a month, and we can't afford her. Now I'm left to do all the washing myself, and Mama in her condition too. That arthritis is still bothering me. Ah, it's worthless being a woman. Look at your own mama, not a thing left to her name, not even a decent dress to go out in. And all that jewelry I came with, Mama's trousseau, all gone, all taken away to the pawn shop by your papa. Ah, bitterness, it's a woman's fate. I guess I'd better be getting dinner on."

He sat there at the kitchen table, his face all twisted up.

"Do you want to come with me to the kitchen? It's all smoky in the kitchen, though. I think you'd better not come, okay?"

He didn't say a word.

"Okay? Why aren't you saying anything? Oh, don't upset Mama. Mama's going to have another fainting spell . . ."

He leapt up all of a sudden and, brandishing his arms, swung out at the multitude of paper monkeys on the table-top, sending them flip-flopping into the air.

30

He, Papa, and Mama, together with his *erh-ko,* were on the steamer heading for Taiwan Province. It was crowded and chaotic in the cabin; people were strewn everywhere, each person staking out his own sleeping area. The ceiling and walls of the cabin were rocking and swaying up and down and from side to side; people were throwing up every-where; the dangling lightbulb was swinging to and fro.

31

Their family settled down in a house a stone's throw from the seacoast. In front of their door grew a variety of flower-ing plantain whose brightly colored petals looked like yel-low tongues with red birthmarks on them. There were also some stubby coir palms with spiky trunks. Whenever they passed by their house, the villagers would stare in at them through the windows. This was because not many people from other places had yet come to this island territory. Since their arrival, his papa had worn a brand new khaki suit in the early Republic style; he was working at the town hall.

His brother was working at a fishermen's union and had moved into a room above the union office.

32

When he had time to himself, Father liked to recite poetry. He could often be heard intoning the verses of such poets as Su Tung-p'o, Li Ch'ing-chao, and Li Yü, last emperor of the Southern Tang. One of his favorite lyrics was Su Tung-p'o's "River City Lament":

> Ten years we've parted not knowing whether the other's
>   dead or still alive,
> No use hankering,
> Hard to forget. . . .

His voice, drawn out in a singsong, was melancholy and sorrowful, yet it also sounded extraordinarily beautiful and sweet.

33

Father's desk drawer was kept clean and tidy, with a pile of ten-lined letter paper and envelopes, his name cards in a box, a red ink-paste seal box, and some writing brushes all arranged in an orderly fashion, side by side.

34

On the bamboo bookcase was an old book, a copy of the *Autumn Water Pavilion Letters.*

35

In the corridor at the back of their house was *A Guide to Morse Code.* He had no idea how that book had got there.

36

Father seemed statuesque. His head was at a level with Father's waist, and he had to lift up his own face before he could see Father's face.

37

When his papa came home from work, his whole face was suffused in a warm smile: the shape of his mouth like a half-moon, his eyes all crinkled up as if he had something up his sleeve, his cheeks all rosy red.

In fact, he had that same look on his face when he went off to work. Leather briefcase under his arm, he would leave the house with that smile on his face.

That smiling face made him happy whenever he saw it; it was as if the sun were shining on him.

38

Whenever he had the hiccups, Mother would say, "Go get some chopsticks, crisscross them on top of your glass, and take a sip of water from each of the four spaces." But he couldn't remember a single time when it had worked.

Then there was the time she had scolded him for putting a white handkerchief on his head, saying that white was the color of corpses, not an auspicious color.

39

Mother kept an account of their daily expenses in a ledger. When she wrote in the ledger, she always used a peculiar kind of numeral:

| 〡 〢 〣 Ⅹ 〥 〦 〧 〨 〩 十

For the number twenty-four she would put

40

It was when they had their bath that he and Father spent the longest time talking. He still needed Father to help him wash; that was why they took their baths together.

The sight of Father's naked body invariably gave him a start: his naked body was pure white, the white of a lily. He couldn't remember ever seeing flesh this round and smooth, yet solid and firm at the same time. Like Papa, he too had taken off his clothes: his delicate, small white body was next to that imposing, masculine white body.

Father always gave him a wash first and then washed himself. He always launched into stories about his school days in Paris when he started scrubbing his own body. A feeling of exceptional pride suffused him as he listened. He always wanted his papa to say a few words in French. For example, he would ask, "In our garden we have a papaya tree and a banana tree. How do you say that?" Then a look of embarrassment would come over Papa's face, and he would say he had forgotten it all, that it was a long time ago, and he had not used it since.

"How long were you in France?" he'd ask. And it wasn't as if he hadn't heard it many times before, but he liked to ask anyway.

"About a year," came the anticipated reply.

"Um, Papa, you graduated from college in France, right?" he inquired in the most reverential manner, peering up at his father.

"No," he answered hesitantly, "I only studied there for a year before I came back."

"Why was that?"

"Your grandpa was ill; he told me to come home."

"Oh." He felt deeply sorry for his father for not being able to finish.

"In that case, you graduated from a Chinese university, right, Papa?" Again, he reverently solicited a reply.

"Yes. . . . Put your clothes on quick, before you catch a cold," he said, and folded up the wet towel as he spoke.

Their conversations often took unexpected turns, like the time he asked Father as he was wiping his back, "Which country is the strongest in the world?"

"First comes America, second France, and third place Spain."

"Which country is the weakest?"

"Burma is the weakest."

He listened in wide-eyed wonder.

"When I was in France, everything was done by machines. For example, take washing clothes – they had clothes-washing machines. Or ironing clothes – there were ironing machines. For shoes, they had a shoe-polishing machine. Even for washing your face – there was a machine that washed your face for you." Father told him this as he was washing his own feet.

"Today, though, the most technologically advanced country is America. In America, they have a machine – all you have to do is think of a place you want to go to, and it will take you there right away, in person."

Father was standing with one hand against the wall to steady himself while he used his other hand to dry his toes.

He listened in rapt attention, his eyes opened wide, nodding his head.

"The Americans have just finished making a thing called the Killer Flash. All they have to do is push a button, and the whole world, everybody, will be killed in a flash."

41

On the low wooden shelf alongside the tatami, Mother had arranged a number of small objects. For example, a little alarm clock, a vase, two oval mirrors with handles (these were among the things Mama called her trousseau), and a shallow china plate on which were many plastic animals, such as little birds, little rabbits, and little elephants, bright green, pale pink, and pure white.

42

At home and relaxed, Pa was in the habit of cursing, "His mother's!"

For example, while fanning himself in the cool of the evening just before the sun had completely set, he would often say something like, "It's so hot, this weather, and my office has to be facing west. When that sun strikes in the afternoon, why – his mother's – ! It's no different than a furnace. . . ."

43

Once in a while, in the evenings before they went to bed, they would have a singing session, Papa and him. They would lie on their backs on the bed mats laid out on the tatami. Then Father would take off his watch, fold up his fan, and put them beside the hard, black patent leather headrest. Looking up at the ceiling, he arched his legs and got into position. Following Father's lead, he took up this same position. The songs Father taught him were all those he had learned in the days when he was a recruit at the People's Three Principles National Training Camp. Father taught him:

> Red hot, passionate youth and heroes,
> Red hot, passionate youth and heroes,
> Like the billowing waves of the river,
> Like the swelling tides of the sea,
> Ever, forever raging in my heart. . . .

And sometimes:

> The howling wind,
> the whinnying horses,
> the Yellow River roars out its command. . . .

Or:

> The Great Wall is ten thousand li long,
> Beyond the Great Wall. . . .

44

One night, late into the evening, Fan Yeh was watching, waiting for Papa to come home. He went all the way out the front door and into the street to wait for his father, but he did not come. On other days, he was home by about five o'clock; that day, however, it had already gone past six, and still he had not come. He expressed his profound concern, asking his mother, "Why is Papa so late tonight?" To which his mama, her face turning a sullen shade of yellow, replied, "How on earth should I know? Why don't you go outside and look for yourself?"

Thus rebuffed, he went outdoors to wait for Papa. He strained his neck till it grew stiff. He waited and waited for he didn't know how long. Every time someone appeared he was again disappointed. Before he knew it, night had come on, and he was forced to go back inside the house. The frosty look on Mother's face had by now turned to ice. By contrast, he could barely contain his own burning anxiety. Inside the house the lights had been switched on. He headed for the kitchen window, the one that looked out the back, and gazed longingly toward the bend in the road, but all he saw was the pitch-dark night. Time ticked away like slowly dripping water. Finally, he heard the voice of someone at the door. It was his father's voice. It made him feel so warm, so safe. He leaped up, ran to the door, and threw himself into Father's arms, crying, "Pa! Pa!"

F

SEARCH
For Father

Father, since you left on April 14th, Mother and I have been worried sick. Hurry home please when you see this. Everything will be resolved according to your wishes.

Your son,
Yeh

Inside the compartment of a train: an elderly man, very old, sat opposite him. He had a kindly face, bestowing warmth and mercy, radiating happiness. In this search for his father, he had developed a particular fondness for old people; he especially liked to be near those who were about the same age as his father. Thus, ever since this old man boarded the train at the stop just after T'aichung, he had been drawn to him. The old man had taken the seat facing him when he got on. With both hands resting on the handle of the basket and the basket resting securely on his lap, he sat there with a smile on his face that bespoke kindness, peace, and contentment. That was when he promptly set aside the paper he had been reading to look at him. This part of the journey passed, and the old man got off the train at the stop right before Changhua.

45

Since that first time that his papa came home late from work, there had been several other similar episodes. He was often subjected to the burning anxiety of late-night waiting. It was during this period, too, that he often had to overhear the shouting matches between his parents behind the closed door of their bedroom, after which would follow Ma's hysterical crying. One day, shortly into an argument, Papa accidently smashed one of the pair of Ma's hand mirrors. Mama was shocked into timidity; she said scarcely anything for several days afterward. In the end, not long after that incident, Father came home straight from work.

46

Mama too would occasionally say, "Screw his grandmother's . . ."

47

He felt the dark shadow cast over their household, the same shadow of poverty that had left its indelible impression on him once before. He recognized it by the severe silence and the sullen cloud over Father's and Mother's faces. He saw his parents sitting face to face with the abacus between them, trying to make ends meet. This was how he came to identify it.

When he asked Papa to play ball with him, he would half-heartedly roll the ball around a few times with him and then say, "Papa has a headache just now. Leave Papa alone. Go and play by yourself." Then Papa would deftly make his escape.

Mama still had in her possession an emerald jade ring. It was the last piece of jewelry she had left, given to her by her own mother when she was still a young girl living at home. She refused to let Papa take it from her. She kept it wrapped up safely in layers of paper, the way other people stored herbal pills.

Papa took her aside one day and said, "Eh, Ch'iu-fang, there is one thing I need to discuss with you. These last few months have really been tight. I was thinking, perhaps you might consider lending me that jade ring of yours for a bit, just to tide us over this difficult period. Soon as we get back on track I promise I'll redeem it for you. What do you say?"

"Nothing doing. Redeem it indeed! Which of my pieces would you redeem first? My earrings, my necklace, or my gold bracelet? When you have the money, whenever that might be, you'd find other more important things to attend to. Once you've pawned them, my things are lost forever and ever. I'm not going to let you trick me again this time. Among the many things Ma left me, this is the dearest to me. Don't you be looking at it with those hungry eyes of yours." Her tears came pouring down with this torrent of words.

"All right, all right, don't give it to me then!" Papa lashed out at her in bitter resentment.

"I won't give it to you no matter what. If you need money, go borrow some. Or ask somebody to help you out. Don't pin your hopes on my letting you have my ring. Go wait for whatever you like," she answered back.

48

It was an ordinary Sunday. Father was at home, in the room out back doing whatever he was doing, probably writing letters; Father was sending out a great number of letters these days. Mother was in the kitchen washing and picking out bits of sand from the rice. It was nearing midday. He had been in the kitchen for over half an hour already, giving her a hard time.

"Just stop it! Go play in the front room," she said.

"Hm hm hm hm. . . ."

"Did you hear me?"

He watched his mama with an asinine expression.

"Go out front," Mama repeated herself with deliberate calm.

"Go out front," he said.

"Don't be a nuisance. I'm asking you nicely now."

"Don't be a nuisance. I'm asking you nicely now."

"You're not trying to aggravate me, are you?"

"You're not trying to aggravate me, are you?"

"Don't do it again; don't say any more!"

"Don't do it again; don't say any more!"

"O you shameless thing – "

"O you shameless – "

"Now you're really asking for it," she said.

"Now you're really asking for it!"

Her palm came down hard on his backside; it felt hot and tingly. He held in the scream. His papa was standing at the door.

"What's up? Huh? What are you doing in the kitchen? Get out of the way now!"

"What's up? What are you doing in the kitchen? Get out of the way now!"

"What's that? You're probably itching for the rod. You won't give up till you've had a good, sound beating, will you?

"What's that? You probably . . . blah blah blah blah blah blah!"

"You shut your mouth!"

"You shut your mouth!"

"I'm going to get the cane!"

"Give him a good thrashing, Min-hsien."

"I'm going to get the cane – give him a good thrashing, Min-hsien."

Father swirled around, turning to look for a cane and simultaneously issuing the command for Mother to drag Fan Yeh to the rear of the house. His mother grabbed his hands with her dripping wet hands and tugged and yanked at him till they reached the back.

His father came back in triumph with a bamboo cane in his hand. Father flourished the cane in the air and gave the tatami a heavy whack. His hair had not been combed that morning, and now it stood on his head like a cock's tail in preeminent disarray. The boy was transfixed with fear, but at the same time he was trembling with hate. His father had never been stern or harsh with him. What's more, he had never laid a hand on him, not even during the times when his mama had hit him. Papa had always been the one to stand in her way and speak up on his behalf. How had he become such a bloodthirsty fiend all of a sudden? Look how hateful he'd become! At that very instant Father brandished the bamboo cane and charged him. He turned tail and ran. His mama spread out her arms to trap him, and with both hands offered up her catch to the murderer in hot pursuit, who was already a hair's breadth away. "Hurrah! Ha ha ha ha," Father cackled! Father wrestled him onto the tatami and. . . .

They flung him into the room and locked the door. His scalp, both shoulders, the backs of his hands, and his thighs and legs were covered with cuts and bruises. He had calmed down by now, but even so his eyes gleamed with sparks of leftover hatred. He hated his father so much that he was ready to kill him. He also hated his mother, but not to the extent that he hated his father. He considered how he could seek revenge: drive him out of the house and not take care of him when he's old. That's right. The father who had abused his son should be made to suffer. He would bide his time till then and pay him back as he saw fit.

So thinking, he was eased into a more comfortable frame of mind, and even his tears dried up and became stains on his face. The heaving in his chest subsided. It occurred to him that maybe he should be leaving home even now. He could leave this household, he could run far, far, far away, and let them look for him. Let them regret beating him so hard that he had to cut loose and run. He wouldn't come home for anything. He would wander and drift from place to place; perhaps eventually he would settle down as a minor office worker in a faraway city. There was no telling what might happen. He might even get very sick. He would be lying somewhere in a little room all by himself with no one to look after him. And he wouldn't let them know, either. And he might even die, just like that. He would have nothing to do with them up to the day he died. His grief was now tinged with a sort of pleasure and satisfaction.

Just then the door was pushed open, and his father and mother were standing outside the room, looking much more kindly and gentle now, as if they wanted to come in and comfort him.

"Don't you come in!" he shouted. "Out! Out with you!"

49

There was a small round mirror on the wall above the bed by the tatami. He often leaned in front of this mirror and studied himself. He developed erratically fluctuating emotions toward the face that looked back at him. He made faces at this face, by turns hilarious, weepy, or ferocious. He often spent the better part of an hour there, engrossed by his own reflection. Every day he would come for one of these clowning sessions.

In the mirror, that familiar face looked back at him: a pair of impassive brows, two light brown pupils, a large mole on the left side of the nose, and a smaller mole at the tip of a sharp chin. He tried on different faces. After fooling around for a little while, as happened every time, disgust for his own face slowly welled up inside him. Every time this farce of his turned into a real-life tragedy. He became self-conscious of the big flaps that were his ears. He pressed hard against them with his hands. His mouth was too small. He pulled at his lips, trying to stretch them out. But what he resented most was that pale, white color of his face. This, it seemed, was an immutable fact. And he despised the shape of his skull. He lifted up his ma's compact mirror to look at the back of his head; it revealed itself to be in the category of the long, flat type.

He was consumed by unmitigated hatred. He detested those great, big ear vanes that he got from Papa, that tiny mouth that came from Mama, that snow-white complexion that Papa gave him, and that brain shell of his that had been razed flat in the back by his mama's carelessness when he was a baby in letting him sleep too much on his back. He sank into the depths of depression as he continued to stare into the mirror.

50

He often requested story sessions with Father. His father would first meditate for a while, as if he were searching in his thoughts for a place to start. Then he would throw his head back, grin, part his lips, and close them again in silence, only to say in the most gentle manner, "Once upon a time. . . ." Then, half-embarrassed and half-teasing, he would say, "Can't think of anything after all."

51

Papa had been trying for a long time to find a way to persuade his company to let him take a business trip so he could make some extra money. Generally, it was possible to clear up to half a month's extra salary by going on one of these trips. But since the work he did had nothing to do with "business," there was no chance he would ever be sent on a business trip. Thus, even though he had put in his request five times in the last two months, nothing came of it. That he was finally picked for a trip was due to the special consideration his supervisor accorded him – the job was taken from someone else's section. He was very grateful for the assignment.

That day, both Papa and Mama got out of bed long before

it was time for him to go. Father had a special breakfast of minced meat fried noodles, and even before there was light in the sky he was ready to leave. Approaching the front door, tipsy with excitement, he remembered to turn round and say to him engagingly, "Pa's *going* now. See you *soon,* Sonny." Pa cast Mama a sideways glance as he left the house. Ma closed the door behind him.

No sooner had he turned away than there was a knocking at the back door. Papa had returned.

"Ch'iu-fang, don't forget to put out the fire in the stove before you go to bed at night."

"I know. You go ahead, or you'll miss the train," Ma answered him with a chuckle.

Papa said his goodbye one more time. "Heh, Sonny, Pa's going now. See you soon, okay?"

After Papa left, the morning dragged on. A long time passed before it was even seven o'clock. Every so often that morning, Mama would say, "Papa's been gone for two (or three) hours now. Another ten (or nine) and he'll be there. Pa said this morning that it's twelve hours from here to Taipei."

It was just him and Mama alone at lunch that day, looking at each other as they ate. It felt very strange. In the afternoon, Mama again said, "It's three o'clock already. Papa will be there in another two hours." He imagined Pa walking farther and farther away. He pictured Pa having a good time in the belly of the train at that very moment, eating. Pa had told him before he left that they served complimentary meals on these trips. It was now five o'clock in the evening. Ma announced excitedly, "Pa has arrived!" Mama was gazing straight ahead, as if watching his pa make his arrival.

That night they locked up early. Even though Papa would be away from home for only six days, he heard Mama crying that night. Even as he was falling off to sleep, that odd feeling was there: Papa's absence from the house . . .

It was still there the next day, that sensation of unfamiliarity; he felt it as soon as he woke up. Thereafter, every minute seemed to be ticking away, saying, "Papa's not here, Papa's not here." In point of fact, during these hours – except for Sundays – Pa was never here during the day anyway. Now, however, he felt Mama's shadow, vigilant, all day long, hovering around him!

He was indeed drawn close to his mama that day. He helped Ma sweep the floor, set the table, bring in the clothes. Mama told him that she had especially bought the fish he liked best, his favorite bream, "a feast for just us two, mother and son." But he had the distinct impression that their daily fare was scantier than usual.

In the following days, Papa sent them a letter with every Taipei post; Ma tore open the letters and, in a trembling voice, read them out loud to him. She seemed always to be on the verge of tears. Then she would immediately pick up a pencil, laboriously write out a letter in reply to Papa's, and send this in the self-addressed envelope that Papa had sent with his letter. In the six days Pa was away, she received a total of three letters. She saved every one of them, putting them away carefully, as if she had some vague fear that she would never ever see Papa again. During these few days, Mama would often proclaim, "Another (however many days) and Papa will be back!" In the evenings, if he had a warm feeling around the rim of his ear, Mama would say, "Pa must be thinking of you."

On the sixth day, Papa finally came home. He was much thinner, but he was beaming with delight, and his spirits were high. He appeared with a bunch of bright yellow bananas held high above his head, joyfully shouting, "Oh, my Sonny, look what Pa has brought you!" Then from his case he pulled out a pair of lady's silk panties and, flapping them in front of Mama, turned solicitously toward her, saying, "Look here, look here, what's this, Ch'iu-fang?" And Ma, she was so very happy. Then there was that notebook that Papa had used to record the proceedings at his meetings – that too was given to him. Mama also got two pencils. Then Ma saw a leather wallet inside the flap of Pa's leather case and wanted to know, "Who did you buy this for?"

"For Lao-erh," Papa said, for his second son.

Ma didn't say anything.

Nonetheless, the mood in the family was a joyous one.

"Poor Papa, everyone came out of this with something, everyone but you," Mama said.

"That's as it should be. So long as you all have something, I don't matter."

"And you slaving away all by yourself out there, Min-hsien, look how thin you've gotten. You've been having nothing but steamed buns every day, I'll bet?"

"No, no," Papa said, obviously lying.

Going away on this trip had netted them a tidy profit. Papa and Mama counted out the dollar bills next to the black leather case where they kept their money.

Then they switched to a topic he knew nothing about.

"Did you get to see Po Li?"

"Yes, I saw him," Papa said. "I met with him the first morning."

"What did he say?"

"He said there was no problem. 'Why, Min-hsien, of course, you've been with us for such a long time, of course, of course,' he said. And I said, 'I've had the benefit of the director's guidance from the start. I'd be more than happy to work under the director once more, to be of service to the director the best I can!' And he gave me his word he would help; he was very positive."

"Did he appear then to look favorably on you, would you say?"

"Very much so. He treated me with exceeding regard! The moment I stepped into his office, he came forward with hands extended to shake my hand and insisted that I sit down first, and then immediately ordered tea. He was *extremely good* to me. And later, when I was about to leave his office, he accompanied me all the way to the door. I literally had to beg him to stay behind before he turned around to go back."

Mama was *exceedingly* happy.

Just then there was a loud banging at the door. Papa went to open it. A letter had been slipped in under the door. Papa said, "Who can this letter be from?" He picked it up, and, lo and behold, it was a letter he himself had sent home!

G

FATHER

Papa, it has been half a month since you left. Please come home right away!

Your son,
Yeh

On the T'ainan highway bus. A newspaper spread wide across his lap. Rubbing his eyes, feeling his eyeballs move round and round under the lids. During the three days in T'aichung and the three days in Chiayi, Fan Yeh had been in touch with Mother via express mail, asking her if Father had returned; both times Mother's reply came back negative. He opened his eyes to look out the window and was greeted by a beautiful mountain scene!

Two whole hours after he got off the bus, he was still climbing that mountain. In Fan Yeh's search, this was shrine number ten. He had just wound his way through to the other side of a damp and densely wooded area, and emerged onto a patch of green in a valley. In the distance, high on a hill, he saw the cloister nestled among the trees.

Fan Yeh was greeted by a kind, mild-mannered, hoary old monk. He declared his purpose for coming and described the appearance and characteristics of the elderly man he was looking for. The old monk said, "Ah, yes, an old gentleman, not too tall . . . so you are his child."

"Yes," Fan Yeh said.

"Ah." The old monk closed his eyes and nodded his head a few times in silence. "A week ago there was an old gentleman fitting the description you give who left my humble door." After a short pause, he added, "I wonder if he was your old sire?"

"Did he leave anything behind?"

"I'm not sure that he has. We didn't notice anything when we swept out his room. Why don't you come with me and have a look? Perhaps there might be some small article he left."

He found himself following the old abbot to the rear of the building. They arrived at the room. The old monk threw open the doors and walked in. Fan Yeh saw before him nothing but vacant space surrounded by four blank walls; he was to come away empty-handed.

"How long ago was it you said he came here?"

"A month and a half ago."

"Then it couldn't have been him."

What was this other old man running from to come to this mountain retreat? He too must be hiding out, running away from his family.

The old monk spoke again. "Two days ago, a young man very much like yourself came here. He, too, was in search of his father. When I brought him here to this room to have a look, he also denied that it had been his father who was here. His reason was that the other's accent was different."

Fan Yeh proceeded to leave his address with the old monk with a request to please write and let him know if he took in some other guest who might look like his father.

"Try not to panic," the old monk said. "Why not have a little rest first?"

"No, thank you."

52

The train sped forward. They were finally moving to Taipei, where his father had procured a position. The whole family, including his *erh-ko,* was moving there.

They were in the sleeping compartment of the train. He climbed onto his mother's berth; it was the upper bunk. Father came to see that they got settled in, then left their compartment. He and Erh-ko had tickets for seats only.

All the lights were out. He was ushered into his dreams by the *humpety-humpety thrum-thrum-thrum* of the moving train. Each time he awoke he saw lights outside the window, lights and a whole lot of people milling about, and through the window came the singsong cries of hawkers selling their wares, before once again he was pulled back into sleep as the train moved away and station lights flitted past his sleepy eyes.

53

There was a serpentine river behind their house in Taipei. The water in the river was an ashen gray-green.

Their house stood in the shadow of a big building. The building was a three-storied, Japanese-style boardinghouse, open and desolate. Even though he was on the ground floor, he could hear the noise through the floorboards whenever the third floor was being swept.

Their family was allocated a rectangular-shaped apartment. Stepping inside for the first time, he felt as if he had entered the long corridor of a train compartment. There were two bedrooms with a wide corridor running in front of them and a row of glass sliding doors in front of the corridor. Behind the rooms was another corridor, much narrower, with two windows looking out onto two cassia trees.

A rock had been placed at the foot of the center pane of the sliding doors to form a step into the house. A cement trough filled with sand had been provided in case of fire; it stood at the far end of the front corridor, to the right, on the outside. Two flat-leaved Chinese fir trees stood tall in the front yard, and beneath them was a great slab of stone. Not far off were two ample azalea shrubs.

54

The river ran alongside a causeway. He came often to the embankment, turning right out of the alley in front of his house. At the west end of the causeway was a long bridge. Not far from this road was a sanatorium for tuberculosis patients. An awful, haunting silence filled the air. Half of this road, to the west, was leveled out in gray concrete, and the other side, to the east, had been left as a dirt road. When cars drove through, clouds of gray dust rose to fill the air. The betel palms by the roadside were all coated with a veil of gray dirt and dust.

Under the stinging rays of the feverish sun, the office workers who lived in these company quarters, decked out in straw hats and white, short-sleeved, open-necked shirts, waited by the telegraph pole for their bus.

Noontide on the river brought out millions of shimmering stars over its surface, sparkling like crosses. In the middle of the river stood a dredging boat – like a floating pavilion – with a smokestack pointing skyward and hoses on either side of its bulwarks, one with water coming out and the other pouring sand; it made a continuous popping noise. The riverbed was shallow and wide; numerous little islands broke the surface of the water, looking like schools of fish; by the riverbank were two deltas of bamboo, jutting out from the dike. Between the dike and the causeway was a large plot of farmland.

55

He was once again registered for school.

56

To keep thieves out at night, they nailed shut the windows in the back corridor. Piles of old publications, magazines, newspapers, and the like were stacked up at one end of this corridor; at the other end stood a big earthen barrel of rice. The slanting rays of the setting sun fell across this corridor.

He often played ping-pong on the wooden floor here. There was a ping-pong craze at school, but, unfortunately, when he came home, there was no one to play with. Even though Mama was no match for him, he forced her to play. They sat on the floor at opposite ends of the corridor, hitting the ball back and forth.

Every time he hit the ball to his mama she would miss it, or else she would hit it wildly and send it bouncing off the walls. All the while she'd be mumbling under her breath, "Mama's no good at this, you've got to take it easy with Mama . . ."

This invariably made his blood boil. Every time they played they ended up quitting in a huff.

Behind the rice barrel was a gloomy, dank, dead-end corner, full of spider webs. Ma had pasted an amulet here, and this was where she made her sacrifices to the gods. He dreaded this corner and kept away from it as much as he could. In fact, he had never dared look directly into it. Of all the corners of the house, this one aroused the worst fears in him.

57

An airplane tore across the sky, flying low; he dashed out of the house to peer up at it. He was now eight years old. He shielded his eyes with his hand so he could follow the trail of the aircraft. It was a double-winged trainer. He watched it form the figure *1* – which it then turned into an *H* – and followed it till it flew out of sight.

58

One day his *erh-ko* came rushing in to invite Mama and him and Papa to go out to the country and take pictures. When he heard this, he jumped up and down with excitement. "Ma! My brother wants to take our picture!" But Mama didn't look too happy; she merely said, "Why, what for? Why go to so much trouble?" He felt completely let down by his mama's lack of enthusiasm and her cool tone of voice. "Ma, oh, *do* go. *Do* go!" he pressed her.

His *erh-ko* was working at a tax-collection agency in the Twentieth District. He came home only on weekends now, and he didn't stay overnight on Sundays. When he came home, he stayed in the bedroom that faced east. There was a bamboo couch, which was where he slept on these occasions; bedclothes were spread over it for his use. On this particular day, his brother had borrowed a camera from a friend at the tax office and came in high spirits to get them to go take pictures.

Mama eventually agreed to go, and went into her room to change. After Ma changed, Papa also went to change. His brother told him he didn't have to change; his school uniform was good enough.

It was nine or ten o'clock on a sunny, mild spring Sunday morning – shirtsleeve weather. In front of the house the azaleas had reached full bloom. On the grounds outside wild ducks were quacking away, making a great commotion.

Camera in hand, his brother was giving directions. He told everyone to come out in front of the house and had them turn to face right, toward the sun. Pa and Ma were placed on either side of him; he stood in the middle.

His brother moved sideways, took a few steps backward, stooped down; from behind the camera held up against his face came his voice, giving a string of instructions: "Everyone smile! Don't anyone move."

He didn't dare move a muscle – a smile froze at the corners of his mouth. . . . Still no picture. It felt like forever – the sun stung his eyes, making him see stars; even the smile on his face was going funny.

Erh-ko lowered the camera, adjusting the lens once more, twisting it back and forth, and called out, "Don't move – stay where you are!"

"Hey, Lao-erh, give us the okay before you take the picture, eh?" his papa said. He didn't dare look – though he knew that Papa had moved only his lips and nothing else.

The camera moved back up to his brother's face. "Papa, turn a little more to the right!"

Dead silence.

"Sonny, don't stick your chest out like that! Relax a little."

"Almost ready."

Ke-lick! He let the camera hang down in front of him. "All done."

Papa let out a sigh of relief. Mama was smiling still. Sonny jumped about and started running round and round.

"I think I blinked," his mama said.

"Let's take another one. This time stand in front of the azaleas," Erh-ko said, as he turned to face the other way.

"Sonny. Come, let's change around a bit. This time Sonny will stand in front of me," Mama declared.

"Stand in front of Mama! Stand in front of Mama!" Sonny sang. His happiness was beyond description.

"Right, Sonny, stand in front of Auntie. No, squat down;

squat in front of Auntie. Papa, stand beside her. Now everybody lean to the right a little; let some flowers show through," Erh-ko said.

He moved back and squatted down as he was told. Again, that sharp pain in his eyes. The sun. The waiting. . . ! Nose itching. . . ! Ke-lick!

"Ah," Papa said.

"Another one. Stay there. Just change positions," Erh-ko told them.

"How about me and Sonny going over there by the fir tree, and you take one of us sitting on that slab of stone?" Mama asked.

"No good, you'll have your backs to the sun over there," his brother said. "Let's stand over here and include everyone."

Mama didn't say anything.

"Let's take one over on the other side of the azaleas," his brother said, showing them where they should stand.

They did as they were told. Sonny stood in the middle again. He reached up and took his mama's hand.

His *erh-ko* moved backward and squatted down again.

"Okay, I'm ready."

Again, the wait.

"Auntie, give a smile."

Ke-lick!

"Right," Erh-ko said, bubbling over with a rookie photographer's enthusiasm, waiting to show off his skill at every opportunity. "There's a lot of film left. Let's take a few more here. When we've had enough of this place, we can head for the embankment and take some more."

"Oh, to the embankment," Sonny said. "Mama, let's go."

"No, I don't think so. You'd better save some for your own use," Mama said.

Sonny looked up at Mama, not yet ready to relinquish hope.

"No, there's a lot of film left. Let's take some more, it doesn't matter," Erh-ko said.

"No, no, don't waste it on us. It's too much trouble for you," Mama said.

"No trouble at all!" Erh-ko called back.

"I have to go get lunch ready," Ma said.

Dead silence.

Erh-ko gave Mama a blank stare.

"We'll take some more next time, Lao-erh. Next time we'll all take some together," Papa said.

"Fine, all right, next time." Erh-ko closed the camera case with a snap.

"Lao-erh, I'll buy another roll of film next Sunday and get you to take some more for us," Papa said.

"Don't go buying any more film," Erh-ko said. "Next week's no good. This is someone else's camera; I'll have to give it back tomorrow."

"Okay, then we'll wait till you can borrow it another time," Papa said.

"Another time's another time," he replied.

"You will have lunch with us today, won't you?"

"No, I'll eat at the dorm."

59

On a beam in the passageway were markings of his height. Every other week he made his papa measure him with a ruler placed flat on his head and then mark the place. Recently, he had remeasured himself. It had been three months since they made the first marking; he had grown by four centimeters, all told.

60

In the bedroom where he slept with his parents was a closet. One day he looked into this closet and thought to himself how comfortable it would be to sleep inside. There was a plank across the middle, just like a bunk bed, and when the paper door was pulled to, it was just like a room with an area the size of a bed – still and peaceful, dim and dark. That night he took the clothes down off this shelf and moved them to the bottom tier, then carried his own bedding into the closet. He didn't sleep under the mosquito tent with his papa and mama that night. He lay down and fitted his body snugly inside the closet. It was just the right length, just the right width, as if it had been made to order. He slid the paper door across and shut himself in. All cozy and relaxed, he soon fell asleep.

It wasn't until his ma warned him that rats might scurry about in there while he slept that he returned to his parents' mosquito tent.

61

In the interval between getting out of bed and waking up completely, he liked to sit, resting his chest against the back of a straight back chair, in the front corridor. With his eyes half closed, gazing out through the glass doors before him, for several minutes he would lose himself in a stupor, lingering until he heard his papa call to him – "Hey you, off in the clouds again?" – which would finally bring him round and wake him up.

62

A row of bottles stood at attention, some tall, some short. There were green bottles, dark cocoa-colored ones, and brownish yellow ones. They were bottles of oil, some half full, some less than half, and some that measured two-thirds of the way up. Some of them had thick black sauces in them. Sunlight penetrated the smoke-covered, sooty window, infiltrating the greasy bottles. These bottles were in the kitchen. The kitchen was on the bottom floor of the big building; to get to the kitchen from their family's quarters they had to make their way under the eaves. This kitchen was shared by their family, the maid who cooked for the workers on the meal plan, and two other families.

63

On summer afternoons, when the torrential rains that came with the frequent tropical storms had exhausted themselves, a clear, cool stillness soaked the air. Indoors, his mama tidied up, unhurriedly picking up clothes and other things left scattered about.

On these evenings, feathery smoke rose up in waves from the "Moonlight" brand incense set out to ward off mosquitoes.

In the middle of the night, unseen swarms of insects made shimmery, quivering sounds, echoing in his ears.

64

Beyond the east window of the bedroom on the east side stood a spreading banyan tree. In the autumn, countless sheaths of gosling-yellow leaves intermingled in its foliage like the beginnings of white roots entangled among the dark in a middle-aged person's hair. When the wind scraped across the landscape, the yellow leaves fell; like a lute unstrung they fell, strand upon strand, sinking to the ground.

65

During winter nights, after all the windows and doors were tightly closed, warmth filled the house until everything looked flushed and toasty. At these times, he longed for snow to fall. On waking into the clear, cold morning after a severely harsh winter night, he would look out the glass sliding doors, hoping to see a pure white world, but all he saw was the same world of shadowy greenery.

66

At the beginning of spring, the first green shoots of the banyan tree appeared here and there on the tips of its branches, silky green like the baby seeds of broad beans. At the end of spring, the tree was dressed in a full cloak of green leaves, each looking like a piece of emerald jade, like jewels on the fingers of ladies.

The azaleas in the compound, ablaze with blossoms, stung the air with their sharp, spicy scent.

67

He was the recipient of two theater tickets.

They were given to him by one of Papa's office mates who had come for a visit. "Ask your pa to take you," he had said on his way out.

Never had he ever been so happy in his life; on the tickets were printed the names of two famous actors whose pictures he had often seen in the newspapers. "Co-starring Hsia Pei-li and Ch'u Cheng-wei," he read. The thought of seeing these two people in the flesh made his very pores tingle with excitement. It was like being granted an audience with the president of the United States of America. On the ticket was also printed the name of the show: "Yueh Fei." "In celebration of the March Twenty-ninth Youth Festival, the Associated Members of the China Theater Company will present a Five-Act, Seven-Scene Epic Drama, capturing the luxurious grandeur of the Imperial Court." As his eyes passed over the word *luxurious,* they lit up with the sparkle of glittering lights.

Even so, his father refused to take him. It would be very late by the time they got home, he said, and then they'd still have to worry about having a bath and what not. It would be midnight before they could even think of going to bed, and then he'd have to get up early for work in the morning, he said. It would be entirely too much trouble and too exhausting to go to a play that's not even any good. That was what he said – which of course upset him no end.

He then tried to get Mama to take him, but *she* said she didn't know the way, and started off, "What amusement have I ever had? Wouldn't *I* have liked to go to the theater? It's just too bad no one's ever offered to take me. I still remember that one time we went, when we were still in Fuchou, to that play at your big brother's school. What fun that was! Real people moving about on the stage; even more fun than going to the movies! But then that was the only time I've ever been. Now I'm stuck at home every day. Cook and wash, cook and wash. I'm just an *old maidservant, no fun and games* for me. I'm just a deaf and dumb idiot taking up space. Ridiculous really. Who'd believe it, almost three years we've lived here in Taipei, and I don't even know how to ride the bus on my own. From the beginning you had no intention of ever teaching me how to take the bus! . . . The sum total of the matter is, I may be here in Taipei, but I might as well be living out in the boondocks!"

Mama fumed in resentment and rage. Papa remained passive; his face showed no expression, and he made no reply. He, on the other hand, was moping and making whiny noises in his corner.

"Let's do this," Papa finally said. "Let's ask if Erh-ko will go with you, okay?" Mama's eyes widened perceptibly, but she didn't say anything.

"Okay," he replied; this was going to be a *new experience.* Mama left the room then.

"But we really can't be sure if your *erh-ko* will agree to go," Papa said. "We'll have to wait till he comes home and ask him."

Thus began his vigil of waiting for his *erh-ko*'s arrival. He should be coming a little before seven o'clock, which meant they could just about make it on time. He waited for his brother with bated breath.

Finally, Erh-ko came! He could hear him getting off his bike and parking it. He was a little earlier than usual today. Fan Yeh could hardly contain himself as he watched his brother come into the house. He kept his eyes glued on him, even though he was careful to keep his mouth shut. The moment Erh-ko entered his own room he nagged at his papa to go speak to him. But Papa seemed to have already forgotten his promise. All he had to say was, "Wait a bit. Let's wait till your *erh-ko* has had a chance to rest. We'll talk later." Once again, his hopes were dashed; teardrops were ready to fall from his eyes.

Papa approached Erh-ko. "Uh, Lao-erh, would you by any chance have some time to spare this evening?"

"What's the matter?" Erh-ko grunted.

"If you don't have any plans, would you like to take your little brother to see a play?"

"See a play?" he exclaimed, obviously unenthused.

"Somebody gave us two tickets."

Erh-ko took the tickets handed to him.

"It's got Hsia Pei-li and Ch'u Cheng-wei in it," Sonny interjected.

His *erh-ko*'s expression softened as he glanced at the tickets. "Better go soon if we're going. Won't make it if we don't hurry," he said.

"Yes, sir!" Sonny said with unreserved happiness. "I'll go tell Mama to get dinner. Mama!"

The brothers emerged together, his *erh-ko* wheeling the bike with Sonny sitting sideways on the crossbar. Erh-ko looked up at the sky and said, "Looks like rain," and sent Sonny back into the house to fetch raincoats. He dashed in and back out. The two of them headed out into the evening.

The streetlights shone on the pair of them, projecting their elongated silhouettes onto the pavement: one big, one small, one back arched over the other. They rode on in silence. The little brother was filled with respect for his big brother. He was taking him to the play after all (that conferred a kind of honor on him as his little brother, he felt).

He wasn't a bad brother, after all. He couldn't understand why Mama disliked this brother so much. She had beckoned him into the kitchen before they left and said to him, "Oh, Sonny, my son. Listen to me. If, later, your *erh-ko* suggests that you go somewhere else with him, don't go, no matter what. You understand?" He said, "Um, why not?" Mama looked momentarily embarrassed, recovered quickly, and said, "Nothing really. Just in case. . . . You and him, you didn't come from the same belly, you know. I'm just afraid he might take advantage of you." But as he raised his face now to peek at his *erh-ko* he couldn't believe his big brother would harm him. He had complete faith in his big brother.

They arrived at the Town Hall. His brother deposited the bike and took him by the hand, hurrying on in long strides. He tried to keep up as best he could; this was the first time ever he had let Erh-ko take his hand.

They showed their tickets at the door, and his brother was handed a program as they entered. His brother led him up the stairs, into the dark, and then up another flight of steps. A huge auditorium, endless space, emerged in front of them. What an enormous place! He had been to the assembly hall at Papa's office to see a movie once before, but this was the first time in his life that he had ever seen anything the size of this arena. If you wanted to look at the ceiling, you had to strain your neck and tilt your head back as far as it would go. As he was thinking this, a peculiar odor entered his nostrils; it was almost tasty, a sort of spoiled-sweet smell that his nose found rather pleasant. Erh-ko walked on ahead toward the rear. He followed, feeling all those faces of the people veiled in the semidarkness watching the two of them. They turned and entered a narrow aisle between the tiers and continued on down. Erh-ko kept going as he checked out the seat numbers on the backs of the seats, until he reached an aisle seat in the second to the last row. They finally settled down here.

Now he had a chance to take another look around. The houselights were dimmed, all the seats in the audience were taken, and everywhere he looked, he saw the rustling of white program sheets. On the walls on either side of the stage round clocks were hung; both had their hands pointing expectantly at four minutes to eight. At the center was the great expanse of the stage curtain, gleaming an orangy gold, and on its folds were hung sheets of paper with the following words: "Presentation by the Associated Members of the China Theater Company in Celebration of the Tenth Youth Festival." Erh-ko was reading the program. He sidled over and, from the corner of his eye, caught a glimpse of Hsia Pei-li's smiling face in the program.

A loud buzzing rang through the hall; it was the electric bell announcing the raising of the curtain.

"The show's about to begin; it's show time!" he shouted.

"Shush; don't shout, Sonny."

He squelched his enthusiasm, staring hard at the stage. But the curtain refused to go up. After another two minutes, the electric bell was sounded again.

This time it's got to begin! Yes, the lights were really fading out. Only a row of little lights at the front of the stage was left on. The curtain was gradually rising . . . revealing yet another set of curtains. Then the little lights, too, were killed. The curtain was split down the middle, and, as it slowly parted, a glittering, lustrous, glorious world came into view. A revelation, a world of magnificent and multitudinous colors! Gold dragons and red columns. Behind it, the glassy blue of the night sky and the hook of the crescent moon. On the stage floor, to the left, was placed a palace censer, and on the right was hung a pearly, sea-green blind; this was an efflorescent manifestation of "the world of dreams."

"Hooray!"

"Stop it; stop shouting! Hush!"

He stood up.

"Sit, sit down," Erh-ko ordered. "What's there to be so excited about now?" Erh-ko exclaimed, laughing.

Onto the empty stage stepped a figure, dressed in dazzling regalia. A warrior. He had never ever seen anyone so splendid, so bold. Two more actors followed, dressed in classical costumes of blue brocade, with yellow robes and red sashes tied around their waists. Behind them came a bevy of maidens in long gowns with flowing sleeves. What a fantastic sight! The actors began to speak; the performance had begun.

"Has the general arrived?" "Yes, Your Majesty, the general is on his way."

The actors strutted about the stage ceremoniously, their wooden clogs resounding on the floorboards like a percussion accompaniment to their ceremonial dance. Their eyes, catching the glitter of the stage lights, sparkled like the eyes of little animals peering out of the dark. Presently, the male lead, Ch'u Cheng-wei, arrived. He was dressed in full battle gear, a rich purple costume complete with headpiece and mail. Of all the actors on the stage he was the most awesome. And, as he unsheathed his sword. . . . Ah, what a flash of light! Next came the leading lady, Hsia Pei-li. She had the classical "goose-egg" face, all made up in rouge and powder; she was an extremely beautiful woman. When she spoke, her translucent voice rang out like bells of light. He was startled and transfixed by her beauty.

"Madam, we were just telling General Yueh that we wish to confer on him the title of supreme commander of the northern front. He will expel those barbaric thieves from this great land of Sung."

"Thank you, Your Majesty."

"The general will have to take his post first thing in the morning."

"General!"

"Honorable Consort," Ch'u Cheng-wei said after a moment's pause, "I shall have to take my leave immediately, but I am called to arms in defense of our great Sung fatherland. I am ready for my destiny, my duty from heaven, and I am deeply grateful for this highest honor. In this time of our country's need, China's youth must by rights repay their country's benevolence with loyalty and valor. That I have been granted this fulfillment of my deepest desire to serve my country is indeed my ultimate joy."

"General."

"Honorable Consort," he said, "you should be happy for me. Please do not grieve. Stay home and look after my parents and our children so that my heart will be at ease and that I may slay a greater number of Jurchen bandits to repay king and country for the benevolence showered on us."

"My dear General, take care of yourself."

By this time he was enthralled: he had fallen in love with the leading lady. He thrilled to every flutter of her eyelashes, every lilt of her silvery voice, the way she moved her hands, every step she took. His eyes pursued her every movement and rested where she stopped.

During the whole of the second act his leading lady did not appear. He looked for her and waited and waited for a long time. But she didn't come. Finally, at the very end, she came out. She had changed into a plainer costume suggesting everyday attire, which gave her yet another air, a gentler, simpler grace, entirely different from the court dress she had worn in the first act. Yet it was no less impressive. Now she and her male lead gave a most tender and moving performance of a lovers' scene. She laid her head on his shoulder, and the two of them murmured to each other under the crescent moon. This was the best scene of all; Sonny nearly swooned with desire.

Before the final curtain came the climax of the tragedy —

she was left all alone on the stage, sobbing, her tiny shoulders heaving. Words could not express how this pained his heart. At that moment he felt he was transformed into an adult. He wanted to climb onto the stage and say to her, "Don't you cry, aw, please don't cry." His own eyes were welling up with tears. He leaned forward, resting his chin in his hands; he had entered entirely into the world on the stage.

Next to him, his *erh-ko* stirred, shifting his weight about in his seat. Erh-ko's attention, too, was totally fixed on the leading lady, who was now the only figure on the stage. Erh-ko craned his neck, keeping his eyes on her until she disappeared behind the curtains; then he let his head drop onto his chest, staring fixedly at some spot before him. The stuffy air in the auditorium left him with flushed cheeks and a dry, tight feeling in his throat.

After the final curtain, he trailed out after his brother, feeling wistful, as if he had lost something or had left something behind. She was all he could think about; he was hankering after her, sighing for her, all the way out of the auditorium. Erh-ko, too, was in a bad humor. "Hurry it up, will you!" he yelled at him. Just as before, his *erh-ko* led him by the hand; the difference was that this time his brother's hand was hard and stiff.

As they stepped down off the last flight of stairs, he asked him, "Erh-ko, that leading lady, Hsia Pei-li, is she that leading man's, Ch'u Cheng-wei's, wife?"

"How's that?" Erh-ko sounded puzzled and surprised. Then it dawned on him what Sonny was after. "Kids have no business asking such questions!" he snapped, staring straight ahead.

Like a tidal wave, the crowd behind them pressed forward, breaking their grip on each other's hand. He heard his *erh-ko* call out in a loud voice from far away, "Wait at the front door. Wait for me at the front door!"

After that he lost him. He arrived at the front door before his big brother. Then together they went to pick up the bike. Erh-ko walked on in front of him. When they got to the parking lot, his brother said, "You wait here; I'll be right out." Not long afterward Erh-ko came out with the bike. "Get on!" he ordered. Sonny climbed onto the crossbar, and they left without another word to each other.

They wound back past the front of the theater and rode into a quiet street behind it. Suddenly Sonny cried out, "Erh-ko, we forgot our raincoats!"

"Oh. Left them under the seats," Erh-ko said. "Why didn't you say so sooner?"

"I forgot, too," he replied. Erh-ko cursed. They had to go back again. Erh-ko went in to retrieve the raincoats while he waited outside.

Again they rode around and reentered that quiet street. This time they saw a small crowd of people gathered round a brightly lit noodle stand. Erh-ko's curiosity was aroused, and he steered over to have a look. The brothers saw that the crowd had gathered to watch those same actors in the play they had just seen. Traces of stage makeup could still be seen on some of their faces around the brows and cheeks. His *erh-ko* parked the bike in a hurry and joined the circle of onlookers. He, too, squeezed in. He saw that these actors had on rather shabby clothes; the men were wearing old jackets on top of khaki pants, and the women were wearing old sweaters. He searched among them for Hsia Pei-li. He almost missed her. She was wearing an old black sweater. Her face appeared a scummy yellow, making her look much older than before. Then he heard her say:

"My stomach's killing me. This stomach acts up whenever the belly goes empty. Hey, big boss, give us some more of that beef! And don't stint on the MSG!"

Just then a gust of wind swept past, and she let out a

thunderous sneeze. Wiping her nose with the back of her hand, she flung the snot onto the ground.

A man in a blue cotton jacket entered the picture. On closer inspection, he turned out to be Ch'u Cheng-wei. He heard him say to the others, "That son of a bitch. What a waste of time putting in those extra hours. That skinflint won't pay us a cent over fifty dollars. And he won't even give that till tomorrow!"

The whole cast was in an uproar. Hsia Pei-li's shrill voice was heard above the din, shouting, "Fuck his goddamn forefathers and their fucking sons! I'll give him a good thrashing, that pig of a fat Chu and his chicken prick! That lousy asshole with his slimy, sugary eyes thinks he can fool us with his sweet words and honeyed phrases and then turn around and stab us in the back. Well, I'll go have it out with him if it kills me!"

"Okay, okay, old mother hen, the noodles are here. Have some before you go killing anyone!" one of the actors said.

"Right you are. I'll have my noodles first, and then I'll go settle accounts with him!"

He and his brother left after that remark. Right then and there his love for her vanished. It was as if the play had never been and his feelings for her had never been. He felt as if a great load had been lifted from his shoulders; he was traveling light on the journey home.

His *erh-ko*'s composure too had somehow returned, and he seemed much more peaceful and relaxed. He could hear it in the way he spoke: "Sit a little more to the front; don't sit so far back." Nevertheless, this was not the tone of voice he had used inside the theater either. It was more like the way it was before they went to see the play.

"It's raining." Two drops of rain fell on his face.

Erh-ko didn't say anything.

"Should we put on our raincoats, huh, Erh-ko?"

"No need."

"It's going to pour," he said.

"We're almost there!"

Erh-ko pedaled faster. The shadow of their two elongated figures slashed across the middle of the street.

68

A sea of green radiance, the rice fields moved in waves like the backs of a flock of sheep as the wind swept past. Up close, they looked more like the concentric circles of a maelstrom. The wind brought with it surge upon surge of a reverberating *humch-dum, humch-dum.* A tiny speck appeared in the distance, lengthening out into so many sections of a black-colored folding rule, being pulled huffing and puffing along, rousing the air in its wake. The train was made up of several compartments, each completely boxed up, except for the last unit, where at the tail end was an open platform on which a man stood. The train puffed away and gradually vanished into the forest. In the vacant sky, like a cloud of dust, a fit of black smoke was left behind.

The sparkling river lay by the side of the railroad.

69

With the advent of rain came the plaintive cries of wood pigeons, surge upon surge, whirling round in concentric echoes.

70

The first thing he did on coming home after school was to go to the rear hallway and check the wicker basket hung high up on the wall to see what was there. The basket had come with some litchis his mama had once bought. After the litchis had been eaten Mama had saved the container and used it as a fruit basket. Every day, on coming home in the afternoon, he would always find in this wicker basket a couple of bananas or an orange.

7 I

He stood at the open door blowing soap bubbles. He had removed the cap from his writing brush for this purpose, and now, dipping it a couple of times in the soapy water, his face bent forward, he carefully blew into the cap. The soap film bubbled up and took the shape of a goose egg, clinging to the tip of the brush cap, protruding like a nipple. He was going to make this a big one, to transform its shape and size – to make it as big as a balloon. He was transfixed and tremulous. He watched the curve of the bubble's surface. It was adorned with the rainbow colors of gasoline films. He peered into its interior and wished he could go and live inside it – that would be the most beautiful wonderland ever, not unlike the place he had seen when, a few days ago, he had climbed onto the dining table on which Mama was doing her ironing and looked inside the yet unlit little bluish bulb on the iron and imagined how he would live inside the blue dawn of the glass casing of this bulb. His timorous fear was mixed with exhilaration – he didn't dare stop blowing, but he knew that whether he stopped or not the bubble would sooner or later explode. All of a sudden, it blew up and evaporated into thin air.

He tried again and again to produce another one as big as that one, but to no avail; that one time was his only success.

He gazed far into the distance, recalling that beautiful round shape. He was filled with regret and despair for not being able to reproduce another one like it. Then, as he lifted his head absentmindedly – wonder of wonders – the sky was full of lovely, brightly colored balls. These were the small bubbles that had not burst.

Thus spurred on, he blew nonstop. Within the hour he had blown upwards of hundreds, maybe thousands, of bubbles; like flying catkins in the spring they were everywhere.

Tired out, he finally slowed down. He put the brush cap into the cup. He was completely exhausted and felt that sapless feeling of the letdown. There was a soapy taste on the insides of his lips.

72

At home, his favorite dishes were chopped scallion and eggs shallow-fried with bull oysters, pan-fried bean sprouts with beef strips, and salted eel slices in red vinegar. He didn't like tomatoes cooked with greens, pan-fried pickled cabbage, fried eggs, or steamed shark's liver.

73

It was finally subsiding. After over two weeks of unremitting rain, the downpour just now showed signs of having spent itself. The muddy ground appeared a brownish orange. Excess rainwater oozed from the tips of boughs of the blackened trees. The bamboo thicket turned a wine red color in the rain's aftermath.

74

The air was filled with a balmy, sweet scent, like that from the soft, ripe core of an apple. On the horizon was spread a dizzying array of stars, glowing in the dim light, much like the glow of the streetlamps along the misty road. By contrast, the lamplight over the bridge was clearly discernible, and its shaft of light was like a golden drill speared into the water. On the embankment you could hear, coming from the far reaches of the other side where the fields had been flooded by the spring rains, a chorus of frogs, roused by the rain.

He ran along the puddly strip of land between the plots where the mud showed up white and made his way through an almost impassable stretch of wasteland overgrown with tangled weeds. Then he crossed a small wooden bridge; under the bridge, the little brook gurgled as it flowed toward the river.

Crossing over the bridge, he walked through a bamboo thicket and saw coming toward him an acquaintance of Mama's from the neighborhood who was just returning with an armful of wild greens to feed her ducks; she said hello to him. Further along he ran into some fishermen on their way to make the night's catch. They were carrying flashlights and fishing rods and had creels strapped around their waists. Coming out of the woods, he caught sight of someone taking a shit in the vegetable plots. He then passed by a farmhouse. He could see all the way inside it through the lamplit square windows.

By now the countryside was completely deserted, not a soul in sight. He continued on until he arrived at a stretch of murky swampland, brimming with spring rain. All around him he could hear the bright, piercing sounds of the chorus of frogs, springing up from all directions in rhapsodic reverberations high and low, yet each with its own distinct timbre. But you couldn't tell where these frogs were. You couldn't see them. This medley of frog voices was earth's own great choir. As he looked up at the shimmering, starlit sky, their singing voices seemed to him to be as distinct and as numerous as the silver stars above.

He forged on, taking a byway into the fields that opened out into an even more forsaken and chilly place. He had left the lamplit farmhouse far behind; he had left his own home even farther behind. He looked around but could see neither lamplight nor the long bridge; he was surrounded by ink-black darkness. A breeze crept by, sending a shiver down his back. Soon after he heard a fit of dry coughing, like the raspy cough of an old person, coming from the fields. Fear gripped him. What was that noise? Was it the loud cry of some kind of big toad? Or was it the retching call of the egret? Or was it the wailing of a field snake? But no, it didn't sound like any of these. What if it was the noise of some nameless thing? No . . . it was probably a person, or maybe he had merely imagined he heard the noise. He cocked his ear to listen. Nothing. Not again. Only the breath of the night wind, flitting past. In that instant, terror rose up in him. He turned and ran like the wind.

75

The milky mist of dawn cast a blurry haze over the whole courtyard. It was 6 A.M., early morning. Papa had been up for quite a while already and had flung open all the doors and windows to let the brisk, clean air into the rooms. Just then a deep scent, the rich odor of manure, passed under his nose. It wasn't a nasty smell. On the contrary, it had a kind of hypnotic effect that was comforting. Papa immediately ordered them to shut all the doors and windows to keep out the stink of the night soil. But, even after everything had been closed, the smell seeped into the rooms, and the house was infused with a faint stench. Outdoors a coolie hurried by, bearing his heavy load across his shoulders with a carrying pole.

76

From the window in the rear hallway you could see the embankment on the other side. The Number 12 bus passed by here, and right outside this window was the bus stop. This was a dirt road with few pedestrians. There were two straight, skinny betel nut trees, gray with dust, standing next to the bus stop. Every time the bus passed by, the shrill voice of the lady bus driver could be heard issuing a string of instructions, followed by a blast of dust as the bus drove away.

77

Outside the house, the sun was at its most ferocious. He came indoors to escape the blaze.

"Sonny," his papa said, "go gargle with some cold water from the flask. You've swallowed a great deal of the sun's heat. Get rid of it so you won't have heatstroke."

He stepped outside and spat the cool water onto the ground in front of the house.

78

He suddenly developed an interest in old-style verse. He memorized many poems at one go. He selected the ones he liked best and copied them out onto a clean sheet of white paper. The greatest pleasure these poems gave him was that of resonance and rhyme. Of course he was also delighted by the worlds of pictures they evoked, but these too were brought about by the painting in sounds. The delight he found in these old poems was much like the fondness he had for the military bands not so long ago.

The poem he loved most passionately among these was

Moon sinks, crows cry, and frost fills the sky.
River maples, a fisher lamp: sleep comes in fits and starts.
Far from Gu Su's city wall, Cold Mountain Shrine
Tolls out the midnight hour, reaching my borrowed raft.

Another one he really liked was

Red beans thrive in the Southlands.
Spring delivers a few new sprigs.
Pick and gather your blossoms now,
Of gifts, this is the most nostalgic.

He couldn't really understand some of these poems, but he still found them extremely beautiful, like the lines

Clouds dream up her dresses, flowers dream her face,
Spring wind wraps the balustrade, dewdrops embrace.

Some lines were particularly captivating in their musical composition; from dawn to dusk they ran around the portals of his brain, like

The same bright moon of Ch'in, the mountain gates of
    Han:
Ten thousand miles, the long march, no one has yet come
    home.

Another favorite was

Dappled steed so fine,
Sable coat of mine,
Take these to market, my son, and buy the best wine you
    can find.

He liked especially the last line: "Take these to market, my son, and buy the best wine you can find."

There were also those most perplexing poems in which he could not find a single strand of meaning to latch onto, such as

The phoenix tail on her thin silk gown
breathes perfume through the many layers;
emerald waves crown the carriage canopy,
embroidered into the thick night sky:
the half moon hides her half-opened fan,
cannot hide her blush of shame;
like a thundercloud it came and went,
not a word uttered between us.

79

He walked down the meadowy bank, the air misty and the ground moist with dawn dew, and halted among the tall spears of the goat's-teeth brackens. With their long stalks and crescent fronds, they looked like ancient halperns. From here he commanded the vista of the grassland. Dawn mist took on the appearance of spiky white fuzz, oozing from the ground, hovering over the green blades. In the last month or so he had begun to appreciate a great many scenic marvels: the fold upon fold of hillocks receding into the remote horizon, like the famous peaks of China found in classical paintings; the aura of twilight as the flares of the setting sun fanned across the sky; late at night the somber darkness of the shrouded sky suddenly came alive with numberless starry constellations. They thrilled him with immense excitement. He strode forward, taking the path to the right, and saw a shrub with a folded leaf holding four or five crystalline pearls of water inside it. Not far from that spot was a flowering plantain; it had brought forth a dazzling bloom that looked like a bright yellow handkerchief draped on its branches. Soon after this discovery, he happened upon the most graceful and lonesome little river and ventured onto a stepping-stone to bow down and take a closer look at it. He had expected to feel sorrow and heartbreak at the sight of it, but instead the quiet stream lent him a fresh, clean, tranquil sensation. Far off, to the right, was a bridge. In the daytime, this bridge was like a huge abacus on which black counting beads slid back and forth, back and forth in fast motion. There was no traffic on it now. Everyone was elsewhere, fast asleep.

Abruptly, the yellow sun peered out and rose from behind the mountain's shoulder; a wild profusion of golden radiance poured over the earth its sheen of gold. The arched canopy of the eastern sky was crowned with a rainbow. What a fantastic touch! Everything was gilded – gold shore, gold islands, gold trees, even gold water. "Awe . . . woo. . . ." From somewhere came a voice calling, no telling whether from the earth or from the water. He listened hard for it to come again, but it didn't. At that moment a flock of white birds flapped their wings and flew into the open space above. At the same time a rowboat slipped into the scene. On the boat was a boatman, plying the oar – the whole boat was a glittering gold; the man on board also shone gold. This golden boat and the golden man swayed up the river, and the arched crown of the sky shone in golden glory.

80

Deep autumn and the season of incessant rains arrived. They were now in the middle of the drizzly phase of the rains. He saw several schoolgirls all dressed up in blue frocks and round, white hats. They were taking a shortcut home via the embankment behind his house. One of them craned her neck to look down the slope; the other girls looked on to see what she would do. The one in front took a couple of steps forward; the others followed close behind. The one in front plopped down and slid down the side, and, one after the other, they all slid down behind her.

81

"Don't you go outside. I'll be coming home as soon as I get the groceries. And keep an eye on the doors." That was what his mama said on leaving the house. When it got quiet, a lot of meaningless things and phrases popped into his head. Mama made sure the closet was closed up tight. This was her habit – she did this every time she left the house. When Mama went out grocery shopping, she locked up behind her since usually there was no one home. Today, however, he was home because of the fall break school picnic; his teacher had taken everyone on a hiking trip to Wulai, but he wasn't allowed to go. Mama said she was scared he might fall off a cliff and kill himself. Since this morning she had been after him to do his calligraphy; he was to practice his small-character script. Even now his copybook was opened up and left on the desk in the other room; the inkwell was still wet, and he had copied out only a few columns of characters, but he didn't want to write any more. In any case, tomorrow was Sunday, and he could finish it then. The assignment wasn't due till Monday. Still, maybe he should really be doing that rather than coming out here to stare at these boring photos hanging on the wall.

He didn't go back to his desk, though. He gazed at himself as a little boy in an old photo that was turning quite yellow. Then he stooped down to look into the mirror. He saw his own face in the mirror, and he also saw the light shining brightly through the white paper door and a bit of the front hallway as well. He grew suddenly apprehensive. What if some stranger's face were to appear from behind the white paper door. A chill crept up his back. He then remembered that the front door was unlocked, and that the window in the next room was flung wide open, and that the shutters in the rear hallway too were left open. He was vulnerable to attack from all four corners of the house.

Feeling thus threatened, he went to the glass sliding door in the front and pulled it shut. Having done that, he went into the next room and closed the window there and to the rear hallway and pulled that window to as well. Even then he did not feel safe, so he went to fasten the latch on the door and also the ones on the windows. He was reminded of the rumors he had recently heard about how some of the houses in the neighborhood had been broken into in broad daylight and of the story in the papers about how one family was robbed, also in broad daylight! Hooligans simply knocked down the front door and forced their way in. What if they did the same to his house and simply came in and snatched him away? He stacked some chairs one on top of another against the back of the door; this was going to be his first line of defense. And, if the hooligans were to break down the door, he could use these chairs to fend them off, for a while at least. Having more or less satisfied himself with this area of fortification in the event of an enemy attack, he turned his attention to the windows in the next room and in the rear hallway. He made a barricade behind each window by first buttressing it with a wooden stool, then heaping biscuit tins and fruit baskets on top, which were in turn held up by a bamboo rod that was shoved up at an angle against them.

In the solemn stillness of this state of siege, the ticking of the clock sounded menacingly clear. He truly feared for his life. He suspected an intruder had come into the house when he was absorbed in looking at himself in the mirror. This person was now in the room he shared with his papa and mama, and there might even be others in his *erh-ko's* room. He listened with all his might and heard an unmistakable movement – a rustling, creeping noise, that of somebody putting his foot stealthily onto a tatami mat. He knew that the only way to put this petrifying dread to rest was to go to the other room and take a look for himself. He nerved himself for the confrontation. But there was nothing unusual. The desk on which he had been practicing his small-character script and the couch that his *erh-ko* used for a bed on the weekends were where he had left them.

Nevertheless, he was not convinced that there wasn't an intruder in the house; he felt, instinctively, that the security of his environment was seriously threatened. He suspected that while he was in this room that person had slipped into the rear hallway. Once again he drummed up his courage for the task. He charged, shouting at the top of his voice. Not a soul in sight.

Perhaps the intruder had already bolted into the front hallway and was by now spying on him. He didn't dare turn around to look; he was afraid he might be greeted by a white face with a cold smile leering at him. He was sure that the enemy had penetrated his territory. The only safe thing to do was to retreat into the room he shared with his parents. Thus he withdrew, shutting the bedroom door after him. He backed up into the corner and sat down with a bamboo rod at the ready.

Just as he settled down, a series of violent knocks shook the house; he heard his mama yell out his name. He sprang up, opened the door, and ran out. All he saw was his mother's angry face, livid with rage, flaring up behind the other side of the glass pane, hollering at him, "What do you think you're doing! Open up right now! See if I don't give you a good thrashing when I get in!"

82

Around five or six in the afternoon, bats flew, helter-skelter, in front of the house.

83

It was a cold winter's night; he had gone to a school-mate's house in the early evening to admire his new piano and was thus late coming home. His father went out to search for him. Father headed for the road to his school, hoping he might run into him on the way. The sky was painted crow black. The beams of a streetlamp opened out to form the shape of a gray, dusky fan. His father walked past this and was swallowed by the dark patch beyond the light. Not too far away was another streetlamp. Under the lamppost were parked two pedicabs; the drivers were dozing. Here his father turned back, thinking that perhaps he had missed his son, since the boy might have taken another route home. On reaching home, though, Father decided to leave again, determined to find his son, and took to the original route once more. He walked past that first streetlamp again and came to the second lamppost, where only one pedicab driver was now left under the lamplight. This time, he continued on with the search. A gaping mouth lit up by a row of teeth turned out to be neon lights on top of the entrance to a dental clinic. He strode on and passed a hawker with a wonton cart, then another lamppost, and under its electric light were parked several more pedicabs. He looked searchingly into the face of every child he passed, hoping to make out the face of his own child.

Finally he arrived at his son's elementary school. He was greeted by an empty schoolhouse: lights out, doors and windows shut in the desolate dark. His heart sank. In despair he turned to go. An empty pedicab went by. Stunned and confused, he picked a different route to go home and strayed into an unfamiliar side street, for some reason expecting his child to be out here playing in this neighborhood. He had no idea how he lost his way, but he found himself by a railroad track. He went round and round and ended up standing next to a mountainous heap of rubbish. He didn't know which way to turn to get out of this dirty, deserted maze. A skeleton of a dog slunk past in front of him. He took another turn, entered another alley, and somehow made his way out. In the distance he could see those bright neon teeth of the dental clinic.

84

He took the pair of leather gloves out of the closet and put them on. This was a pair of very old gloves that had once belonged to his father. The leather had gone a bit moldy even, but he thought them really neat, like those worn by pilots. It was mid-July, but he didn't mind the summer heat as he flexed his little hands inside the great cavities of the big leather gloves.

85

In South Garden when walks are green
and half of Spring has still to come –

the sound of horses shrill in the wind,
green plums like baby beans, willows like brows,
days long, and butterflies flit about. . . .

He had forgotten the rest of the song, not just the tune,
but the lyrics. He decided to start singing it over again.
Maybe this go round the whole thing would come back to
him. It didn't. "Days long, and butterflies flit about. . . ."
Then what? What came after that? He repeated the song
another time from the beginning:

In South Garden when walks are green
and half of Spring has still to come –
the sound of horses shrill in the wind,
green plums like baby beans, willows like brows,
days long, and butterflies flit about,
flowers heavy with dewdrops,
grass bathed in smoke,
and every household has left its blinds hung down,
and the swing is idle, and I have unloosened my dress –
home to the gallery a pair of swallows come to nest.

86

He discovered that he liked his mother's face very much;
it was a very pretty face. She had a proud-looking nose, tall
and straight, and thin eyebrows. In fact she had plucked all
the hair on her brows, and a new pair was drawn on with a
stiff eyebrow pencil. There were also a few freckles on her
face. (She called them "mosquito shit." He had them too,
she said, "because you're my son.") And she had little holes
in her earlobes, where once she had worn earrings, but they
had now closed up. Around the house, she wore an old pair
of black woollen slippers and an old dress, loose and soft,
made of a red and brown gingham material. The tiny, neatly
woven curls of her permed hair made the back of her head
look like a round packet of noodles.

In recent weeks their whole family (excluding Erh-ko) went downtown every Sunday afternoon. The three of them walked side by side, with him in the middle between his papa and his mama because they were afraid he might get run over. Hand in hand they crossed the road, running, as if their lives depended on it. By the time dusk fell, their little family would invariably be seen passing under the Little South Gate, the three of them all in a row. A tall steel tower, and on it, a speck of red light, blinking away, appeared ahead of them then, and his papa would say, "The radio station, the radio station. . . ."

Their last stop of the day was always the Shantung Dumpling Tavern. After his mama had finished her shopping for cheongsam material and bought the cosmetics she needed, they would head here for a feast of braised beef and noodles.

Though still quite a way away from the Shantung Dumpling Tavern (having arrived at the Taipei Train Station from the West Gate District), they walked this last stretch. Throughout the work week his mama had sung its praises: "Ah, that Shantung Dumpling Tavern, what great beef noodles they make. So tasty, the beef noodles at the Shantung Dumpling Tavern. What a treat, eh?" He himself could never figure out quite what it was about this beef noodle she found so tasty.

At the entrance to the Shantung Dumpling Tavern sat a big, fat lady. Dark and oily, shiny and plump, like a huge, black date preserved in syrup, sat this store-owner's wife, behind the cashier's counter, filling up the entire space. Behind her stood three strongboxes, arranged in a semicircle surrounding her, and planted securely in front of her was another small money box. All the monetary exchanges, going out or coming in, were handled by her. On her waist was hung a chain of keys. He pictured her there day and night amid the money boxes and iron safes and imagined that, being thus encircled, she too became part of that iron-clad zone. Ma was full of admiration and envy. The first thing she said on going home and for days afterward was, "What a sweet fate, that boss's wife! Ah, to be surrounded by those strongboxes all day long and handle all that money, that's good fortune! That's what I call *fortunate.* That's what living should be like."

H

SEARCH
For Father

Dear Father,
It's been over half a month since you left; everything will be resolved according to your wishes.

Your son,
Yeh

He was in the outskirts of Kaohsiung, walking down a long street flanked by banana trees, his eyes shielded by the two ink-black shades of his dark glasses. He had just now stepped out of a Roman Catholic church. His heart was a jumble of confusion, mingled with the chaos of hopelessness. He had already searched through many, many temples and monasteries as well as churches, but he must also have missed a great many more. There must be countless monasteries and shrines and churches he hadn't yet been to! This search was really nothing more than a tranquilizer for his inner turmoil. He had sent home a letter via express mail every day; today was already his third day in Kaohsiung. In this morning's response his mama had said, "Yeh, my son, thy Father has still not come." He had a vague premonition his father would never come home again. A sob rose in his chest, and tears threatened to follow. Luckily he had on his sunglasses. He wanted to slow down and take a rest, but he was afraid his stopping would somehow call attention to himself; there was no bus stop or anything like that around here, not even a café.

In the middle of the road was an island, and on it, among a jungle of greenery, stood the bronze statue of Premier Sun. It was the center of a four-way crossing. To the right of it, along the wall of an elementary school, was the name of the school in large blue characters. The bicycle traffic criss-crossed before him like marionettes dangling from wires. A native Taiwanese soldier in an olive drab uniform walked past. Around the corner of the wall with the blue characters stood a royal poinciana ablaze with explosions of red efflorescence. He had left his address at every monastery, shrine, and church, so that if his papa should arrive after him they would be able to contact him. Perhaps there was still hope. The thought that his father might already have gone home ahead of him today, or perhaps will tomorrow (he planned himself to go on home tomorrow), kept his hopes up. He ran toward that red royal poinciana. Oh, don't get carried away. Don't hope for too much. The higher the hope, the more likely the fall. Oh, God, please let me not lose even this thread of hope, this slim possibility. . . .

88

One summer afternoon, his papa took them to Grass Mountain. His brother came along this time. That day Papa wore a khaki Republic-style suit. His mama wore a new cotton cheongsam and new shoes and carried a new handbag. He was in his summer Boy Scout uniform and had on a pair of black and white gym shoes. His *erh-ko* wore a white shirt and black trousers.

The family hailed two pedicabs and headed for the train station. They had to go to the train station to catch the bus. His papa and his *erh-ko* took the cab in front, and he and his mama sat in the one behind. All the way there he could see the top halves of the backs of their heads.

The cabs pulled into the station concourse. They found their bus stop, which was shaped like a wooden box, and stood in line. He marveled over what a huge space the concourse was; he lifted his head up and saw an armed soldier standing guard on a battlement, which turned out to be a huge billboard. The line had grown very long by the time the announcement for the arrival of their tour bus came. It was a colossal, dazzling blue splendor, one of those new designs that had no protruding hood. The people behind them swarmed up and pushed forward, heaping themselves on top of them; they were squeezed out and pressed into the back of the swarm. After a long struggle, they finally managed to push their way onto the bus, but by then there were no seats left. He saw the bus driver sitting high up in his seat behind the flat, broad windshield, proud and disdainful, looking down at the world around him.

The bus was now packed. With one hand, he hung onto a piece of his mama's clothing, while his mama grasped one of the chrome bars at the front end of the bus, her body wrapped around him. His papa was somewhere in the far end of the bus and could be heard calling to them on and off – to him and his mama – to ascertain their whereabouts. His mama answered back every time and kept telling Sonny to hold on tight. He was squashed in the middle; all he could see were other people's bellies. A long time passed. His head was wet with sweat when he heard a clear voice announce through the microphone that they were about to head up the mountain; he felt the car tilt upward. His papa had finally secured two vacant seats and called out to him and his mama to come sit down. He followed the direction of the voice but couldn't get to it through the crowd. By brute force, he jostled forward, savagely pushing each body aside, and, amid glares and curses, he made his way out.

When he finally sat down next to his mama, she asked him, "How did you manage to push your way through? Look at you, your hair's all wet, and your face is dripping with sweat."

"I thrust them all to one side and came right out," he boasted.

"What a child," Ma said with approval.

His father was standing next to them. Because he couldn't reach the bar that ran across on top, he tightly gripped the backs of their seats. His *erh-ko* stood with his arms hanging loosely at his sides next to his father, his face stern and cold.

From where he was sitting he could look out the window and see masses of wild plants on rock slabs shooting past like arrows, not more than a foot away; intermittently, patches of grassland appeared. . . .

They arrived at Grass Mountain. He got off the bus and immediately took in a whiff of a toasty, sort of vaporous smell – not unlike that of the night soil that was carried past their house. His papa said that this was the smell of sulphur and that it came from the hot springs. The smooth, clean surface of the tarmac road sloped gradually upward. His *erh-ko* and his papa walked behind them, deep in conversation. A few steps ahead, by the side of the road, half hidden behind the shady woods, he saw a lodging house with red pillars in the front. On the moist, brown surface of the coarse brick wall was written in white the words "Hot Springs Hotel," and there was also a symbol for hot springs that looked like a bald head with three hairs on it. Still farther along he saw a little round hillock in the shape of a wheat bun with clumps of bushes planted on it; it looked like a giant head of cauliflower. He ran on ahead and, coming to a series of ditches and channels, bent down to watch the water flowing past. The water was boiling hot; clouds of steam rose up from it. The rocks at the bottom of the gullies appeared a rusty red, and several of the marshy rocks looked as if pieces of torn rags had been placed on them; they were all covered in slithery, slimy threads of something.

He ran as fast as he could to Papa and announced at the top of his lungs, "Papa, look over there at that water. It's hot."

His papa looked over at him and said, "Yes, it's the hot water from the springs."

He tugged at his papa to come look at the ditches.

"You can bathe in this hot spring water, and it can heal all sorts of skin rashes. Even people who have nothing wrong with them will feel better after they've had a soak in it. That's why so many people come here to these hotels," Papa told him, looking over toward the building on the side of the road.

"Let's go then," he said as he dragged his father toward the hotel.

"No, next time we'll go. We can't go now," Papa said, planting his feet firmly where he stood.

As they walked on, an unspeakably skinny person came toward them. He had a great big box strapped to his shoulders, and he came toward his papa bowing low and full of smiles. "Wouldn't you like your picture taken? Take a picture to remember the occasion by. A discount for you."

"Not interested," his papa said sternly, and dismissed him with a wave of his hand.

On they went until they came to a place where an emerald green hedge encircled a country estate. The shrubbery was studded with dazzling red buds, and each bud had a tassel hanging out from its lips. In front of the house, on the fine sandy path that ran alongside the hedge, was parked a small blue sedan. The house was made of stone, and its roof was a pale red. "A rich man's house," his mama murmured with a knowing smile as she threw his papa a sidelong glance. All of a sudden, a giant dog sprang out, barking and snarling at them. He jumped backward a whole foot or more. Right behind the dog, a man who looked like a servant emerged from the shrubs and glared at them menacingly. "Let's go," his father said. He caught a glimpse of an old man with silvery white hair inside the house.

They continued on their way toward the public park. His mama had gone a few steps ahead and was calling for him to hurry up: "Come along, Sonny." He caught up with her while Papa and his *erh-ko* continued to lag behind. From time to time he turned around and asked, "Papa, are we going the right way? Is it this way?" Papa, talking busily to his *erh-ko,* would lift up his head and wave him on, shouting, "Right, straight ahead!"

Soon they arrived at the park. There were many pine trees, the sort with narrow trunks and pointy needles, and the ground was the muddy color of bare earth. He could hear the crickets chirping and sighing in the trees, but he couldn't tell where exactly they were calling from. Then he saw a solitary leaf dangling on the end of a spider's web, spinning round and round, which made him think that the chirping came from that spinning leaf. His papa stood in the shade of a tree and said, "Ah, it's nice and cool here," and proceeded to undo all the buttons down the front of his tunic.

He and his mama sat down on a concrete bench. Nearby a hawker was squatting by his great big wicker basket full of peanuts cooked in the shell. His papa went over without being asked and bought some plump peanuts for him. Then Papa asked if Erh-ko wanted any. Erh-ko said no, he didn't. So Papa and Erh-ko went over to another concrete bench a little farther off and sat down. Over here, mother and son were cracking and eating the peanuts, then throwing the shells on the ground. When all the peanuts were gone, he leaped up and took off. His mama yelled after him, anxiously, "Sonny, come back here!"

"I'm just going to play over there!"

His mama said, "Don't go any farther. Stay close!"

What had attracted his attention was gushing out from the creepers on the high ground and flowing down to the flat grass plain where a bamboo stick diverted it to some unknown destination. Following the direction of the flow he made a new discovery. There was a pond over there! He called to his mama to come over, but she shouted back to say her feet were killing her (she had just kicked off her shoes and was massaging one of her sore feet) and told him to go by himself. "But don't you go running off anywhere else, and don't fall into the pond!" He took off.

When he got to the pond, he found hundreds of goldfish swimming in it. These little swimmers looked like tiny girls in dancing costumes, waving their long, silky sleeves about in the water. Right in the middle of everyone was the fattest goldfish you ever saw, a giant the size of a carp. He roared with laughter. This startled the watery world and set it into a frenzy of activity. Hordes of tiny fish, like aquatic gnats, were sent reeling in opposite directions, the way swarms of gnats might be blown about by a sudden gust of wind. His eyes darted back and forth as they followed the little fish about.

Jets of water suddenly came spurting up over the other side of the pond. He went to take a closer look and saw that the spray came from inside a mound covered with little black holes like a sponge. One of the water spouts was twisted, so that a single jet of water overshot the edge of the pond. Blown by the wind, a few sprinkles landed on him, tickling his cheeks. He opened his arms out as wide as they would go to catch the spray. His arms felt cool and tingly. He stuck his face in the spray and let the water drench his forehead and his face; the water seeped into his eyes, but it didn't sting. When he broke into exultant yelps of laughter, the water entered his mouth.

Some kids had brought their boats to the pond, and just

as he was about to go over and join them his father called to him. Papa said they were ready to go and told him to hurry up. He couldn't believe it was already time to leave, but he ran back to make sure. Father said they needed to go now if they wanted to avoid the crowds. Then Papa turned toward Erh-ko and said, "You think about what I said. As I've been saying over these last couple of days, when you've established yourself, you won't have to worry about not having any girlfriends. Besides, she's a native Taiwanese; it's really a bit. . . ."

Erh-ko said nothing.

"Well, what do you say, Lao-erh?"

"Yeah, I'll just tell her no, okay!" Erh-ko brusquely replied.

"All right then," Pa said happily, "let's go home. Sonny, go to Mama."

Ma got up from the chair. When she saw that his head and his clothes were all wet, she lashed out at him, hitting him on the back. "How the hell did you get water all over your head and face!" she scolded.

The sun was in the western sky by this time; the slanting rays shone into the forest, coloring everything scarlet. The sighing sounds he heard when they first arrived had now stopped, and that single leaf had also stopped twirling. They walked toward the bus stop. There were not many people waiting in line. The bus came on schedule. As it started up, his excitement was once more aroused. He looked out the bus window and saw the grass plain, the clumps of grass sticking out from the rock slabs, speeding past like shooting arrows, and then, straining to look back, he caught sight of the low hedge with the red flowers and their dazzling tassels. The bus went round a curve, and he saw once again that hillock that looked like a head of cauliflower receding into the distance. Papa, Mama, and he were sitting together. His *erh-ko* sat all by himself at the back of the bus, staring out the window.

89

Another notch had been made, a little higher up, on the column in the hallway where they marked his height. His papa now used his fingernail to make the markings; between this mark and the one they had made last month he had grown the length of Papa's thumbnail.

90

Before falling asleep at night (he now slept on a wooden plank attached to the wall in his parents' room), the thought of his parents' impending death haunted him as he stared into the murky dark – his father turned fifty-one this year, and his mother was already forty-nine. He kept his eyes opened wide in the dark for fear of what might happen. Being superstitious, he reasoned that if he punished himself hard enough he might be able to forestall their death. He slapped himself violently on both cheeks, clap upon clap in loud chastisement, testifying to the earnestness of the punishment.

91

He learned to wrestle in elementary school, in his physical education class, but there was nobody to practice with at home. He tried to talk his father into practicing with him, but Papa refused. Eyeing him now as he stood in his undervest and shorts at the center of the tatami, his father appeared enormous compared to himself. Here was an opportunity, he thought, to sneak up on him and take him unawares; maybe he could even knock him down. He decided to pounce. He wrapped his arms around his father's waist and with all his might tried to pull him down onto the tatami. Father didn't budge. Solid as a rock he stood, imposing and unmovable. Well pleased with himself,

Father gave a triumphant laugh and, with a look of utter disdain and derision, taunted him, saying, "Come on, show us what you've got." And with that Father dealt him a blow right in the chest, throwing him off balance onto the tatami. His leg ached from the fall. His papa tossed his head back and broke into a loud guffaw. He protested that Father's move shouldn't count because he didn't know that they had started and appealed for another go-round. His father agreed. He scrambled up from the floor and lunged forward once again for the attack.

They each did their best to throw the other off balance, and were for a while going at it head to head. His heart was enraged; he wanted so badly to pull his papa down, but his papa once again threw him out of the ten-foot circle and again tossed his head back and laughed at him. He dashed forward, pretending to laugh it off, but inwardly he was overcome with hatred for his father. Bout after bout they fought, but Father seemed *invincible.*

By and by Father grew tired, and said, "Enough, enough, Sonny. Let's stop now." But he kept his head in position and was still trying to ram into him; this time, to his own surprise, he felt Father move a little. "Ha-iiee," Papa exclaimed as he actually stumbled forward. Using this movement to his advantage, however, Papa lifted his foot and kicked him in the belly, saying, "Out with you!" As a horse might send a little dog flying with one kick, his father sent him tumbling onto the tatami. Papa roared with laughter. With his hands on his hips, he planted his bare foot firmly on his opponent's chest. "Will you ever again wrestle your own father? You actually think you can whip your own father? Just take a look at yourself, see how puny you are! How dare you wrestle with me?"

"No, never again." He lay limply on the floor and smiled sheepishly.

"All right then, I'll let you off this time," Papa said, and took his foot off him. As Papa turned around to walk away, he swung his leg out and hooked him. At this unexpected swipe his father tripped and crashed to the floor. He jumped to his feet and, prancing about his father, cheered, "I won! I won!"

"How can you treat your papa this way?" His papa sat cross-legged on the floor, fuming.

He was still jumping for joy.

But as he watched his father languishing on the mat, failing, several times, to get back onto his feet, he was overcome with compassion and felt compelled to stretch out his hand to his father.

"How can you do this to your own father?" Papa said.

92

A colony of termites flew indoors, circling the room. Papa filled a washbasin with water and lifted it toward the ceiling lamp. Teased by the light's reflection, the termites dove to their death, destroying themselves in the water. Father's hair stuck out like a bird's nest torn apart.

93

"No doubt about it, the child has no respect, no filial feelings whatsoever. People say, 'Store grain for the lean times, rear sons for old age,' but from what I can see, neither of us can count on this son for our future. We've fed him for nothing, this son. Brand new, top quality gym shoes bought especially for him, but does he appreciate it? No!"

"I know. That's just it. Stubborn and rebellious, he was born to oppose his parents. Won't listen to a word we say. No hope for us, no counting on him, I'm afraid," Mama said.

"No counting on him. Can't count on him, you and me. I can see it coming, two lonely paths before us, one heading for the monastery, the other the nunnery. That's where we'll end up."

Hearing them talk like that was like being stabbed in the heart; he was pierced by the pain of immense guilt, of having committed a deep wrong. It all started this time with the new pair of gym shoes his papa bought him. He was hoping for a pair of cream-colored ones or ones that had black and white stripes, but his papa had bought him a pitch black pair. He refused to have anything to do with them and put up a big fight until his parents' reproaches and harsh accusations finally wore him down and he gave in. But that was not enough for them. They kept at him, recounting the instances of his disobedience and rebelliousness. He was racked by guilt and remorse. Under their indictment he hung his head in repentance for his crimes.

94

At the end of the seventh month by the lunar calendar, at the epiphany of autumn, as night died away, lying still on his pillow, he could often hear wave upon wave on the dark wind, pressing through the air from far away, bringing with it the rumblings of the trains on iron rails, by turns resounding near and retreating far away, returning on the autumn wind, like sheet upon sheet of music scores blown toward him.

95

A faint scent slipped into his room. It was his mother passing by on her way out; it was the lingering fragrance of the newly washed jasmine flowers pinned against the right side of her braided hair. Jasmine flowers! Each bud looking like a rice-yellow soya bean. Before putting them on, his mama would first let them soak in a soy sauce saucer brimful with water to prevent them from closing up and withering away. Then, when she was ready to wear them, she would pull a hairpin from her hair and stick the pin through each one of the still unopened jasmine buds, forming a string of pierced blossoms, and pin them in her hair.

96

"Shush, shush. Don't say such things. You must never talk like that outside the family. Do this for me if nothing else. Remember what I said, eh, Sonny?" His papa would thus warn him, in great fear for no apparent reason.

97

A beautifully patterned, multicolored butterfly darted in through the open window. Ma chased it down, caught it, and nailed it to the wall, like a trophy.

98

The ink-black slabs of the tiled eaves had faded to a slate gray in the blistering sun. He stared at them from across the alley through his window. Their heavy shadows cut deep into the earth, as if someone had carved the pattern out with a blade. On her way to do the washing at the public faucet outside their boardinghouse, his mama warned him, "The sun is wicked just now; it's late autumn, Season of the Autumn Tiger. You're not to go outside and run about in that sun, you hear me?" He couldn't fathom it. Shutting him up like this, did she want to turn him into a pale, white thing, nothing more than a slip of moldy fungus? He had wanted to go catch some sun, scorch his skin a little and make it darker, so his schoolmates wouldn't keep jeering at him. Last weekend he ran into Shen Yen-t'ing, who immediately pounced on him, saying, "You're so *white,* whiter than Snow White herself. You've never been out in the sun, I'll bet." He dreaded going to school because of his conspicuous whiteness. But no matter what he did, for some mysterious reason his skin simply wouldn't take in the sun. All the other kids needed to do was spend a couple of hours in the sun, and they'd be nice and brown, whereas with him it took weeks and weeks before anything happened, and then, if he didn't keep it up, it'd all fade away to nothing within days. Thus, his baby white skin gradually took on symbolic proportions. It signified weakness and became for him a daily torture, especially when the nickname "white mouse" got around — just thinking about it made his earlobes burn with embarrassment. The boys at school were forever teasing him about it; even his closest friends ridiculed him. What really got to him was how those smarmy girls would laugh at him to his face, pointing out his conspicuous white skin to each other. And he would never forget the day when his favorite teacher, the lady who taught them music, teased him in front of the whole class: "So very white you are, my, just like a little girl. You should get out in the sun more often. A boy should be shiny black all over. Dark and shiny, that's what a boy should look like." And she was right too, no doubt about it. Just look at all those boys at school showing off their tans, brandishing the forearms they've scorched black in the sun, saying, "Take a look at that, so black, so brave!" And sometimes they'd pull up the ends of their shorts and, pointing to their knees, say to him, "Right there, you see that? Even here I'm darker than you." Consequently, the moment the sun came out he would run out and roast in it whenever he could. Several times that year he managed to toast his arms till they turned bright red, and his chest swelled with pride whenever he surveyed his thin arms, red like the shells of cooked crabs. This solar treatment left his eyeballs dry and turned his breath hot. Even so, the moment he stopped the violent exposure the red would vanish, just like that. He often thought that if only he could keep his arms tanned he wouldn't mind if his face, his legs, and his body remained as they were. All he wanted was to have one part of his anatomy to show for his efforts in the sun. He wished for a medical miracle; if only there were a kind of ointment he could rub onto his skin and make it turn a raven black. Ah, what a shame there wasn't any such medicine, just as there was no miracle cure to fill out his rail-thin body – for that, too, was for him a measure of his inferiority. . . .

The tall coconut palm tree was parched and split, like a trunk made of straw-mud bricks. In its shadow, on the sandy ground, hens were busily showing their few little chicks how to scrape the earth and dig for worms. Out of a corner of the window frame came Ah Fang, just back from picking crickets in the trees, a long bamboo pole hitched across his back. His skin baked to a crispy brown, like a coarse, ripe, dark brown olive, Ah Fang was free to do as he pleased, to come and go as he liked, for all the world to see. He looked down at his own body in disgust. He detested his smooth legs, so delicately white they looked like bleached tofu, and under the satiny skin on his bony knees were criss-crossed strand upon strand of fine, blue veins. And the skin on his feet was worse than white; it was just about transparent. At that moment he hated his mother for what she had done to him. She was the one who was forever saying, "You, with a body like yours, you don't think you can go dashing out into the blazing sun, do you? You come right back in here. You forget how easily you get sick the minute the sun gets on you." If only he could go outside, let the sun shine on him, he knew he would get stronger, healthier, more resistant to disease. But his mama wouldn't even let him go outside to play basketball, not even in the winter when the sun wasn't even out! O how stupid, how ignorant she was! Didn't she know that by being shut up like this, his body would only get weaker, that the less he exercised, the weaker he'd be? It was entirely her doing; his mama was the one who made him this white; she was responsible for his daily shame and embarrassment. He decided then and there to go out. See if she could stop him! He would go down by the river for a stroll and take in half an hour's worth of sunshine. He got up and went.

99

His mama loved to get dressed up when they went downtown on Sundays, all made-up in the most vulgar and flashy fashion. She'd whitewash her face with snowy, powdery stuff, and on top of that she'd smear a thick layer of rouge, and then she'd put on (totally unnecessarily) glossy silk stockings, after which she'd pick up that goose-egg-shaped mirror to preen herself some more, looking closely at what was left of those neatly plucked brows of hers and, ever so carefully, tracing out another pair, and when that was done, she'd gaze and smile at herself in the mirror. Then she would slide the paper door shut and go into the bedroom to change her clothes; she'd try on one outfit after another, making him wait outside that flowery paper door, getting more annoyed and more outraged at her. His papa too was waiting on her. After a while, his mama pushed open the paper door, and lo and behold she appeared, all aglitter, cloaked in silver and draped in gold! "Ma, please, can't you change into something a little less gaudy? That dress is really ugly," he had once said, from sheer anguish and shame, at the very end of his endurance. One time, he even blurted out, "You look *just* like a hooker!" That time his mama was wearing a brilliant, blazing red cheongsam. "You go fart!" she erupted in fury, launching into a tirade. "Mind your own business. I'm free to wear what I like; I can do what I damn well please. Who do you think you are to talk to me like that? You're really getting out of hand these days, you know that? You'd better watch out, young man. Mind your manners in front of your elders and betters!" The ferocity of her language gave him a real shock. Moreover, she had ranted at him as if he were another adult. He hated her totally and without reservation. He was going to reply in kind and curse her out with the foulest words he knew, but that murderous look on her face left him tongue-tied and petrified. On occasions he had indeed answered her back, and then she had flung her handbag away and slammed the sliding door shut with a bang, saying she wasn't going to go out at all. That stopped him in his tracks, leaving him dumbfounded. In the end it was up to his papa to cajole her. Thus, Papa often restrained him and stopped him from answering back. Why did Papa have nothing to say at such times? It was as if he agreed with Mother or something. That one time, they did eventually go out, and Mother had actually worn her bright, red cheongsam into the streets, flaunting herself like a big, fat sow on parade, all decked out in red cloth, readied for a feast. Everybody turned to stare at her, but she reveled in it, holding her head high.

100

Father had accumulated over ten volumes of notes, bits and pieces from proverbial sayings and classical aphorisms, written in black ink with a goat-hair brush on rice-paper stationery. Father said they represented the best of his writings, his choice selection; he also said that in the future he was going to compile them into his autobiography to be handed down to his little boy. Fan Yeh felt both proud and exalted by this work that Father was doing. He felt that he couldn't possibly inherit this great task; he didn't think he would ever be able to live up to it, not even when he became an adult.

101

He liked watercolors best. One day he spent all morning drawing a still life of fruit. He drew a tabletop on which he placed their white clock, a long, yellow, speckled banana, and a round, red tomato. He filled in the background with a flush of luxuriant, deep azure, making this the main tone of the piece. He was extremely fond of this dark blue watercolor drawing. He propped it up and stood back to take a good look at it, admiring it from different angles. In the end he pasted it in a high place, way up in a shrine on the wall, against the white background.

102

The fountain pen he had was leaking ink from its black bug belly, smudging the top joint of his middle finger with a great big wet patch like a dark cloud. He wound some cellophane paper round the reservoir and used the pen for a few more days. In the end, this coil of transparent tape fell off. A huge puddle of ink flowed out. When he told his papa, he promised to replace it with a brand new one. One morning his father presented him with a new pen. The new, Japanese-made pen had a long, slim, apple green trunk and a cap that was glittery gold, but when he slid it across the paper and tried to write, the nib was too pointy and scratched the paper. He wished he didn't have to part with his old companion. He developed a sense of immeasurable pity at having to part with his old pen. Its trunk was maroon, like the color of ripe red dates, and the tail end of it had traces of his teeth marks. It had been with him for two whole years. It was like a dear friend, to whom he was now saying goodbye forever. He caressed it, turning it about in his hands, unable to part with it.

103

It was his mama's idea. They too could have chilled watermelon if they went and bought ice to put on it. They had often seen cyclists with blocks of ice strapped to their bikes, a heavy block of ice with a thick jute rope wound round it, making the bike sway this way and that. They didn't own a refrigerator. They didn't even have an ice chest. But now, by means of this method, they too could experience the pleasure of ice. He was sent on the errand. When he came back with the ice, Mama would use it to chill a great big bowl of fresh, red melon, and with what was left over they could make another bowl in the evening. So thinking, he headed for the ice store nearest home, which was twenty to thirty minutes away.

The store owner opened up his ice cabinet and hauled out a gigantic block of ice. A large gunnysack was draped over it, and it looked like a big mother pig with a mass of cloudy white material in her belly and fumes of smoke rising from her steamy body. The store owner took a huge blade and sawed into the ice, as if he were sawing into a wooden log, bearing down on it, sending sparks of white debris flying in all directions. Eventually he dislodged a chunk of it, and with a piece of jute made a noose round the ice and handed it to him. Dangling the block of ice by his side, he walked home under the bright sun. The ice emitted a grayish, cold smoke from its sides, and pretty, delicate crisscross patterns showed through its transparent body.

He came to a shady patch of ground and stopped to wipe the sweat off his brow. He noticed that his ice was already melting a little and that its surface was turning slippery, looking like a smooth layer of lard. He quickly lifted it off the ground and ran, afraid that the whole thing might melt before he even got home. As he ran, it kept dripping, dripping, under the blast of the blazing sun. Every once in a while he would have to stop and kneel against a telephone pole to tighten the rope around it, but the crystal block got smaller and smaller. Despite his efforts to save it, the crystal became so small that the noose could no longer be tightened enough to grip it. He had no choice but to hold it in his hands. When he arrived home and opened up his hands, there was nothing left but the tiniest ice splinter. His mama took it and barely managed to produce two small bowls of cold watermelon, which they divided among the family. Everyone felt the disappointment.

Two weeks ago he was given a new pen, and once in a while he would almost succumb to the desire to take it out and use it, but each time he stopped himself, afraid he might use it up and thus have to suffer the pain of deprivation. Later on he had a revelation: from that moment on he would "use" what he "wanted" and not think of "use" as "waste." On the contrary, the use of the pen increased its function: it conferred happiness on the user. Were he not to use it, not only would he be unhappy, he would be making himself suffer for no reason at all, because even if he were to wait another two days before using his new pen, he'd still be using it in the end, and by then he would have lost the satisfaction of his initial desire and would have missed out on that portion of happiness as well. Thus he came to understand the significance of his ice-bearing experience and the similarity between it and the significance of his use of the fountain pen: to hold fast to the enjoyment of the moment. That year he was eleven years old.

104

Often he would see his mama mending his papa's socks by the lamplight; sometimes they were his socks. She generally took a scrap piece of cardboard paper cut into the shape of a foot and stuck it in the sock and then, by placing a piece of blanched white cloth of more or less the same size on the sole, make tiny stitches all the way around it. In so doing, she ended up with a sock with a white pad on the underside. He loathed having to wear such an ugly thing on his foot; he felt that being made to wear it was a form of intense humiliation. One time his mama even took his Boy Scout shorts to the small family shop round the corner to have the so-called Western-style tailor fix them up. His shorts came back from that tailor's with tiny lover's knots stitched like artwork all over the buttocks; those tiny stitches that wound tightly round and round, one on top of another, looked like the markings of a cattle iron branded on his backside. Naturally he refused to wear any such thing, but his mama yelled at him, saying, "What a wastrel you are! How you despise heaven's gifts. And to think I've gone to such trouble, spent ten whole dollars at the tailor's to get them sewn for you." This time, he didn't budge; he refused to put them on, not even once.

105

One afternoon, late into the summer holidays, his papa was stretched out on the tatami in his room taking his afternoon nap. Before going off to sleep, he propped himself up on his elbow, turning the pages of a small volume entitled *Erotic Tales from a Flowery Grove.* His papa held up the book to him and said that this was a very entertaining book, a good read, and handed it to him so he too could have a look at it, after which, his papa laid down and fell into a deep sleep. He squatted down alongside him and leafed through the pages of this volume. He had the sudden sensation that his body was gripped and whirled into an eddying frenzy. It turned out that this book was full of descriptions of the sexual activities between men and women. His hands were trembling, and he could hear his heart knocking against his chest. Descriptions of lechery followed hard on each other, page after page. He sped through the pages, picking out only the passages with such scenes in them. He was so caught up by these assaults that he almost fainted away. Finally, when he couldn't bear it any longer, he returned the book quietly to his father's side. Father was still snoring away; he would now sleep till four in the afternoon before he awakened.

For the rest of the afternoon he was in a daze, staring out the east window.

106

The next day, he woke up in high spirits and set out to inspect his brother's books, to see if he couldn't find some more of those juicy passages. All the books in his brother's possession were kept in a narrow drawer of a small desk, except those that were kept in a secret compartment in the wall cabinet (in a coffer near the ceiling). He began by rummaging through the desk drawer and found some four or five books, but these turned out to be nothing more than translations of famous works, such as *Eyewitness Accounts of the Second World War* and *Memoirs of the Duke of Windsor.* At the bottom he finally found a volume with a green dust jacket that promised "sentimental tales of a passionate nature from everyday lives," and on the back cover was sketched the bewitching silhouette of a woman in a cheongsam, combing her long hair. He immediately took this one out and opened it up to look inside. To his dismay, it was written in "classical prose," which he couldn't read. He reluctantly returned the volume to its place. He then went to the small unit on the wall and slid open the panel of the coffer, inside which he found six hidden texts. This time, all six were novels, and they were romantic novels. He went through them one by one, looking, looking. But all he found that even came close to what he wanted was written in the following vein: "He held her tight and kissed her passionately. Her whole being melted into the heat of their two bodies." Teased into eager expectancy, he was left high and dry.

107

At year's end he started keeping a diary. His *erh-ko* had won it at a New Year's party last year; Erh-ko gave it to him because he himself already had a diary. It started with his cousin's visit three days ago. She was a little older than him and left him with such a deep impression that he was moved to recall his memory of her in a diary. His cousin was now a secondary school student and was taller than him by a head. Her clear, bluish-black pupils, her chin-length hair parted in the middle, and that mouth of delicate teeth that looked like little white stones aroused in his heart such a honey-sweet feeling that he could taste it even in recollection.

He entered the most minute detail of that day's visit into his diary. At one go he wrote eight pages nonstop, on and on for three hours or more. Then he was afraid his papa might find out if he were to inquire into the contents of his volume (his mother would probably not go into his drawer), so he planned to buy a padlock and lock it up. With this in mind he went to his papa with the request; his father responded with a look of disapproval and did not consent. He kept on and on, pleading pitifully, until the next day, when, to his great surprise, his papa produced a little padlock and gave it to him. He thus secured his drawer with this precious lock.

108

He was mindful of the fact that his aunt had not come for a visit in a long time. His concern was of course brought on by his cousin's long absence. He waited for a whole month. Still they didn't show up. It was then that he went to ask his mama why, why it was that his aunt and his cousin had not come round recently. His mother stammered before saying something about his aunt and his cousin probably being too busy with other things these days, which was why they couldn't come. Another good while passed, and still they didn't come, so he suggested to his mama that perhaps they should first go and pay a visit. At which point his mother made the following reply: "You mustn't let your papa know I told you this, but three months ago he borrowed five hundred dollars from your aunt. Your papa had said at the time that he would repay her in a month, but as of this week he's still not repaid the money. Your papa thinks he can just get away with it. More than likely your aunt's angry at us for this reason. Your papa's to blame for this mess, showing us up and making me lose face in front of my relatives. He's cut us off from even this good family connection now."

Her words stung him to the quick, and, as he listened, his face grew progressively redder, and his eyes flooded, becoming reservoirs of tears. He bellowed at the top of his voice, "Mama, you must repay her! Ma you go pay her back right now!"

"Mama can't do anything about it either. My good boy. I want for nothing so long as you're a good boy."

"No *way!* Papa must pay!"

109

They hired a servant to come wash their clothes. This servant was a middle-aged widow of Taiwanese descent. She had a bony face, worn and wasted, and wore her hair in an old woman's bun at the nape of her neck. Every morning before it was even light out and the house was still lit by the night lamp, she'd already have arrived and collected together the clothes, the large laundry basin, and the washboard from the house and settled down to the wash at the public faucet located at the other end of the corridor of the boardinghouse. The clothes she washed came back much cleaner than they'd ever been.

This past month his mama seemed to be in a bad temper all the time. He often saw her, greasy cheeked and jaundiced faced, her dry, scraggly, disheveled hair flying everywhere, and she often picked on him, rasping at him in coarse language. On this particular morning he was still in bed when he heard her shouting at someone. He got out of bed to see what she was screaming about and discovered that his

mother was upbraiding this washerwoman, telling her off
for losing some piece of her clothing, accusing her in no
uncertain terms of having stolen it. What his mother was
missing, it turned out, was an ordinary light green handkerchief. His mother was just now using her broken Taiwanese
to scold this washerwoman. His mother was holding a sliver
of wet soap in one hand and had on a pair of filthy pajamas,
sloppily worn, with the top tucked halfway into the bottom,
yelling at the top of her lungs, "You thief! You think you
can steal from me? . . . Do you have any idea how much it
costs, how much money a handkerchief costs, any idea?
Dirty hands, foul habits – I have no use for your sort. You
stop coming here as of tomorrow. I'll get you your money
right now, pay you for the rest of the month is all."

The woman stood there, her face consumed in misery. She
defended herself, claiming that in the last two days' laundry
she had not once seen any such handkerchief, and what
would she be doing taking something like that anyway?
Despite that, his mama insisted on fetching a month's pay
right away and forced it on her. She stood with her hands at
her sides and wouldn't take the money; but Ma stuffed it
into her collar. The woman stood in mute resignation. His
mama said, "I've come up with a full month's wages here.
I'm even paying you for the three extra days left over in the
month. In our house we always treat our servants right;
we're never harsh with our help. I'm perfectly willing to
give you a few more dollars just to be rid of you, the sooner
the better. So just go, go away now. Everything in my
house, *everything* is worth top dollar. We can't have you making off with anything."

The washerwoman set her jaw and replied, "If I have
really stolen your handkerchief, my fingers will rot with
boils and fall off! But if I haven't stolen it, then you – "

His mama was really stung by this talk and flew into a
fury. "Are you trying to curse me out? You'd better get out
of here! You have no shame. What do you think you're

doing standing there like a dead rat stinking up my house? If you think I'd go on using a rotten thing like you, you rotten thief, you've got another think coming. Well, what are you standing around for? If you don't go right this minute, I'll call the police. I'll call them right now, tell them to come and take you away and *lock* you up!"

That was how she finally scared the woman away. He saw her come in with the washing board and lean it up against the wall at the end of the hall. Then he saw her weeping, her hands covering her eyes, sobbing and gulping down her tears.

Before this washerwoman had even left their front yard his mother was already spreading the word around the boardinghouse that she was no good, an evil person who went around stealing other people's things. It didn't look like many people believed her story, though. Then she came back into the house and made him listen to her version of the story.

"She couldn't clean at all. And on top of that she was heavy-handed; perfectly fine clothes came back all torn and ragged after just a few washes. She certainly knew how to bleed us for our money, though. Twenty dollars each time, and for what? Just last week she was mumbling to me about a raise. Something about how Mrs. Wu had already upped her wages and what not. It doesn't even occur to her that our washing is so much lighter than other people's, and besides, we always give her three whole days off for the New Year in our house, and if she wanted to she could even drag it out to four. I couldn't have been more generous with her; ordinarily when I'd give her a bedsheet or a bedcover to wash I'd throw in an extra dollar. Even now, I've given her an extra three days' pay. Tell me, where else can she hope to find a better employer than me? But what can you do? People like that are totally incapable of gratitude; they have no sense of loyalty! Coming back at me like that, with a curse on us. You tell me, is she evil or what? That's why I had to snarl at her and order her to scat. She got the message then. That gave her a real fright. What a wretched sack of bones — won't budge till you kick it. And then she had the gall to cry. What's there to cry about? Stupid idiot! Puts on this slithery-slobbery, creepy-crawly act and thinks she can soften me up. What did she think she could get out of me anyway? No way. It wasn't as if we had the money to use her to begin with, and now, since the opportunity presented itself, I turned it into a good excuse to get rid of her."

She cackled with this last confidence, which filled him with indignation. He burst out with, "You mean the theft was part of your scheme to get rid of her? Was it?"

"Well, not exactly. I didn't mean to say that. I just wasn't going to risk letting her wash our clothes anymore. What if she ripped up some more of our clothes in the wash, what then? It just so happened that as I was considering what to do it dawned on me we might as well do away with having the laundry done and save ourselves a lot each month! The money situation these last few months has gone from bad to worse. It's a crisis. Your father's taken another cut in pay of several hundred dollars. That was what made me decide to let her go."

"Who can believe anything you say?"

His mother shot him a lightning glance and began ranting, her voice cracking as she raved: "That thief, she *stole* my things. Don't I have the right to ask her to leave? Are you telling me we should keep a thief in the house and be responsible for her upkeep? You just wait and see if she doesn't take everything of yours away from you!"

"But when did she take any of your things? Why would she be stealing a silly little handkerchief from you? What for?"

"But this wasn't even the *first* time. She's done it before!"

"Couldn't she have lost it in the wash?"

"No, losing it in the wash is not acceptable! She still has to go!"

She was out of breath, and, if anything, he was probably

even more infuriated than she. He turned his back on her and went straight to his room. His papa, on the other hand, behaved from beginning to end as if nothing much had happened; his expression was relaxed and calm. He couldn't understand how his father could stand by and watch as if none of this concerned him.

That night, as he was getting ready for his bath in the kitchen and was looking for some underwear in the closet, he inadvertently came upon that green handkerchief. There it was, the very one in question, lying there plain as day. He grabbed the handkerchief and dashed out to cross-examine his mother, who was just then rinsing out some clothes in a small washbasin in the dim hallway light. He ran up, stuck the handkerchief under her nose, and shouted, "Look! What's this?" His mama lifted her head and looked closely at the handkerchief. "Oh. It was your *papa* who said it was lost, lost it. . . . To hell with it! It's just as well we ran her out. I was going to take over the washing myself in any case. See, at this rate I can save over a hundred dollars a month. What could be better?"

With that his mother went to hang the clothes to dry on the bamboo rod. Her face was the color of straw, her hair looked like a tousled lion's mane, and on her tightly drawn lips was etched the word *viper*. That night his papa continued to behave as if nothing had happened. If anything, he acted as if he had never been cheerier – he was humming a Peking Opera air. It was then that he realized why his father could be so unperturbed, so cheery; it was because he had just dispensed with a huge expense. That's it – moral values may be worth a few cents, but what a bargain to trade them in for several times that every month in real money. Moral values be damned!

He ran into that washerwoman in the neighborhood alleyways a few times after that incident. She was now washing clothes for some other families nearby. He thought she looked grievously hurt. Every time she would lower her head and avert her eyes so as not to look at him, while he, heavy-hearted, hung his head and dared not even sneak a glance at her.

I IO

It was his father's fifty-third birthday. As always on such occasions his mother set out an array of delicacies arranged on the shelf of the kitchen cabinet at the end of the front hallway. On the wall above it she had pasted a piece of red paper on which his father had written, "The Altar of the Fan Family Forefathers"; two fat candles were lit on either side. The whole of the cabinet area was aglow with brightly glimmering light. At school, he had heard about the need to abolish superstition, and he was already a convert to the theory of overthrowing idols and spirits. Just this last Mid-Autumn Festival he had had a heated debate with his mother over this very issue. Therefore he now stationed himself in his *erh-ko*'s bedroom all by himself, hoping that by so doing he could wait out the possibility of being summoned to pay his respects at the altar. During the last Mid-Autumn Festival he had lifted a meatball from a similar altar arrangement at this very table and was about to eat it when his mama intervened. This had led to an argument.

"Why can't I eat it?" he asked.

"Because your forefathers have not had any yet, that's why," Ma said.

"Then why did I see you eating it in the kitchen?"

"I wasn't eating it from *this* dish."

"You mean once it's been placed on this dish it becomes something else? Then what if you took some of this here and placed it on another plate? Could you give me some then?"

His mama hesitated for a second. "That's okay."

"What difference does it make, then, if I had eaten that meatball I picked up just now?"

"It's *just . . . different.*"

"Then give me some now!"

"If you had come a little sooner, it would've been okay, but now we've already started to make the offering, so we can't take it back."

"Hah! Do you want to hear what I think? I say there's no such thing as gods! None whatsoever! If there were a god, what shape or form would he take? How is it that I've never seen him? You seem to have *seen* him. Tell me, if you would, what does he look like? Ask him to come out and let me have a look at him!"

"Shut your mouth, shut your mouth! God will punish you for that!" She was almost trembling with fear.

"Okay, okay, I won't go on. Just let me ask you this. Why have our forefathers not eaten this food here? How is it these dishes are still full?"

"Don't talk about it here. Let's go into the other room if you want to argue."

"Okay, let's go into the other room then."

"Our forefathers are satisfied simply by the smell of the food," she said after they had entered the room.

"Is that right? Then our forefathers sure have rotten luck. They can't even eat what they want to eat. All they can do is smell. But if you've cooked these dishes for our forefathers, then why did you ask me yesterday what it is I would like to eat? Shouldn't you have asked our forefathers instead what it is they would like to eat, or, rather, would like to 'smell,' hm?"

She was silent.

"Hah! It's clear that all such offerings, wine and meat and so on, are merely what people themselves want to eat. Offerings made to the gods are merely an excuse for a feast; you've shifted the responsibility for your own desire to eat onto the heads of these so-called forefathers. Now you can eat all you want and at the same time congratulate yourselves for revering gods and honoring ancestors. You hypocrites with your false piety! Hypocrites! Hypocrites!"

She was still silent.

"And besides, you don't really think that by writing *forefathers* on a piece of crumpled up red paper you can summon them to come live here with you, do you?"

Mama was wracking her brains, but she couldn't come up with a retort. Since his father was willing to listen to his mother and wrote these words on the red paper for her, it must mean that, in his heart, he, too, was fearful of such gods and spirits. This led him to despise his father just as much. Father, too, was superstitious. And to think that he had been abroad to study in Europe!

Despite the debate, his mama still insisted that he bow down before that strip of red paper. He refused. She persisted. Thus ensued a brutal shouting match. In the end it was he who had to submit that day and suffer himself to make one kowtow.

Now, once again, the threat of his mama making him bow at that altar was before him. He curled up in a bundle, with his eyes shut, in his *erh-ko*'s room, waiting.

When the time came for the burning of the gold paper offerings, his mama summoned him in a loud voice. "Sonny, come." Her voice resounded through the corridor.

"Uh," he answered sluggishly.

"Come here, come make a bow at the altar!" Her voice sounded charged and testy.

He had no choice but to come out grudgingly. Holding his head up high, with the proud expression of one who will not submit, he dragged himself forward, his slippers slapping on the floorboards. Shuffling past the altar, he looked up indifferently at it, hesitated for a moment, and then stiffly bent forward and made the merest gesture of a bow.

"What's this wishy-washy nod of the head? Straighten up and give me an honest-to-goodness show of respect. Go on, bow down again!"

"I've done it once already. Why do you want to make me – "

"Do you hear me? Bow down right now!"

There he stood, engulfed in the blaze of the raging pyre of paper money, holding himself erect before the name plaque of his ancestors. He hung on for another second, and then stiffly, rigidly, he bent his body forward thirty degrees and bowed.

As soon as he made the bow he turned round to go back into the room, but his mama managed to block his exit. "Wait, wait just a minute. Haven't you forgotten something? What about paying your respects to your papa and wishing him a long life on his birthday?"

"Another bow for the birthday?"

"Of course. You've forgotten? We do this every year."

He kept his thoughts to himself.

"What's *with* you, anyway? Let me tell you right now. Don't think you can get away without giving me another bow today. Do it, now!"

So he had to go before his father, and, with a tortured expression, eyes drooped, he directed a pathetic nod at the old man. His father for his part could not but show his disapproval even as he acknowledged his nod with an even slighter one.

"And? You still have to say you wish Papa a long life on his birthday. Go on, say it!"

"Let it go," his father said cheerlessly. As soon as he heard that, he scurried back into the bedroom.

Encircled by the candle's flickering radiance, his mother, in a stern voice, began her lecture. "Today is the day of your own father's birth. How dare you *defile* such a day as this? I'll tell you once and for all that if you refuse to be filial and obedient, your forefathers will not let you get away with it.

Anyone who dares thwart his parents will be dealt with by the heavens and eradicated from the earth! You mark my words! If you are not filial, your father's fathers and their forefathers will punish you severely. They'll have your body crushed and your bones ground into powder, and your soul will not recover for aeons to come!"

He retreated into the bedroom and crouched back into his corner, deeply wounded by the shame of having submitted, twice, to the indignity of bowing down. This sort of superstition should never have been allowed to exist! This kind of filial piety should never have been allowed to prevail! Then an idea came to him. There was no one in the hallway; both his parents had gone into the kitchen. He slipped out of the room, headed toward the cabinet for the pair of candles, and blew them out.

Part Two

I

SEARCH
For Father

Dear Father,
It's been over half a month since you left.
Everything will be resolved according to your
wishes.

Your son,
Yeh

Darkness wrapped round about him. Looking in through the gaps of the bamboo fence, he saw one dim light inside the house. It was the light in the front hallway, the only light left on. The rest of the dark hallway was covered up by the shabby old curtains that had been drawn almost all the way through the front of the house. From this he could tell that his papa had not returned. It was now close to ten thirty. The entire neighborhood had turned in for the night. His mother, he was sure, was waiting up for him alone in the house. He knew she was waiting because he had written two days ago saying he would be coming home today. He tapped quietly on the bamboo gate and waited. He could feel his mother being roused into activity inside the house. She came to the window and drew the curtain aside, peering out, staring into the darkness, before she headed for the glass sliding door with the wooden paneling and pulled it open. His mother came down the stairs and reached for the latch at the bamboo gate.

"Who's there? Who is it?"

"It's me, Sonny."

"Ah!" She sounded disappointed. Perhaps she had thought, at first, that he might have been his father.

"Mama," he called to her. The bamboo gate swung open.

"Sonny."

He walked on ahead, across the yard and up the steps, and, bending down to undo his shoelaces, asked, "Any news?"

"Nothing. Except the District Registrars did come round once, day before yesterday, but all they did was ask a few questions, nothing more. And you?"

"Nothing." He paused before asking, "Any letters come for me?" He thought of the various places he had been to in the South.

"None at all."

He picked up his briefcase, the suitcase, and the umbrella.

"Have you eaten?"

"Yeah, I have."

Out of the blue, his mother started sobbing quietly to herself.

"Don't cry. Don't upset yourself."

"Go in and have a rest. Rest up now. You must be tired out."

"Okay."

"Will you be going straight back to work in the morning?"

"I'm going to put it off another day. Tomorrow I want to see if I can't find out anything more from the District Registrars."

"What do you think should be done from here on out?"

"I'm afraid the search will have to be put off for a little while now. We'll just have to sit tight and wait."

She became quiet and just stared at him as he went on.

"I'm thinking we should stop the ad in the paper tomorrow; it's getting too expensive."

III

A twin-engine plane zoomed past, flying low. The propellers protruding from its wings looked like two spinning tops. The booming noise it made initially sounded as if one huge piece of sheet metal had collapsed on top of another. Then, as it gradually faded away, it was like the rumbling of hundreds of empty, echoing petroleum barrels tumbling over a stone pavement. A youth came dashing out, barefoot, into the courtyard, but by the time he got outside and looked up into the sky, the airplane had already covered its tracks and disappeared. All he saw was a mass of scrambled clouds that resembled tender, white tofu-jelly flakes, scattered across the sky. This youth was sixteen years of age. At the moment, he was standing behind the bamboo fence that had been erected around his house about two years ago; he was looking out at the world beyond the bamboo, at sky and green branches, when it suddenly occurred to him that he had no shoes on his feet. He leapt back into the house.

Their home had changed a little from the way it had been before: real steps, made of concrete, had replaced the stepping-stones that used to serve as the front steps, and a great many wooden clogs and old shoes were littered all over the top of the stairs. In addition, an extension made of wooden planks covered in black asphalt was built onto the front of the house; this was now their kitchen. Both the bamboo fence and the kitchen were put up two years ago, when the whole boardinghouse underwent repairs. He went inside the house. The interior of this house looked much older now. He entered the room that belonged to his *erh-ko*. His brother's bamboo couch was still there; he plopped down on it and started turning the pages of a novel he had read many times before. It was a Russian novel, *The Nest of Gentlefolk,* by Turgenev. He had fallen in love with the simple, leisurely life of the small farming community and the Russian bourgeois landlord of the period. In the last month he had plunged into Gogol's *Evenings on a Farm Near Dikanka,* Turgenev's *Smoke,* and Chekhov's *The Steppe* and read them all in one breath.

Into this world that his reading had created the shrill voice of his mother came crashing through, bursting in with the bright sunshine, like the noise of cups and platters being smashed onto the ground outside. She was scolding somebody in her stiff, broken Taiwanese, sputtering in incoherent rage: "Who the hell. . . . What unreasonable person can it be this time, leaning this pole full of soaking clothes on my bamboo fence? My fence will topple over under the weight of this load. Don't you know that, or are you too dumb to understand?"

He flung his book onto the bed. His face flushed bright red. His mother was at it again. It wasn't as if she were really worried about the fence – a bamboo fence didn't fall so easily as all that. It was just that she couldn't stand it that the tip of someone else's clothes pole had been propped up on it. She took this as a personal affront. To think that she couldn't even bear to lend someone else that bit of space, couldn't give someone that little support. How mean, how narrow-minded could she get? He blushed with anguish and shame; he ran out to the front hallway and looked out, wringing his hands.

"Min-hsien! Come out here and help me talk some sense into these savages. These bossy types have no respect for anyone or anything. Look at this, they've just come right out in the open and plunked their stuff right down in our space. You tell me, is she beneath contempt or what? I will never allow this! There's *no way* I'm going to let her do this to me. I'm not going to lend it to her even if she asks me. My space is not for lending!"

Because she was shrieking at the top of her voice, a crowd of small children had gathered on the other side of the bamboo fence, peering in through the stalks to see what was going on inside. These were kids from the rundown buildings across the way, and could even have been from that family that had hung the clothes out to dry.

"Hey, you! Beat it!" Mama yelled at them. "Didn't you hear what I said? You've come to see how else you can help knock down my fence, *have* you?"

Then, all of a sudden, from behind her came: "Buzz off, you! *Beat it!*" It was Father, charging out of the kitchen, raving like a madman, his eyes glaring so hard they looked like two big circles.

His war cry made his own son jump and fall back a couple of steps. Several of the children who had been hanging onto the bamboo fence let go in fright, and some were so shocked that they started to cry. The shame and contempt he felt for his father was something he had not experienced before. Oh, Father! How could you treat children that way? How could you be so cruel to little children? But of course the very reason he could abuse them so was precisely because they were little and therefore weaker and he knew it; he knew he could bully them into submission.

Just then a skin-and-bones woman with a face as white as a sheet of paper stepped out. With a look of utter disgust she yanked her clothes pole away and left. Fortunately she did not choose to start a quarrel. Mama, however, wasn't about to let up and wagged her finger after the woman. "You totally unreasonable person, taking up my space like that, you have no right, you know? What would've happened if you had toppled my fence? Do you have the money to pay for it?" His father was standing right behind his mother, staring daggers at the woman with those great big brass-bell eyes of his.

"Min-hsien, you go in and fetch those two forked poles for me. Let's bring out our own clothes and hang them out in the sun. Better take up the space before someone else decides to come take advantage of us again."

Oh, Ma, didn't you just say that fence would fall over from the heavy weight of the clothes?

He paced up and down the hallway, seething, his face feverish with indignation, his hands sweaty and cold.

His father came out of the kitchen carrying the two makeshift clothes poles that had been fashioned from two broken-off tree limbs. Normally they would hang their clothes out to dry by fitting these two forked branches across the trees in front of the kitchen. Now they were trying, with difficulty, to prop the branches up against the fence. He watched the two of them under the bright sunshine, his own parents, acting like two "aborigines," swaggering and strutting about as if they had recently emerged victorious from out of the Flood.

As step by step he paced the floor, he pressed his face harder and harder into his hands. From the beginning to the end of this fierce row, he had not had the *courage* to show his face, and even several hours afterward he was still unable to bring himself to go out.

112

His father's financial situation deteriorated; he was demoted from the secretarial position he had originally held to that of a mere assistant, which also meant the loss of two hundred dollars each month. This state of affairs filled Father with rancor and resentment. He was sure that his "adversary," a Secretary Hsieh, was behind it all. This Secretary Hsieh was Father's public enemy number 1. He knew that his father did not get along with quite a large number of people in his office because at home he often heard his father bad-mouthing this person and cursing that one. More than likely someone or other had overheard him talking like this in the office as well, and, because of that, Father had killed his own chances of ever being sent on those much coveted business trips. Consequently, he was left sitting at home day after day, eaten up by envy over other people's good fortune.

His monthly income was in fact far short of the family's expenses. And by now the child was well acquainted with the predictable scene at the beginning of each month when the pay arrived. His papa and mama would shut themselves up in their bedroom, each crouching on one side of the small crow-black money box, counting out the money. His mother's sickly looking face would look sicklier still, and her already short temper would become even shorter as she sat on the tatami with her legs spread wide. By the twentieth of the month or thereabouts they'd have run out of money, and his papa would have to go borrowing from this person or that at the office. And these people, who had been the targets of his indiscriminate envy and vituperation, whom he had called "wheeler-dealers" and "manipulators," and about whom he had even come right out and said that they were "on the take," these same people were all quite willing to help him out and lend him money.

He had once asked his mama how they could ever hope to dig themselves out of this hole if they went on borrowing money and getting into debt month after month. But his mama replied that by borrowing money this month in order to pay last month's debt, and then borrowing again next month from someone else, they could go on forever. His father's attitude toward poverty might even be called philosophical, a sort of go-with-the-flow kind of attitude. Each time, after he had counted out the money, he would light up a cigarette, pour himself a cup of tea, lean back against his chair in the corridor, breathe a sigh of relief, and say, "Aigh. Take 70 percent here and 80 percent there, and this month's pay is as good as nothing." He behaved as if a great load had just been lifted off his shoulders. Sometimes he would take somebody else who was even worse off than he and make fun of that person instead. "That Cheng I-kang, not only didn't he get a cent in pay, he ended up owing the accounting office two hundred dollars!" One time he caught sight of his mama counting a big stack of dollar bills. He had never seen so much money in all his life, and, though he was just a child, the sight of it aroused in him such wild rapture that he couldn't help exclaiming, "Wow! What a lot of money!" But his mama turned on him, saying, "What are you so happy about? This is other people's money. It's just our turn to collect the savings club money this month, that's all!"

His father had tried to get some overtime, but opportunities eluded him. He cursed his coworkers for keeping these small advantages among themselves; it was always the same few people who got the perks. "It's a dead-end job this, nothing but a dead-end job," he huffed.

Papa had taken him, once, to his workplace. It was the time Sonny needed help with a math problem from one of his father's colleagues. He had taken the 1:05 company bus with his papa to the office. The bus was parked and waiting at the entrance to their alley. It had been converted from a delivery truck. The passenger compartment was like a matchbox; it had no windows, not even a peephole, and no doors. The office workers climbed in by grabbing onto a short metal chain and swinging themselves aboard. The older ones had to be helped on by others who hauled them in by the hand. As the truck pulled away, a latecomer dashed out, waving his arms, and barely managed to get on. Half in and half out, he hung on as the truck accelerated; his glasses had slipped onto the tip of his nose. Several workers came to his aid and with great effort finally got him in by dragging him in over the side. During the bus ride, the younger workers jostled about, playfully punching one another, while the older ones closed their eyes for a snooze. One old man kept his eyes shut throughout the trip and opened them only when the bus came to a full stop at the end of the journey.

When they arrived at the office building, he was greeted by an old, tumbledown, wooden structure. Climbing up the first flight of stairs, he was assaulted by the smell of dust, the musty smell of stagnant dust accumulated through the years. Turning the corner at the top of the stairs, he came upon a rickety skeleton of a rattan chair that had been parked on the landing since who knows when. They arrived at Father's office; it was a small room shared by five people. Against the wall, at the end of the room, a towel rack had been provided, and on it were hung some soppy, soggy facecloths; several mosquitoes flew out from behind them. His father's work station turned out to be an old writing desk, its surface marked with the circular impressions left by hot teacups. There was nothing much on it at all – just a squat copper ink box and a box of paper clips. The person who sat opposite father had not come to work this particular afternoon. Father mumbled something about his having "gone moonlighting" and told Sonny he could sit at that man's place. Presently, they realized that the young man he had come to seek help from, the office worker who could help him with his math problems, was not going to show up either, and he was left with nothing to do except read the newspaper.

During this time a well-dressed man in a Western suit, middle aged and with the fine looks of a learned gentleman, entered the room. He greeted Father warmly as he passed by, and Father greeted him back. This man went over to another person, said something to him, and then left again. He asked Father who that was. His papa told him that he was the Secretary Hsieh he had heard so much about. Naturally his curiosity was aroused, and he asked where this man's office was situated, but to this question his papa gave no answer. At around 4:30 in the afternoon, everyone in the entire office was ready to leave. As a group they boarded the bus that had been waiting for them outside the office building, shooting the breeze and telling jokes while waiting for quitting time. When the bell rang out at 5 o'clock, the bus started up, and the whole workforce was on the way home, he among them, riding on the communal bus that transported them to and from the workplace.

113

His *erh-ko* had recently got himself a new girlfriend. His father was even more violently opposed to this one than to the one before. He heard his mother say that this woman had once been a barmaid at some hotel. For this reason, his father was already up in arms about the liaison, but to make matters worse his *erh-ko* announced that he was determined to marry her. The fact of the matter was that, beyond these differences of opinions, ever since he had hooked up with this woman his *erh-ko* had brought home less money with each succeeding month, so that the family was plunged into even worse straits than ever before. In the last two months he had not given them a cent because he figured that since he was spending less and less time at home there was no need to further supplement the family income. For this reason family quarrels broke out at the slightest provocation, and every quarrel turned into a storm. These stormy scenes transformed the household into a living *hell*. These battles usually took place at nightfall because his *erh-ko* didn't come home till late in the evening. It was inevitable – the moment his *erh-ko* stepped into the house he was bound to get into a fight with his father. Were it not for the fact that he kept his trunk of clothes here, his brother would probably not come home at all. He could vividly recall one horrific scene.

It was some time past the fifteenth of the month, and it had occurred to his father that two weeks and so many days had already gone by and his *erh-ko* had not handed over any money for the month. As was often the case, it was closing in on nightfall, even though, in order to save on electricity, the lights inside the house remained unlit; the darkness was filled with the buzzing, brooding noise of mosquitoes flitting about. As soon as his *erh-ko* approached the bamboo fence his papa caught sight of him and immediately parked himself in a straight-back chair out in the hallway so as to waylay him at the entrance. His brother approached, walking past his papa without even acknowledging his presence. Thus ignored, his papa riveted his unblinking gaze on him all the way as he walked into the room; Sonny followed suit, similarly looking daggers at his brother. Regarding this particular issue, he stood on his father's side. This was because his mother had already biased him against his *erh-ko* for not helping out with the family expenses, for not taking care of his own family.

Seeing that Erh-ko was not going to initiate the conversation, Papa roared out at him as he walked away, blustering, "Hey, you, Lao-erh! Answer me this one question. Let me ask you this. Do you or don't you give a damn these days whether we live or die?"

Erh-ko glared back at him with an astonished expression, as if it had not until this very moment occurred to him that such a question might be put to him. "What's that?"

"It's not that I want to ask you for money. You know I'd rather not have to spend one cent of yours, but have you no regard for your own little brother here and your aunt and what is to happen to them?"

His mother immediately retreated into the background and, grabbing him by the arm, tried to yank him away with her. He, however, had too much curiosity to be thus dragged away from the scene. He lingered on. He remembered the deadly look his brother shot at him just then.

"Didn't I already tell you that I've got to have a suit and that for that I've had to put money into two savings clubs? I've very little money left over the last few months. Wait till the terms are up, and we'll see what I can do."

"Hah!" his father sneered. "My foot. The way I see it, all you have to do is spend less money on that girlfriend of yours, and you'll have more than enough to spare!"

"Pa, Papa. . . . Please, I beg of you, don't bring up that subject again, will you? What's the use? No matter how much we talk about it, it'll still be the same. It's no good. Might as well leave it unsaid. But let me tell you formally right now that I and I alone am responsible when it comes to my money. It has nothing whatsoever to do with her. She has *never* asked me for one cent of my money. Besides, this is money I have earned on my own; I don't see why I can't spend it any way I damn well please. And, what's more, when have you ever given me money to spend – ever?"

"What? What did you say? What's this attitude now? What kind of an attitude is this you're taking with me? Is this the way you should be behaving when you're talking to . . . me?"

His brother was silenced.

"You look to me like a different person altogether! In your eyes, do I even exist anymore? When you came in just now, you didn't even cast a glance at me. Have you no manners left at all?"

"The moment I came in the door your face clouded over. How the hell do you expect me to start chatting with you?"

"How's that? You're not telling me you expect me, your own goddamn *father,* to come fawning with a smile on his face to greet his own son, are you? You must be joking! Don't you think you can just come back here and treat this home like a hotel. Eat and sleep, that's all you do here! We'll see about that, see if there's any dinner here for you tonight! So you think you can just barge in here expecting dinner to be served? No dinner for you! There's no dinner for you tonight!"

"That's fine with me, just fine! I don't need your dinner. I'm gone!" Erh-ko turned sharply to go.

"Stop right there!" Pa yelled out in a mad rage.

Erh-ko halted involuntarily.

"You *traitor!*" Papa hollered.

Mama reappeared at this critical juncture.

"Since it has come to this, I may as well finish what I have to say. Under *no* circumstance will I ever allow you to bring that filthy, immoral, mongrel bitch of a lowlife woman across this threshold! If you want to marry her, then you . . . ," Papa said, ". . . you had better wait till I've breathed my last. Talk to me then, when my lids are closed forever!"

"Marry her or not, that is *my* decision, mine alone. If I choose to take her for my wife, I'll take her whenever and wherever I wish!"

"What? You turtle egg of a bastard, you!" His papa slammed his open palm onto the table, and in an instant his face turned white as ash.

"Min-hsien, Min-hsien, you must take care of your own health. You know you shouldn't get so upset. Remember that high blood pressure condition of yours," his mother said anxiously. His father's blood pressure could shoot up without notice.

By now a crowd had gathered all around the bamboo fence outside, watching the spectacle.

"Then let me also make myself absolutely clear to you. I don't care the least about this so-called family anymore. As far as I'm concerned, whether this family exists or not has nothing to do with me. I'm going to leave right now. Just you watch me! See if I come back *ever* again." Having said that, his *erh-ko* shot out of the door like an arrow.

"You stop right there! Come back here!" His papa suddenly covered his eyes with his hands, stumbled forward, and doubled up in pain, saying, "My head's spinning! Spinning round! . . ."

"Min-hsien! Min-hsien!"

"Papa!" he shouted.

Erh-ko had vanished long ago beyond the bamboo fence.

"Min-hsien!"

"Ah . . . don't worry. . . . I'm better now. . . . Don't be afraid!"

Mama hurried off to get his father a cup of hot tea. He rushed off into the front hallway and drew the curtains around.

His father sipped his hot tea and said, "He . . . he. . . . What kind of a son is that? He'll make me spit blood!"

"Don't you upset yourself over a son like that," Ma urged him. "It's not worth wasting your breath over him. Better watch out for your own health. Besides, it's your duty to look after us two, mother and child. If anything should happen to you, you tell me, what will the two of us do, all by ourselves?" So saying, real tears began to roll down Mama's cheeks.

Just then Father stared straight in front of him, his eyeballs stiffening. The color drained from his face; in an instant it was as white as a sheet of paper.

"Min-hsien! Min-hsien!"

"Papa, Papa!" He was completely terrified by his father's blank expression.

"Nothing . . . it's nothing. . . . I'm okay."

"Min-hsien. . . ." His mama went on with her plea for calm.

His hatred for his brother was complete!

114

The typhoon struck with virile abandon. Through the murky turbulence of the night he listened to its riotous assault as broken beams were knocked about and doors and passageways violently attacked. He was inside the house, but the tumult outside filled him with dread. He couldn't be sure whether the scary noises came from the howling wind or from the thrashing rain. Or perhaps the fury was not created by the rain but by the boisterous complaint of the leaves and branches as they were crushed into each other. He was conscious of the noise approaching from a long way away, like great billows crashing ashore, drawing near from afar, gathering momentum. The closer it got, the more menacing it became, closing in on the many banyan trees from all sides, so that with each bout of the tempest he imagined the trees and leaves coming at him, terrorizing him, till he tossed and turned in bed, tormented by these hideous shadows. With every new eruption of the typhoon he expected the whole wooden structure of his house to be uprooted and swept away, with him in it; together they would be reduced to nothing. This boardinghouse was very old indeed. From some obscure corner there came a creaking, dripping sound: leak-creak, drip-drop, drip. Another giant wave of the typhoon mounted, ready to pounce.

115

In the silent, noonday heat of the city street, a father hurried along in swift strides; the Observatory building could now be seen in the distance standing tall against the hazy sky. This father was wearing a stiff, white gauze, open-necked summer shirt above a pair of trousers made of a dark, winter-weight material. This disregard for the changing of the seasons was due to the fact that he had no money to buy a new pair of summer pants. Wound around his waist was a thoroughly worn leather belt, so limp and twisted it looked like a tailor's cloth tape measure, particularly as the extra length of it had to be looped around to the back of his pants and left dangling. The tarmac street had been melted by the blazing sun into a molten rubbery sheet, and as he walked he had difficulty keeping his shoes on because with each step they stuck to the black, gooey surface. Each time he lifted his foot back up again he had to be careful that the sole was not left behind; these were extremely aged shoes indeed. The soles themselves were worn perilously thin, and the sticky, rubbery tarmac felt like hot coals under his feet.

The company bus had broken down and had been taken to the shop for repairs; thus transportation was not provided during lunch hour. Most of the workers had chosen to take the public bus back to the boardinghouse, but he and two other guys insisted on walking. After ten minutes or so under the blast of the sun, one of them abandoned the idea and went back to take the bus. Another ten minutes passed, and the other guy also decided to give up, but he couldn't locate a bus stop nearby and had to hire a pedicab instead. A smug little grin crept onto his face as he watched the other man being taken off; he continued on his solitary way, limping happily along.

Straight ahead, not too far off, was the towering red building of the State Monopoly; he was almost halfway home. His face was toasted scarlet by the fiery sun, his mouth hung open, and he started to pant. To protect himself from the savage sun, he had covered his head with his handkerchief, which he also used from time to time as a sweat cloth, wringing it out and wiping himself, wiping himself and wringing it out again. His mouth was getting very dry just as he walked past an ice-water stall. The hawker beckoned to him invitingly, "Come, come, a dollar a cup!" He shook his head and refused the offer with a smile.

By this time he was not only wearing the handkerchief on his head but walking with his hand on his crown. A skeleton of a stray dog wandered by, his long tongue dangling out of his mouth, and God knows why he started to follow him, trotting side by side with him, step for step, stride for stride. In this manner they proceeded on for a while, and then, as if even this down-and-out drifter of a skeleton realized that no good would come of following such a one as he, the dog turned tail and deserted him.

He now came to the spot where he could see the level crossing of the railroad tracks; he was a mere six or seven minutes' walk away from home. What dumbbells, those guys, couldn't even grit their teeth and take a little heat. Aren't I here now, almost home? So what if I'm a little late? Of course, now that I'm half an hour late for lunch, there won't be time for my nap afterward. Wonder if I should walk back to the office? No, I don't think so. I'll probably be late if I do. Too risky . . . the Personnel Department's gotten tight about these things lately.

At long last he arrived home. Ma chewed him out for taking such a long time to get home. How was it that everyone else in the whole boardinghouse had arrived so long before him? she wanted to know. He beamed back at her, still catching his breath, and from the breast pocket of his gauze shirt he pulled out a soaking wet bus ticket, saying, "They issued these free tickets at the office for our afternoon ride home. I've saved mine up, so now *Sonny* can use it for his ride to school in the morning."

116

The kind of pain he experienced during this period was worse than all others. He was made witness to the endless quarrels between his father and his mother. These fights occurred so often that he was unable to separate one incident from another; they were all mixed up and cast into one single impression left on his mind.

The following episode was probably not one single event but the conflation of many such memories, the culmination of them all.

That afternoon, for whatever reason, his mother had found it necessary to call his father at work. But Papa was not there. She called him again after a while, but he was still not there. His mama got mad then and quit calling altogether.

She sat in the hallway and began to spin suspicion into reality. "Look at that now, Sonny, your father, in broad daylight even, has the gall to stay away from his office." From the long-suffering expression she had worked up into her face, it was clear that the monsters of jealousy had been eating away at her.

He recognized the symptoms with anger and loathing; he was absolutely sick of his mother's jealous paranoia. "That's right. Not there. He's not there! What of it?"

"Where do you think he could've gone?"

"*Can't* he simply have gone next door to another office to discuss business with somebody? What's the big deal? Can't he have gone to the toilet for a pee?"

"But I called him twice."

"Just give him another try, why don't you?"

"I'm not going to call him again. Besides, he'd have had time to return to his desk for sure by now."

He didn't know how to reply to that, so he yelled back at her, saying through clenched teeth, "Then that's your business!"

Five-thirty rolled round, and his papa came home. His mother gave him the silent treatment. His father couldn't make heads or tails of it and tried asking her what the matter was. "What's up? Has something happened? Huh?"

His ma merely pursed her lips and wouldn't say anything.

"How's that? What in the world's the matter?"

"*Since* you ask, I'll *tell* you! Where have you been all afternoon? I called you to ask if you would stop at the office co-op on your way home and pick up a bag of detergent for me. But twice I called, and twice you weren't there. Where *were* you?"

"Me, nowhere! I simply went over to Section 1 for a short chat. I came back almost immediately. So it was you! The guys in my cubicle told me I had two phone calls. I wondered who could've called me. I was there all afternoon after that. Why didn't you call again? I'd have gotten you the detergent on my way home."

"I don't go asking for abuse! No thanks. Why should I call again?"

His father had no reply for that.

That night dinner was eaten under a dark cloud; everyone was in a foul mood. Mother didn't say a word from the beginning to the end of the meal. Even after dinner Mother kept her silence. He knew this was the forecast for some extraordinarily severe eruption to occur later on in the evening. Experience told him that this type of condition, this kind of depressive phenomenon, was an ominous signal for that inevitable bitter brawl that would occur in the middle of the night.

Thus it was that he approached his bedtime with fear and trepidation. Perhaps it was the anxiety that hung in the night air that prevented him from falling into a deep sleep, and because of that, in the sleepy wakefulness of this anguished state of alert, he could detect the slightest movement in the dark and distinguish even the noise of a pin dropping, to the extent that he could tune in to the suggestion of his mother's sleeplessness in the next room. Shortly afterward he heard a long sigh. Instantly his nerves tightened and tangled up in a thousand knots. Was this it? Was the critical event he so dreaded about to commence? He strained to listen. As expected, a hush-hush noise started up in the next room. It was all too familiar, the imminent threat that such hushed-up conversations held for him; this was the tone his mother used whenever she didn't want him to overhear, thinking that by whispering other people would not be able to make out her words. He heard his father say,

"But I didn't go anywhere. . . . If you don't believe me, you can go ask the guy I was with."

Out of the hum of silence that followed, he suddenly felt the shudder of the tatami shaking with his mother's kicking and thumping. He could hear her thrashing about, lashing out at heaven and earth, and then he heard her cry out, "My heart, it's pounding something terrible – I'm not going to make it!" His papa was calling after her desperately, "Ch'iu-fang! Ch'iu-fang! *Ch'iu-fang!*"

He sat bolt upright, fearing the worst. Then Father went completely quiet. What was it? Was she dead? He dashed out and burst into their bedroom.

"What's happened? What's happened?" he asked in a panic.

The light was on in his parents' bedroom. No one spoke.

Then, without warning, his mama shattered the silence with a torrent of tears and thunderous weeping.

"Ch'iu-fang, really, you mustn't ever scare me like that again. You scared the hell out of me!" his father cried.

"Good. That's exactly what I wanted to do. You need to be scared!"

At that moment he hated his mother without reservation. He despised her trickery, her vicious and crafty playacting. He detested her for using this utterly ruthless method to achieve her shameless end.

They, the couple who were his parents, were inside the mosquito tent; he remained outside, staring at them through the netting.

"Now let me ask you this. Who the *hell* is she, this no good, filthy woman you've been with?"

"Where in the world would I get such a woman? I honestly went over to Section 1 for a chat. That's all. If you don't believe me, just go ask. Ask anyone."

"Okay. It's clear then that this shameless woman is in Section 1. So which one is it? Spit it out. Is it that Ou-yang Yi-ming? It must be her. That's it. So it's her. That was why she came here over the New Year! A social call, was it? What a bitch in heat, that rotten turtle's egg of a filthy whore. Just you wait till morning comes. I'll charge right over to their house and haul her out, show her up for what she is, and let that wimp of a husband of hers have a good look at what he's got at home! What a live turtle head he is! We'll have it out once and for all!"

"Ch'iu-fang! Whatever you do, you mustn't . . . whatever you do . . . don't. She's a decent, proper, good person. You, whatever, ever, ever you do, you mustn't go casting aspersions on other people in their own home. . . ."

"So now you're taking her side, are you? Have I dared slander your darling sweetheart? Your heart's aching now, is that right? Good. All right then! Now we have all the proof we need right here before us. So you're standing together, protecting each other, are you? You just watch me, see if I don't go charging over to her house bright and early tomorrow morning, haul her out, and show her what for!"

"Ch'iu-fang, you . . . you . . . you really . . . whatever you do, watch out that you don't blow this thing up into one big mess! That husband of hers is in the air force. You go messing around over there, and who knows what he'll do. What if he pulls his gun on you? It's no joke. Don't go fooling around about a thing like this."

"Me? Afraid of him? My life's not worth living anyway. What do I care? Provoke him? Let him shoot me, see if he has the guts to kill me! I've made up my mind. I'm going first thing in the morning to take her by surprise!"

"Ch'iu-fang. Please, please, I *beg* of you! I'll get down on my knees if you want me to!"

"All right then, you go ahead and *kneel* down before me! If you're really sorry for what you've done and will really sincerely repent of all your past mistakes, if you're truly determined to make an end of it, then go right ahead and kneel down for me!"

"But Ch'iu-fang, I've really not done anything. . . ."

"Kneel! Kneel down! You get on your knees! I don't care what you've done or not done. You just get on your knees!"

And indeed Father stooped. Knees bent, body hunched forward, supporting himself on the floor with his two hands, palms down, he crouched on the tatami.

At that moment he despised his father ten thousand times more even than he despised his mother.

"Look at you now. It just goes to show you were up to no good, you and her, doing your dirty deeds. So now you're running scared, afraid I might make a scene and alert her husband about you two! Since you've admitted to your mistake, I'll forgive you this time! But from this day onward you must solemnly swear never to see her again. As of today you are not allowed to speak to that witch of a vixen woman, not a word! And if I *ever* catch you talking to her, humph – ! Tell me, can you abide by this rule I'm setting down?"

"Yes, yes. As of today I will not say one word to her, never speak to her again. Now are you satisfied?"

"So, finally, I caught you by calling in the afternoon. I was going to do that a long time ago, give you a ring at the office to see what you've been up to. I've had wind of these goings-on for quite some time now. Don't you think that just because I'm stuck here at home I don't know anything. Let me tell you now that I have planted *secret agents* everywhere in that office of yours. You just *watch* your step. I'm telling you now, I'll be calling you again, and I don't care what time of day it is, if you're not there, ever again, you just wait and see what will happen to you!"

"Oh, but Ch'iu-fang, there are times when I'm called away without prior notice. Sometimes they need me to go to the other offices to take care of business. What then? Wouldn't you say that something like that is unavoidable? Wouldn't you allow me to go under those circumstances?"

"No. Not even then! You are not allowed, from this day on, to step away from your desk!"

His father twisted his face into a pained expression. "What if I need to go to the toilet? Am I not even allowed to go piss?"

"Don't you try to be funny with me! You think I don't know all your devious, lowdown, dirty tricks by now? No, pissing is not allowed! You want to piss, you piss before you go to work! Or else you can piss after working hours. No pissing allowed in between times."

"Okay, okay. I'll do as you say." Papa shifted his weight from one knee to the other, repositioning himself to ease the pain from crouching.

Infuriated, he turned abruptly from the mosquito tent and left.

He tossed and turned for a long time but was still unable to fall asleep. This was the second of two consecutive nights of sleeplessness. Nothing in particular had in fact happened. The insomnia was merely the result of the general unhappiness of his days. Each time he moved, the bamboo joints of the couch were sent into creaking, crackling spasms. This couch was his brother's overnight sleeper. Some time ago he had moved into this bedroom that had once been his *erh-ko*'s room. Ever since that violent outbreak between his *erh-ko* and his father, his brother had not been home to spend another night.

A small car drove by on the level road outside. The bright beams of its headlights swept across the room. In its wake he heard a clump of plaster, shaken loose, fall from the ceiling. All the walls in the building were peeling, stripped, blistered, and pulpy, rupturing into green, hairy, moldering blotches, with slimy slivers dangling and sliding down the sides, looking like the festering wounds of a leper. He was disgusted and ashamed to live here. He was too embarrassed ever to invite his friends home. All through the term not once had he asked anyone to visit, and even when people came by to see him he would come out into the front yard to chat with them, keeping them at a safe distance on the other side of the bamboo fence. He felt nothing but revulsion for this poverty-stricken environment. He wanted to extricate himself, to be dissociated from everything that had anything to do with it. He suffered *intensely* because of it, and his hatred for his surroundings made him feel it as an evil, so much so that he flatly refused ever to go fetch water at the public faucet for his family's use, despite the neighbors' harsh criticism of him for leaving this chore to his parents. The shame he felt for his own state of poverty far exceeded his filial feelings. It was all very well for people to say that poverty was nothing to be ashamed of. He could not help but feel its insult. Nothing could erase the deep impression left on him last winter when, at nightfall every evening, they had to go through the exercise of preparing for sleep. The flimsy cotton quilt that was supposed to keep him warm was as thin as a pancake; not only that, but it had numerous patches sewn all over it just to keep it from falling apart. On top of this fragile cotton quilt they placed his father's old black woollen coat, and on top of that they placed a piece of a furry material with long, finger-like strands of floppy wool that had once been the lining of a sheepskin jacket, though the jacket itself was nowhere to be found. This piece of dirty yellow fur was so worn and tattered that all the seams had come apart. The bits and pieces of this fluffy mess scattered all over the coat made it look as if dry straw had been thrown on top of the heavy woollen material. He simply couldn't bear to look at this poverty; it was so immediate, so demeaning. But what was even harder to bear was the public toilet they had to use. It was located in the main courtyard of the boardinghouse. It was a concrete outhouse, with a single wooden door and no windows. He couldn't imagine a torture chamber worse than this. On the inside of the toilet door a thick mat of flies lay in ambush. To enter without being overwhelmed by that tidal wave of swarming flies he first had to ram against the door, swing it open, and with one and the same motion rush inside and pull the door to so as to disperse and shut out as many as possible of that buzzing hoard. The putrid smell that came to him on squatting down at the toilet was thick as a wall, and, because there were no vents or windows, he had to hold onto the door and, by contorting himself, keep a slit open to the outside to let air and a little light into the room. Tears oozed from his eyes, brought on by the nauseating stench in the pitch dark toilet; it was even worse when the person before had lit a cigarette in order to counteract the existing odor, leaving the stale smoke to mix in with the other smells. It was enough to knock you over; it was almost like being drunk. Soon some flies would leak back into the chamber through the half-open door, as others came gushing out from the dark pit of the filthy depths underneath. There were simply too awfully many of them to shoo away. Since it was not possible to brush them off, all he could do was let them buzz around him and land on his forehead, around his lips, and on the whites of his eyes. And even worse than that was what he saw when he lowered his eyes to peer into the smoldering pit of the dark grotto. Lurking just beneath his ass were hundreds upon thousands of tiny, white maggots, squirming all over the pool of mushy, yellow, floating shit. It so happened that he was suffering from a fit of diarrhea during this time, which meant that he had to pay many visits to the toilet every day. Every day he had to put up with this torture, not just once, but over and over again. He had, once upon a time, tried to better his living conditions, to ameliorate the deprivation of his surroundings. For example, he had noticed that the light that stood on the big wooden table out in the corridor needed a shade and so had requested that his mama buy him one. She came back with a cheap plastic cover that, even when he put it over the naked bulb, did not seem to make it any better. And then there was the time when he wanted to cover up the windows in their part of the building and asked his mother for some coarse cloth with a green floral pattern to make curtains, but that effort, too, did not seem to have enriched the environment. From then on he resigned himself to let it be and did not bother making any further improvements. He retreated into the solace of music. He had a small yellow transistor radio. (His father had borrowed money from his office to buy it for him, which meant a monthly deduction would be taken from his father's pay for quite a while yet.) He especially liked listening to classical music at night, placing his transistor close to his ear and turning the volume way down so as not to wake his parents in the room next door. He was fond of the music of Mendelssohn, particularly his violin concerto in E minor. The elegiac Adagio in the second movement was his favorite passage. The musical phrases stayed with him always, coming to him like a song, as beautiful as a splash of water lilies. He was at the moment lost in this passage of music – listening intently, succumbing to the magic of the violin. He envisioned a snow-white water lily slowly emerging from the still surface of the pond, floating up and up, the white water lily blossoming petal by petal, limpid and clear, pure and clean – when suddenly, just as he was about to enter into the region of the sweetest of dreams, he was abruptly awakened. The sound of footsteps echoed through the front hallway. It was his father going for a piss. Wide awake now, he followed his father's footsteps from his room to the hallway, heard him slide open the front door and, with a loud swoosh, empty the liquid from the bedpan. Shortly afterward, a melodious stream of music burst forth; it was produced by the jet of his father's piss hitting the pan, from high to low, much like the sound made in the echo chamber of the vacuum flask when hot water is poured into its narrow neck. No doubt the neighbors heard. In the profound stillness of the night there was no way they could have missed it. Words could not express the shame he felt, not only because the neighbors heard this commotion created by his father's piss, but because he himself was implicated. He was feverish with embarrassment. And to make matters worse he was reminded that even his mother went out and pissed in the same way. In actual fact, he was in no position himself to despise others for this practice, for he, too, because of the convenience, used this very method to relieve himself.

The manner in which they had to wash themselves and the very place where they did it also caused him no end of embarrassment. There was a big washbasin that they used as their bathtub; it was kept in the kitchen, where they had to take their baths. Whenever he took a bath, he had to lug the whole thing out to the courtyard in order to dump the water. In front of everyone, for there were always people standing around, watching, he had to tip out his own dirty bathwater. And, as if that were not insulting enough, the bathtub itself was minuscule, barely big enough for him to get into, no bigger than a child's plaything. Beyond that, the greatest source of contempt and shame for him was the fact that his own parents hardly ever bathed. All winter they washed themselves no more than twice. There were other aspects of their peculiar lifestyle that he found utterly unacceptable. For example, just the other day he found his mother placing a sharp knife on top of the gauze umbrella that she used to cover up the leftover dishes on the table. She claimed that this would scare the wild cats away from their food. The room suddenly became unbearably hot; he felt trapped in the smutty heat. His parents always made sure they shut up all the windows and doors in the house before they went to bed. They habitually locked up anytime they slept, even if it was just for a daytime nap. All at once he felt the urge to let go. At the same time the pitiful expression his mother affected whenever she became ill appeared before him. Oh, *how* she managed to make you *feel* for her! She was endowed with the uncanny knack of sharing her misery, giving what was hers to you, pressing her disease on you. He was reminded now of the time when she had diarrhea (her symptoms were just like his), of the oppressive mixture of foul smells, the putrid amalgamation of shit and piss that filled the room. Just thinking about it made him want to puke. And then the thought occurred: What if his parents were killed in an accident? Would he, he wondered, be able to weep for them? He was deeply pained by this criminal uncertainty. He mourned for his own loss of innocence and repented his wickedness.

Another small car went by, and another piece of plaster fell. Like this place in which they lived, his family was simply falling apart, so rotten that repair was no longer possible. His *erh-ko* had just had another tremendous fight with his papa. Erh-ko had made up his mind, asserted his independence by announcing his marriage in two months' time with that ex-barmaid. It happened last evening, when his brother came home and had another fierce brawl with his father. Again his father yelled at him, and again he almost fainted from the exertion, and again the hot tea was poured, and again he feared for what might happen next. In the aftermath of this violent outbreak he stood staring out in the gloomy twilight (the sky had not yet turned entirely black) and watched the mosquitoes dancing around in the half-light under the eaves. At that moment he felt fit to die. The thought of suicide sent a quiver down his spine. He knew he had to seek relief somehow, to squeeze a drop of ease from somewhere. He knew of only one way, the one and only way open to him, the only kind of happiness he could attain. He reached down now with his two hands and clutched at the warm flesh nestled between his thighs. He urged himself into excitement, bringing himself to a kind of sensation that resembled pleasure. In a minute it was over. He had achieved a split second of happiness, though he was not the least bit happy. Nevertheless, he was now utterly spent; it was almost as if he had died. As it happened, the sky was just now brightening everywhere.

seeks happiness through physical pleasure

118

A few months later Father ran into a serious problem at work. There was a new director at his office, and this director didn't think much of his work. To make matters worse, there was no record of any of the certificates or diplomas he was supposed to possess (he said he had misplaced them all, but there was no way anyone could tell whether he actually had them in the first place), and so he was going to be transferred to a small unit far from the city. Father suspected that this was again that meddling Secretary Hsieh's doing, for Hsieh had now risen to the rank of secretary to the deputy.

This transfer to the countryside implied a great number of pitfalls. For example, Fan Yeh would have to give up schooling because what school could there be out in the sticks? It also meant that they might lose housing altogether since this was not a guaranteed benefit and they might not even be placed out there in the boondocks. Furthermore, with this demotion came also a reduction in his monthly salary. But the most worrying aspect of this whole ordeal was that the transfer itself might just be the first step in a scheme to kick him out altogether! These many concerns plagued his father, yet he had to keep them to himself for fear of worrying him and his mother. He was scared they might not be able to handle the threat that the situation posed. Thus, he fretted all alone, keeping it pent up inside himself. It wasn't as if Mother hadn't noticed that Papa often sat in the hallway lost in thought, or that he would stuff down only half a bowl of rice and not be able to eat any more. But when she asked him what was wrong, he would merely say that nothing was wrong. This lasted a week before his father finally broke down. He spat clumps of bloodstained yellow catarrh. The horror of this experience was to throw Fan Yeh yet again into bouts of anxiety. His days were spent dashing back and forth to the hospital for prescriptions or X-ray results, or he had to call the doctor to ask more questions, or he had to go to his father's office for an advance on his salary. He was convinced that his papa had not long to live. (His mother, a mournful expression on her face, drew him aside one evening and said, "Sonny, it doesn't look to me like your papa's going to be able to hold on much longer!") He prayed fervently, beseeching the Almighty to spare his father, to please not come and snatch him away. He made a secret pact with God and offered to repeat a grade in school in exchange for his father's recovery. He even said that he wouldn't mind contracting TB himself. He slept very little during that period, constantly on the alert, listening in bed to his father's bouts of coughing. Each time he heard his father cough he could see the blood brought up with the catarrh, and with each mouthful of blood he felt as if it were he – Fan Yeh – who had spat it out from his own lungs. The sight of blood in the small cigarette tin placed next to his father's cheek left an indelible impression on his mind: each time he saw a new glob of purplish blood in the tin, fear gripped him; each time it was as if he saw blood for the very first time. Luckily, after two weeks of coughing up blood, the symptoms subsided, and finally the blood stopped. The doctor came back with a diagnosis: the cause, he said, was depression. Only then did his father reveal the secret burden he had been carrying all by himself. He spilled it all out to Mother one day, even though he still didn't want his son to know. When Mama heard, she naturally implored him not to worry and told him how *silly* it would be for him to lose his life over a thing like that. "So long as the green hills remain, there will always be wood for fire," she said, and told him that the most important thing was for him to take it easy and watch his health. Then she reminded him that he must remember to think of them. What would happen to them? What would mother and son do if he were to leave them behind? Surely it would be better to move to the countryside than to give up his life for nothing, she had said, and Father agreed, nodding as she spoke, promising to loosen up and not vex himself from now on. And then, after a while, Father admitted that the whole mess with their *lao-erh* might have aggravated his condition. (Erh-ko had not shown his face once during his father's illness; of course, if truth be told, he couldn't have known about it since he had not been home again since that last fight.) Then Mama hurriedly forestalled him by saying, "Don't you go working yourself up over him. You can work yourself into a frenzy and die, and he wouldn't give a damn. You're nothing to him but another old fart waiting to die! You'll be making it easy for him. . . . But why? What for? It's his business if he wants to marry that sort of woman; it's in his stars. He

wouldn't listen to you, so be it, let him suffer the conse-
quences of his own actions! He's the one who asked for it.
It's called *getting what's coming!*"

Another week passed, and, to their surprise, something
good came out of his father's illness. Because of it the new
director was moved to pity and changed his mind about
sending his father to the countryside. Instead he was made
supervisor, a position that existed in name only, and he got
to stay where he was.

J

SEARCH
For Father

Dear Father,
You have been gone a long time. Please come home.
Everything will be resolved according to your
wishes.

Your son,
Yeh

This ad had appeared from time to time in the
paper since his return from that last trip in search of his
father. He didn't place it very often, though, only about
once a week. By now they had gotten used to the phenomenon of not having his father at home. They interpreted the
situation in the following way: Father was probably around
somewhere, waiting for proof of some kind; thus, his decision not to reappear had to do with his not having seen any
proof; so it followed that he must still be alive because he
was purposely hiding from them. What Fan Yeh needed to
do was wait and see if he was going to hear anything from
the various places he had been to, even though, so far, no

one had yet responded to his inquiries. He did receive a letter from one place, but it was only a mimeograph copy of a list of homeless old folks that they had taken in last month, and his father was not among them. Next to each person's name was recorded his or her certificate of identification number. Since his father didn't even have his ID with him when he left, could he perhaps have made one up for himself? That, however, seemed unlikely; obviously the agency would have cross-checked the names against the numbers with some local authority and reported them to their District Registrar. In any case, he planned to wait out another period, and if by then they had still not heard, he would save up some more, marshal his resources, and go on another expedition. As for the notice in the paper, it was truly because he was strapped for money that he could no longer advertise as often as he used to, though advertise he must, because he was somehow convinced that his father was staging a silent war with him; he was certain that his father scoured the papers every day to see if he had continued with the ads, and that it would take a long, long time of this continued advertisement before he and his mother could prove to him that they sincerely wanted him back. Then and only then would he come home. He didn't know why he was so convinced that this silent feud was on. All he knew was that he must continue to believe that it existed and continue the struggle. The current situation at home was one of adjustment; they had a new arrangement and had fallen into a new routine. He went back to work at school every day, and his mother went to the market, bought the groceries, and cooked the meals. No matter how great the changes in life, one still must make a living, still must eat. In addition, the new routine included a trip to the bank at the beginning of each month to withdraw the interest accrued on his father's pension account. He had first ascertained that his father had never been to the bank to claim this money — not since he left home — perhaps because his father figured they wouldn't give him the money without his personal seal. Thus it was that he went to the bank at the beginning of each month with his father's seal and withdrew this money for their use. This sum of money, his father's retirement benefit, was normally used to supplement the household expenses anyway. Besides, it was his mother's idea to do it this way, and she was, after all, the beneficiary of Father's pension account. Of course now that there was one less mouth to feed, the financial pressure they had felt before seemed to be greatly lightened. On the other hand, it had to be acknowledged that his trips in search of his father and the ads he had to place in the paper — all on behalf of his father — cost money, and his father's pension just about covered these expenses. He was thus merely spending his father's money on his father's business. What better use could he have made of it? How extraordinarily tidy and proper. One day he discovered that his mother had taken a photograph of his father to the studio to have it enlarged; later she bought a frame for it and hung it up on the wall. He realized then that his mama did not herself expect his father ever to come back again. And then there was the night he had gotten out of bed and walked smack into his father's writing desk — this particular wooden leg had tripped him up many times before, as the desk was positioned at the entry of what used to be his *erh-ko*'s bedroom. Then and there he decided to remove it when morning came. Early the next day he moved it out into the narrow hallway in back of the house, thinking the moment his father came home he would return it to its place. Then there was the day he was tidying the entryway to the front hallway and among all those shoes came upon the pair his father hadn't worn the day he left home. These were the leather shoes he habitually wore to go out, but by now they were covered with dust, looking much older than before, and he thought, even if his father were to come back, he couldn't possibly wear them again. With that in mind, he picked them up and tossed them into the old wastebasket.

His mother *too* saw him throw them away; she didn't say anything to stop him.

119

He raced down the steps by the bank and ran to the river's edge. He wanted to throw off the burden of his surroundings and the pressures of his daily life, for a little while at least, to drift unfettered like the wild geese in the skies. He handed his dollar fifty to the owner of the rowboats. It was the start of spring. The sky was a pale gray, and the wind was still sharp. A faint smell of fish rose up to greet him as he approached the water's edge. He stepped into the boat that the owner had untied for him and began to row toward the middle of the river. He was the only oarsman on the water. Heading upstream, he passed a grassy bank, green like the shoots of spring onions. Beyond the shore lay a field of vegetables, their leaves fluttering like small animals' ears flip-flopping in the wind. He gazed back downstream; the water was a deep, clear gray, the color of lead. The further he went, the clearer the sound of his oars, dipping and paddling in the water. He drew abreast of a small sandbank, a deserted-looking place. The green here was just as thick and abundant, but it was a dead green, withered by the wintry blasts that cut across the island. In good weather this was a completely different place. He knew because he came here often, especially when it was fine. Then the golden arrows of the sun aimed straight at this island, quickening the yellow blossoms among the sand and grass, transfiguring the sandy mound into a fantastic, huge, multicolored egg nestling in the water. But right now it didn't bear any resemblance to that. He stopped rowing and pulled in his oars, resting his chin in his hands, looking far into the horizon where the mountains were shrouded in the mist. A mountain scene from a black and white ink scroll painting appeared before him, in darkening layers, from far to near. The foot of the mountain range could not be seen, and suspended between the far clouds above and the misty shadows below, the peaks hung in mid-air, as if by magic. In fine weather, this mountain range revealed itself in tints of blue, like lapis lazuli, like a herd of blue horses in swift motion. But not today. Today, as he gazed round, looking downstream to where the long bridge cast its gray shadow onto the dusky reflection of the sky on the water, he felt, in an obscure way, a kind of grief, but what it was, what he was grieving for, he could not say. Even stranger still was that, contrary to expectations, out of this sense of loss and sadness he felt mysteriously comforted, experiencing a kind of relief resembling gratification. . . . From behind a streak of gray cloud, a brilliant silver star suddenly appeared, distant and cold. He gazed at it and imperceptibly, like drawing a breath of cold air into his chest, dispelled the feelings that had long been pent up there. Casting his gaze far out into the distance, he hung all his hopes for the future on this single, silvery star.

120

With the arrival of spring, the coconut trees by the side of the road brought out their baby leaves, shaped like cutout versions of the full-grown fans they were to become, dancing in the gentle breeze like little palms of infants. And the olive trees, too, whose semitransparent, wine-red leaves are capable of growing into big, round ping-pong paddles by late fall, were just now beginning to put out their tender green shoots. Initially looking like little green butterflies perched on its branches, they would grow, in a short week's time, into big, green predatory birds. There was also a kind of kapok tree planted by the roadside, and buds were just now beginning to pierce through their withered branches, fat blades of giant petals pushing out like the slit-open, crimson hearts of the cassava. And because the weather was turning warm, women were coming out in short sleeves, with their arms exposed. And once in a while, when a pedicab went swiftly by, he would catch a glimpse of a pair of lady's calves on the passenger's end of the cab, and think of those naked arms.

121

He watched the continuous dots of light flowing along the length of the bridge downstream, tiny sparks like a meteoric trail of fire, coasting along on his bike with his hands on the handlebar and his back relaxed, resting the weight of his body on the seat. In the daytime the long bridge in the distance appeared like an abacus in motion, the flow of traffic resembling swiftly sliding beads, bobbing up and down, back and forth. These days, whenever the oppressive atmosphere at home became unbearable, he would jump onto his bike and, night or day, take to the streets, winding his way through highway and alleyway, wherever the roads would take him. This had been a wet month, and as he zipped by the rain-drenched houses, the side of the road appeared coffee colored. The rain had transformed the whole street into a misty, poetic country lane colored a dark coffee brown. But when the big, bright sun came out, the seedy streets would be shown up for what they were, and the neighborhood would appear before him like bits and pieces of a tattered and soiled quilt brought out for airing under the blazing sun. Some nights, when he would take off into the quiet streets, newly drenched by the evening rain, accompanied by the swishing of his slippery wheels and the solitary figure of his shadow riding alongside him, he would lower his head and start whistling. And sometimes, just as he drew in his breath, a current of sweet scent from a coconut flower would pass beneath his nose.

One day his father came running in, bursting with excitement. "Ch'iu-fang, Sonny, the strangest thing happened to me today, an encounter you wouldn't believe. You'll never guess what happened. Try and see if you can guess. I'll bet you anything you can't guess what it is."

"What happened?" Mama asked.

"What is it?" Sonny asked.

"Just wait a second, wait till I take off my shoes and come in the house. I'll tell it all to you in good time!"

That afternoon father had slipped out of his office to buy a bun from across the street at the back of the building, and while there he ran into a person he had not seen in a long time. At first Father wasn't even aware that he knew the man, but the man had recognized him and approached Father, calling out to him. It turned out to be an old colleague from Hsiamen back in Fuchien Province. They hadn't worked together for long, though, because this man had left the office within a month of his father's arrival there. At present this person was working at the government's Agricultural Department, and since his office was close by, he invited Father for a visit. After they settled down he told Father that he knew an overseas Chinese who was intending to come to Taiwan and start a business exporting and marketing locally produced dried papayas and that this overseas Chinese wanted him to become his manager in Taiwan. He was at the moment recruiting workers for the business; he went on to ask if Father would be willing to help him out and take on a part-time position. Father, of course, immediately accepted the offer. This person, Ch'en Po-ch'i was his name, told him that the pay was pretty good and added that he himself had already petitioned for retirement from his present position, and that when this happened, in the not too distant future, he would devote all his energy to developing this new enterprise. He then proceeded to urge his father to do likewise, to hurry up and retire from his job so that they could enter into a full partnership and really make something of this business.

Both he and his mother were overjoyed when they heard this news. He in particular was so excited he couldn't keep still; he was clapping and applauding their good fortune. His mother heaved a sigh of relief, saying, "Oh, how wonderful! At last we can take it easy for a bit, haiya, these last two years we've been living on borrowed money every single month. I really don't know how we could've gone on much longer with all the money we owe people. . . . This couldn't have happened at a better time. Believe me, keeping this family going over the last few years has really taken a toll on me." Mama went on and on and on with her endless complaints, putting it all behind her. It was as if he had already been given the new job.

"So how much more money is he going to pay you each month?" Fan Yeh managed to interject.

"He said at least three thousand," Papa replied.

"Three thousand!" He mouthed the sum as he gulped down a breath of clear air, hearing himself gasping for joy, and started to leap about again, yelping and dancing around the room. He looked about him, at the rickety old rattan chairs and tables, the tattered tatami, the paper doors, ripped and torn in so many places, the leprous, pustular walls, and envisioned a complete makeover, an entirely new set of furnishings, now that they could afford it. He could hardly *contain* his exuberance. "Then when are you going to start working for him?" he asked.

"Soon, soon, very soon. He said within three months, give or take. But of course it's not a sure thing yet. It's best not to expect too much, not initially anyway." Father added this warily, seized by a fit of prudence, but even he could not conceal the excitement on his face.

"Well then, we must pin him down right away. You mustn't let him forget his promise," Fan Yeh prompted.

"That's right. You must go after him; go see him often and remind him. Don't let somebody else sneak in and steal the job from you," Mother added quickly, with panic in her voice.

"No, no, that won't happen. He's already told me, promised he'll hire me for sure."

"How often do you plan to visit him then?" Fan Yeh asked.

"Oh, maybe once a month."

"Once a month? That's not nearly often enough!" he blustered, becoming incensed.

"All right then, once a week."

"Once a week is more like it," he said, "and I think you should invite him out. Take him to a restaurant, and treat him to dinner or something." He spoke with the authority of one whose cunning and worldliness surpassed his years.

"Okay, I'll look for an opportunity sometime down the line and take him out."

"No, not sometime down the line. Do it *now*. You've got to get on it right away!" He was waving his arms in an exasperated frenzy.

"Let's just wait and see, wait till we've succeeded. Then I'll take him out to celebrate. It would be more appropriate then."

"Why take him out after the fact? What for?" he railed, infuriated.

"Well, just let's wait, at least wait till success is in sight before I invite him to a restaurant."

Even Mama agreed with this and said they should wait till there was some possibility for success before doing anything else. Then his mother wanted to know more about this Ch'en Po-ch'i. What sort of a person was he?

"He's a *real* good man; quite old now, hair's all gone white; doesn't look too healthy either, extremely skinny.

He came to Taiwan all by himself; all alone he is," Father said.

"I don't remember him at all," Mama muttered. "No wonder you couldn't remember him. Maybe you've never really met him. Even I don't remember ever seeing him before."

After a pause his father started up again, bristling with excitement. "A few years ago there was this fortune-teller who told me that when I reached my fifty-ninth birthday I would hook up with some strange good fortune. This must be it. I'm now fifty-eight plus. In a few months I'll be fifty-nine years old. You tell me, is this fortune-teller accurate or what? This opportunity just came right to my door all by itself, looking for me. Just look at all those people out there in the streets, and among all the people, I run into this man. And I didn't even see him in the first place; it was he who, all on his own, sought me out and called to me. You tell me, am I being chosen for good fortune or what? It must be my turn. You tell me, is this fantastic or what?"

"Fantastic," Fan Yeh agreed.

"Truly fantastic. You keep talking; I'll go get dinner ready. I'll be right back," his mother said, in high spirits, and bustled off into the kitchen.

For the rest of the evening the entire family was in raptures. Fan Yeh could hardly sit still, swinging his arms now and then, back and forth, left to right, round and round, working off the excess energy inside him. His father wore an inebriated grin on his face, the expression of one about to drift off into dreamland, as he moved about the house, tidying up in the bedroom and folding up the laundered underwear. Swept away by the surge of promise, Fan Yeh stared at his surroundings until the dirty old chairs and tables, the beat-up floor mat, and the shell of the leprous, pustular walls were entirely made over then and there. That night he had no stomach for food. After a quick meal he continued to pursue his father relentlessly, interrogating him about the business at hand and this man Ch'en Po-ch'i, pacing back and forth when he was not asking questions.

Soon he, Fan Yeh, would be the happiest person on earth. He sped down the middle of the road on his bike. This time he was not fleeing from some dark cloud and pain; this time he was propelled by happiness and the sheer pleasure of ease. These days, when he looked ahead into the horizon, the sky appeared as blue as the ocean and the clouds like fresh, white bubbles. His ancient bike creaked along, cranking out its familiar squeaky tune. But, as he stared down at its rusty red handlebar these days, he could already feel the sensation of throwing this junk heap of metal away and replacing it with a brand-new state-of-the-art machine, and when that day arrived, he would never again have to suffer other people's rude stares and dirty looks as he passed by them on the road. As he rode along the three thousand dollars were ever present on his mind. Good God, three thousand dollars, what a *lot* of things they could do with that much money. He had already apportioned the money in his mind. In the first few months they would set aside a thousand dollars each month for repayment of debts, thus leaving two thousand to spend as they wished. First of all they might buy a set of new clothes for everyone in the family. The second item on his list was some new paint for the walls inside the house. After that they should think of a way to procure for themselves a somewhat presentable sofa of some kind, like the ones he had seen in the main building, the ones the Kungs and the Shens used to have when they were better off. After a year and a half they would have cleared all their debts, but they should still set aside that thousand dollars and put it into a savings account, just in case, so that if something were to happen at some future date they would have a sum of money to fall back on and get them over the rough patch. During this time, whenever he came upon some kind-looking old man, he would absurdly wonder if this old person might be that Ch'en Po-ch'i. Didn't his father once tell him that Ch'en Po-ch'i was a lifelong vege-tarian, that he was a believer in the merciful Kuan Yin and a "real good, very, very good" elder in his community? Thus, he must naturally be extremely approachable, gentle, and kind. This Po-ch'i (his very name suggesting an elder who sparked new beginnings) had almost become for him the figure of the Messiah!

The first two times at the beginning he was the one who reminded his papa to call on this Ch'en Po-ch'i. "It's been a week now," he would say. "You should go look him up again." Both times his father went, and both times he brought home good news. He was thrilled. Then, the third time, when he mentioned it, his father said, "I've just been to see him, you know. I shouldn't be going too often. This is not something that can be hurried." Nonetheless, that time Father also went. Some time passed before he urged his father to go again, and he was shocked and utterly dismayed when he realized their lapse. "Didn't you say you were going to go once a week? How come you've let three weeks slip by and still haven't gone to see him?" He was angry at himself as well for having let his guard down. In response his father said that an overseas investor was coming to Taiwan soon and that it would be better to wait till he arrived before going to see Ch'en Po-ch'i again.

"When, then, is this overseas investor coming?"

"Soon, soon. In about a month or so he'll be coming."

The month passed, and he was after his father to go again. His father went and came back to say that the over-seas investor had again postponed his visit to Taiwan and would not be arriving for at least another month.

"Another whole month?" Fan Yeh said, dejected and in despair.

"No, no, don't worry. Po-ch'i told me there's no problem whatsoever. The only reason that investor decided to come later, in October, he told me, was so he could come with the Taiwan Homecoming Tour group to celebrate the Double

Tenth. It's more convenient this way." Fan Yeh rallied at this last bit of information. Father went on casually, "Can't think what this guy, Po-ch'i, is up to. I found him at his office. He had spent the night there; doesn't even have a dorm to sleep in. He lives there; I saw his toothbrush and toothpaste beside the tumbler he used for rinsing his mouth, right there behind his seat. What a character." These words sent a chill through Fan Yeh, but he recovered immediately, coming to Ch'en's defense. "Well of course he's living here all by himself. He probably doesn't really care where he lives so long as it's convenient." His father then carried on from where he left off, saying that he (Ch'en Po-ch'i) was not feeling too well these days and seemed to be taking some kind of medication.

October finally arrived, but many days had passed, and Father still didn't seem to want to make a move. He began to complain, calling his father indifferent, lazy, accusing him of dragging his feet. His father finally gave in and said that he would go in another day, on Monday; he would go then and pay another visit. On Sunday he once more reminded his father, and this time his father faltered, saying, in a daze, "Ah, this thing. . . . It's not going to happen any time soon, I'm afraid."

"What?" Fan Yeh froze.

Observing his reaction, his father immediately changed his tone. "Oh, it's just a wild guess on my part. Nothing, it's nothing. Nothing's the matter."

"You, you, you mustn't ever think like that, ever!" Fan Yeh said, tripping all over himself as if running from a raging fire. "If you're going to admit failure and defeat before you've even gotten started, of course there's no way you're not going to be defeated in the end. People must look on the bright side, be positive, be optimistic about what they're doing. That's the only way you can hope to succeed. If everyone were to take such a defeatist attitude, then of course, even if they weren't going to fail they'd turn around and defeat themselves," Fan Yeh rambled on reproachfully. His father gazed at him steadily and, as if suddenly enlightened, started to nod his head, speaking in a voice full of warmth and understanding, consoling him. "Don't you worry; don't go upsetting yourself. There's no problem at all. First thing in the morning I'll go see him." The next morning, his father announced early in the morning that he was definitely going that afternoon to pay this Ch'en Po-ch'i a visit. Fan Yeh then set out for school and had to wait till five thirty before he could come home again. His father was already there. Strangely enough, Father didn't volunteer any information about his afternoon visit to Ch'en Po-ch'i. He couldn't even tell if he had indeed gone to see him or not. The thought that he might not have been at all crossed Fan Yeh's mind, provoking him into sudden fury. "Didn't you even go to Ch'en Po-ch'i's place this afternoon?" he burst out.

"Yes, I've been already," Father replied, looking cheerful.

"What does he have to say?"

"He told me that the overseas Chinese investor will be getting things moving *real* soon. In fact he was in Taiwan just last week and said he would be back here again in the next month or so." Having said that, he paused and said no more. After a little while Father said in what seemed like a happy tone of voice, "Everything's fine. Really, no problem, none at all. He said it's going to happen in the very near future."

Seized with sudden suspicion, Fan Yeh snapped back threateningly, "Have you really been to see him, or haven't you?"

"Yes, of course. Of course I've been. He even gave me this business card from that overseas Chinese, see? See for yourself." So saying, his father pulled out a name card from his shirt pocket. It was a small card with the three characters of a name printed on it. His father, again with extreme delicacy and tenderness, comforted him, saying, "There's no need, you don't have to be anxious, my good boy. This is not something we can hurry. It's no use rushing things."

"But five months ago you said it'd be soon, very soon. You said no more than three months then, and now there's not even a hint of any movement whatsoever. You call this trying to rush things?"

Father drew a deep sigh and said, "It's not so easy to get things done. It's not like eating a piece of cake or drinking tea."

"Okay. What now? When do you plan to go see him again?"

"I think we'll wait another month or so."

"Another month. Okay, we'll *wait* another month."

"It's been another month!" he reminded his father. His tone was accusatory, reprimanding his father for neglecting his duty. For an instant his father looked distracted, almost half crazed, and then wildly exclaimed, "That son of a . . . He's been dragging this thing out ever since the very beginning! I really must get to the bottom of this and find out what the hell's going on." So saying he left. But when he came back from his talk with Ch'en Po-ch'i, racing home with what he had been told, he was once again in high spirits, fully satisfied. He told him that Ch'en Po-ch'i said that the first overseas investor had probably gone bankrupt, but that there was another overseas Chinese businessman who was about to come to Taiwan, and that this one was, if anything, a cut above the other, and that within two months at most, no longer this time, all the preparations would be completed. This time even the location had been found, and this time Po-ch'i once again invited Father to join him there. Father was so fired up by what he had been told that he was almost tongue-tied as he blurted out the news. That evening, that dreamy, inebriated grin found its way back onto his father's face. Flushed with the promise of success, he wandered about the house, doing this and that.

Fan Yeh was to let himself be absorbed in these pipe dreams for yet another month, although, by now, experience had made him smart, teaching him not to pin his hopes "up" too high, knowing now that in this world wishing alone does not make things happen. His mother really surprised him, though. Not only did she not ask for news about the matter, she didn't even seem to want to hear about it. It was as if she had put the whole matter behind her, regarding it as some unmentionable event that had happened a long time ago. His father, thus, became the only one in the family who focused all his dreams on this great promise, although even then he did not go see Ch'en Po-ch'i. And when he did eventually go see Ch'en Po-ch'i, Father couldn't bring himself to really question him, because he saw that the old man had fallen ill, suffering from a bad case of the flu; several medicine bottles and packets of powder were strewn all over his office desk. Papa was naturally too polite to press him for answers.

From then on Fan Yeh conditioned himself to ask about it only at certain specified times and without conveying any sense of threat or irritation: "About that matter of yours, how's it going?" And Father, the lilt of happiness gone out of his voice, would reply bitterly, "He said it's still in the planning stage just now." Without warning a plain white envelope came in the mail one day; it was a funeral announcement addressed to his father, sent out by the Agricultural Department, notifying him that his good friend, Ch'en Po-ch'i, had passed away. Papa heaved a long sigh that sounded like something between a groan and a wail. And Fan Yeh, having guessed the news, reacted as if he had just been struck by the horror of his own parents' death. Paralyzed by the news, he flopped down in the nearest chair – that rickety old rattan chair from his father's office. Father left immediately for the Agricultural Department to see what he could find out and came back with the information that this man, Ch'en Po-ch'i, had had a chronic heart condition for a long time and that he had not been well over the last month or so, when, three days ago, he had a heart attack at his office and died in his sleep. His father's name and address were found in Ch'en's own date book. People at the Agricultural Department also told his father that Ch'en Po-ch'i was somewhat of a schizophrenic, emotionally unstable, and prone to fantasies.

A few days later his father attended the funeral service. Out of what was left of the five hundred dollar salary after deductions, his father had to contribute two hundred to the funeral kitty. This conclusion to the story he kept to himself until after the funeral. When he did tell Fan Yeh and his mother, Fan Yeh listened in wooden silence. For a long, long time he sat, like a clay statue, unable to make a sound, his grief far exceeding his father's. "That motherfucker!" his father cursed, the blood drained from his face. "I'm out another two hundred dollars for nothing!" At this remark Fan Yeh broke into a horrendous guffaw, as if he had heard something terribly funny, although his laughter conveyed something altogether different. With an ugly expression on his face, he said, "Not bad, not bad at all. We have at least been rewarded for our pains. We've been given ten months of *pure happiness.*" As abruptly as it started, his laughter turned into a spasm of weeping. He dashed off to his bedroom (that is, the room that was once his brother's) and shoved the paper door shut violently.

This turbulent roller-coaster ride left him with an entirely different attitude toward his father. No, *not pity,* but rather a savagely contemptuous way of looking at the old man.

123

The prospect of his brother's wedding receded with each passing day. And now, because the bride's family refused to let the marriage take place without the groom's father's consent, his brother had come to ask his father to be at the ceremony as head of the family. Father, however, was adamant. He was not going to give his consent. "Don't even think it. My name next to that person's name in a wedding announcement? Never! I have opposed this match from the *very beginning,* and I'll oppose it to the bitter end. Even if you went to the courthouse on your own, even if you had the marriage certificate in hand, I would not recognize this marriage, so don't go thinking I'm going to let myself be shown up in public with that no-class, low-down sort of person!"

"It's up to you. Don't show if you don't want to! I certainly don't need you there. But let me tell you this. Once I've gone to the courthouse on my own – and don't say I haven't warned you – I am not ever going to come through that door again, you hear? Never going to set foot among this family again, never. No, I'm going to pack my bags this instant, and I'll be gone for good."

"Go ahead! Get *lost!* So be it. I renounce you from this moment on. *You are not my son.* You and I have severed all ties. *I am not your father!*" his father hissed in desperate rage, as Fan Yeh watched in dismay, afraid that this confrontation might trigger another bout of that hemoptysis from which his father had suffered only two years ago. He half expected to see globs of blood spill out of his mouth.

"Fine. You're not my father. I'm not your son. Our relationship ends here!" his *erh-ko* shouted back. "This was exactly what I had in mind when I came!"

"*Out* of my sight!" Father slammed his fist on the table and sprang up in fury.

"I'm gone. But before I go there's something I must make clear to you, one thing I must get through that thick skin of yours." Erh-ko glared out of bloodshot eyes. "You think that my girlfriend is beneath you, don't you? You think she's beneath you because, one, she's a native Taiwanese and, two, she was once a barmaid. Well, let me set you straight. If truth be told, you yourself are far, far beneath *any Taiwanese.* In fact, you don't even measure up to a barmaid!"

"What did you say?" His papa leaped up in reckless abandon, his face sweaty and swollen, nostrils flared. Fan Yeh was throbbing with fright. He could smell the blood that would come spewing out of his father's mouth any second now.

"What am I talking about? How can I even compare you to them? There's no comparison. You're shut up in your own little bigoted, corrupt, *ridiculous* world. How can people like you even hope to be compared to her and her family? She became a barmaid solely because she needed the money to support her sick father. She sacrificed herself so that others could live. And you, how can you measure up? No way, not by half. You who are capable of stabbing your own son in the back, you who wantonly, deliberately try to ruin his entire life, you tell me, how can you hope to measure up against her?"

"Traitor! You turncoat, you!"

"Yes. You're right. I've turned, turned against you!"

"You . . . you say another word, and see if I don't box your ears," his papa shouted, advancing.

In one swift motion Erh-ko reached for the hammer hanging on the wall and responded by swinging it in the air, saying, "As the father lacks virtue, the son cannot be blamed for lack of piety." The scene was set for a bloody patricide.

"Fan Lun-yuan, you must not, no, absolutely not – " his mama screamed at his brother, addressing him by his full name, standing in his way, throwing her body between them.

His *erh-ko* sobered up somewhat and, flinging the hammer to the floor, dashed into his bedroom to pack his things. Three minutes later he came out carrying his trunk. He stood for a second, then headed straight for the door. From that moment on all ties were severed between them. In that second his brother had kicked himself loose and bolted out of the rabbit warren they called home.

His father lurched forward, about to black out again. He remembered going toward his father then and, in a voice charged with sympathy, said, "Pa, had Erh-ko really struck at you, I'd have gone for the knife and stabbed him!"

"Ah, no. . . ." Tears were streaming down Father's face as he looked up at him. Presently, Father asked, "Has he taken all his things?"

"Everything," Mama replied.

Part Three

K

SEARCH
For Father

Dear Father,
You have been gone for nearly three months. Please come home. Everything will be resolved according to your wishes.

Your son,
Yeh

He was on the train going South. A notice had come from a shelter in T'aichung two days ago with the description of an old man who had recently arrived there, a man without an ID, who had lost his sight in both eyes, and was unable to speak – most likely the result of a stroke. Hence this trip down to T'aichung to make an identification. And inasmuch as this chance offered itself to him as a reason, he simply followed it to the logical conclusion of picking up where he left off and putting into action that long-planned-for search a second time. It also prompted him to revive that newspaper advertisement.

He undertook this second search with the same mindset he had adopted for his first trip. Then as now, he harbored little hope of success – after all, the Taipei police alone had called him several times to see if they had turned up the right person. Each time, however, it had turned out to be a waste of energy. He had shelved the whole business of the search for far too long. Since this opportunity to go South presented itself, he took it. Besides, it also gave him a way, momentarily at least, to salve his conscience.

The low drone of a plane in flight drew closer and louder.

The young man closed the book he was reading. He was now twenty years old. Last year he passed the university entrance exam and was admitted into the History Department at C University. The addition of a pair of thick, black-rimmed glasses changed the appearance of his milk-white face only slightly. Of late, however, the face itself had undergone subtle changes; it now appeared more resolute and self-possessed, perhaps even a little aloof and withdrawn.

Fan Yeh waited till the boom trailed off into the distant sky before picking up the book again and, after a short pause, resuming his reading. Fan Yeh recoiled from loud noise and excitement of any kind, particularly when he was reading. Often, at such times, the slightest little ripple would distract him, disrupt the flow of a sentence, and when he tried to pick up where he had left off, the atmosphere in which he was previously immersed would have dissipated; to continue his reading thus was like trying to fuse the bottom half of a body with the top half after a person had been cut in two. This extremely fastidious habit was not likely to be appreciated by others. If he were to explain it to others, they were sure to cast him as a fanatic, acutely sensitive and abnormally picky.

Abruptly Fan Yeh put his book down yet again. Vaguely aware of the proximity of commotion, he had been unable to concentrate for quite some time. It turned out to be the presence of his father in his room, coming and going in and out right behind him. He didn't know how many times he had told him already that this puttering about was a huge annoyance to him. And it wasn't just the shuffling alone. The very quivers sent through the tatami mats in his bedroom as his father lifted and pressed his feet on the floor were insufferable. And here he was again, that Pa of his, coming in to start up a racket once again.

He decided to give up, to forget about getting back into the reading altogether, and to put the book away for the duration. And he wasn't going to say anything more about it either. He was sick and tired of the squabbling. The feeling of weakness and the very thought that he still felt that he ought to be quaking in fear before his father each time they quarreled was enough to tire him out. He was hoping to wait this one out, let his father make his noise and have done with it. These last few days, and in fact the last few weeks, his father had managed to drive him up the wall in numerous and sundry ways. What happened the day before last was a typical example. That afternoon he had unstrapped his wristwatch and laid it on the level armrest of the chair in which he was sitting, thinking that in this way he could tell the time while he read. Before he knew what hit him, his father, who had been watching him, came rushing up and snatched the watch away, claiming that he was flirting with danger, placing the watch in such a precarious position that it would surely crash to the floor. And just today he was struck by the absurd way his father summoned them to wash their faces in the mornings. His father would call to them, as if inviting guests to a banquet, saying, "Come, come, the hot water's ready, right here. Come while it's hot, Sonny, Ch'iu-fang. Come now." Father would then tap his fingers against the rim of the washbasin, flicking off the water drops from his nails in this ridiculous manner. But perhaps more ludicrous still was the morning exercise that the old man called brushing his teeth. First he would fill that tiniest of tumblers, which he used as his rinsing cup, with water, and then each time he gave his teeth a brush he would dip his toothbrush back into this small pool of water, stirring it around each time into who knows what sort of a mucky mess, and then, finally, when the tiniest little mouthful of water was left, he would stick his brush in for one last jiggle, rolling out the drumbeat to his cacophonous fanfare and concluding it with a flourish. Throughout the process, he had paid no attention whatsoever to cleaning his teeth, the ostensible object of the exercise. He was intent only on the observance of a ritual, much like the way a monk mouths his liturgies in the morning.

Just then Fan Yeh heard a scratching noise, like a cat clawing at something. It was his father, of course, who was at the moment dusting the windows in the back hallway, combing the window sills with a small handheld brush. Here was another case in point. It simply made his blood boil. There could not possibly be a single strand of thought in his father's mind at that moment; it had to be a complete and utter void. This sweeping, brushing activity was, to the old man, the way to nirvana, no different from what Buddhists achieve through meditation. His father did not sweep and dust for the sake of cleanliness. These activities were only pretexts, means by which he escaped from mental exercise, singularly instigated by his sloth, his unwillingness to use his brain, opting to spend what life he had in him on these asinine, hypnotic activities. Fan Yeh felt a sudden surge of fury straining for release.

With considerable effort he managed to control himself, and was just about to reach for the book he had been reading, when there he was again, his father, barging into his room. "Hey, Sonny, I'm going out with your mother now. Will you come out and lock up behind us now, okay?"

Another wave of fury, blinding, torrential, gathered momentum, ready to gush forward. Lock up, did he say? What the. . . . Here he was, sitting right there at home in broad daylight, and from where he was sitting he could see all the way straight out from his room to the bamboo gate. What's the great fear?

He did not make a reply.

His father repeated his request.

He still did not answer him.

His father asked once again.

"I heard you," he said, after a pause.

"Then why didn't you answer me just now?"

"Haven't I just answered you?"

"Aigh...." Father stamped his foot, wagged his head, and dragged out a long sigh. Of all the variety of his father's sighs, this was the sort he detested the most; it called up the image of a dying man heaving the last and final drop of breath left in him, and, worse, like the pitiful cry made by some whiny, helpless infant girl.

Not long after his father left his bedroom, much as he had anticipated, he came pattering back in again.

"Sonny, if you're not coming out now, you must remember to lock up the front door with that heavy padlock when you go out. The lock is hung on the other side of the kitchen door. Don't forget now."

"I'm not planning to go out at all!"

Father stood there like a jackass, at a loss for something to say.

"Ai-ya, Sonny, this child has changed so much recently. He's an entirely different person from even just a year ago. This tone he's taking with his own father, this kind of behavior is totally unacceptable...." His voice trailed off in mournful lamentation as he turned to leave.

In the wake of this commentary, Fan Yeh was suddenly struck by one immediate and insufferable reality of his situation. He became aware that all the windows and doors in the entire house, even those in the front and back hallways, were closed, each and every one of them, carefully shut and locked by his father. On top of that, he, Fan Yeh, was supposed to stay home and stand guard after they left. After a brief pause he looked around again, only to see that by now even the paper doors to his bedroom had been slid shut. What purpose did that serve? Was it supposed to secure the house against burglars and intruders?

He could no longer contain his wrath. He lashed out, shrieking, "Look you, you, you. . . . Look at. . . . The paper doors are all shut." But it came out all wrong. What he said did not express what he wanted to say at all. He wanted to express anger and indignation, but what came out seemed more like a polite remark. He tried again. "These paper doors, they're all shut!" No good, even worse than before. Losing restraint altogether, he cried out. "Open the door! Open the doors for me now!"

"What?" His father reappeared with big, round eyes like two balls of burning coal about to pop out of his head. "Who, just who do you think you're talking to?"

"To you, of course!"

"How's that?" His papa nearly hit the ceiling, jumping up and down, and then started to hold his head, striking hard at the right temple, saying, "You're going to be the death of me! Oh, my head . . . ah. . . ." Father was holding his head with both hands now, swaying this way and that, stumbling forward, about to fall.

"Min-hsien!" his mama screamed, lunging forward to catch him.

"Papa!" he, too, blurted out before he could stop himself, and instantly felt ashamed for the outburst. But his papa had already, distinctly, ascertained the terror in his voice, and within seconds seemed much revived. It was all too clear that his father was convinced that the yelp he just let out indicated submission.

Nonetheless, there was no denying the fact that, when his papa looked as if he were about to faint away, his own blood turned cold. The threat of high blood pressure was his father's weapon, and it was by this weapon that he was forever to be defeated. It didn't matter how much anger he bottled up inside of him, it didn't matter how airtight a case he was prepared to make for himself, in the end he simply could not express himself. What could you do? You couldn't disregard the fact that your father had high blood pressure, now could you? Thus, he must suffer forever and ever, go on suffering in this situation forever!

And then there was the unanswerable question: Were his father's fainting spells real, or were they merely for show?

125

He had gone to a schoolmate's house for a visit and was therefore later than usual coming home. When he finally came in that night, it was already past eleven. The minute he stepped in the door, his temper flared. There they were, his parents, looking pale and mournful, looking as if someone had just died. His father even went to the extreme of covering up his eyes, saying, "What you put your parents through! Why are you bent on frightening us this way? Look at that, can you see what time it is?"

"What time is it? So what? It's not even twelve yet. Who told you to stay up anyway? I've got my own key. I'm a grown man now. You've no business poking your nose into my affairs."

"Just look at him. This is all the good it does to be concerned about him!"

"Who needs your concern?"

"Okay, okay, I told him so. That's exactly what I said. I told him not to worry, not to get anxious, but would he listen?" his mother was saying. "Since nine o'clock he's been pacing the floor, up and down, this way and that, turning in circles, muttering to himself, 'Look what time it is. So *late*, and Sonny's still not home. How come Sonny's still not home, it's so late already?' And then he even went out looking for you. He's been out all this time looking for you. He didn't come home till almost eleven. He's just stepped in himself."

"You went out looking for me? Where did you go looking for me? Did you even know where I was?" He flew into such a rage he was almost beside himself.

"Hush! Lower your voice. Don't yell like that. The neighbors are all in bed; everyone's asleep already. Frankly, it's not that I'm worried about anything else, it's just that, those cars, and, oh, you on that bike, the roads and those trucks. . . ."

"Again, again, it's the cars again. Those *cars!* I'm not a little boy anymore!" He started to shout again — but immediately remembered about the neighbors and stifled himself.

"Okay, okay, enough said already. Don't say any more. Enough. Go on, go to bed now, everyone, go." It was Mother who spoke next.

Fan Yeh strode toward his bedroom, but before he got there he heard his father let out a long sigh:

"Aigh . . ."

126

It was during this period that he discovered how peculiarly short, abnormally short, his father was, and for the first time in his life he registered the fact that his father was a cripple. He was bewildered by his own capacity for blindness, his ability not to have discovered the lame foot for such a long time.

It was also during this time that he discovered, retrospectively, the many mistakes his parents made, the wrongs they had committed. He recalled, for example, that utterly laughable practice his father imposed on him as a small child when, after each meal, his head and face had to be wrapped in a steaming hot washcloth so that, according to his father, at least, his blood would quicken and thus his health improve. And then there was that other thing he was made to do. On hot days, whenever he came in from the outside, his father would make him rinse his mouth with cold water, claiming that this would rinse out the heat. His mother was the same way. He was forbidden to place a white handkerchief over his head because this was, according to her, asking for bad luck. In addition, his mother wouldn't allow him to sunbathe because, as she would have it, too much sunshine is bad for you. And when you had the hiccups, you should put a pair of chopsticks crosswise over a glass of water and drink from it like that. Especially absurd were all the crazy, far-fetched, fantastic tales his father told him, making them up as he went along, about how France was the strongest nation on earth and how they had this incredible machine that could take you wherever you had in mind to go the instant you turned it on. In fact, even the way they used to praise him, calling him a little scholar and so on, even that appeared now to him an insult, because it stemmed from their low expectation of him as their son, someone who must, like them, be dumb, dull, and common. And as for the Confucian teachings that had been drilled into him from a young age, that inculcated notion of filial piety, that too was no more than the perpetuation of the *selfish* custom of rearing sons as old-age security. And his mama positively enjoyed bad-mouthing his brother. Not only that, but she loved to deck herself out in a mix of the loudest colors, the tackiest, most whorish clothes imaginable. Then there were all those words his father taught him to read when he was little, all those words he had mistaken or misread to him, many of which were mispronounced in the Fuchien dialect. It wasn't until recently that he realized how poorly educated his father really was. And to think he had looked up to him all this time – what a mistake that had been. His father had told him he had studied abroad, in France. Well he now knew what this studying abroad amounted to; his father had merely gone to France for a brief tour and was not even able to utter the simplest, most rudimentary greeting in French. If you came right down to it, his father had probably never even finished reading a book in all his life. In fact, there *was* no collection, they had *no* books *at all,* unless you counted that *Autumn Water Pavilion Letters,* which was just a model text for formal correspondence. Come to think of it – and even the thought of it made his blood boil – all his father ever gave him in this regard was a porno paperback at a time when he was just becoming aware of such things. The only other "scholarly interest" his papa had was that collection of proverbs and clichés that he copied into his stack of notebooks. What was the point of copying out a few stale phrases and useless sayings?

What was worse, far worse than these, were those foul habits that this father bequeathed to him by way of influence, so that he was repeating his father's mistakes without even knowing it, bringing ridicule on himself. Take, for example, the idiosyncratic way his father had of peeling bananas, the way he peeled the skin off the entire fruit all at once and held the naked banana in his hand when he ate it. To this day Fan Yeh ate bananas this way. And his mother must have similarly corrupted him. For example, she held to the belief that *plums* were bad for you because they *plumbed* the depths of your innards and caused dysentery. This was of course a theory founded on extreme ignorance. Obviously, plums were not the culprit. More likely, she merely overheard people talking, saying that plums caused dysentery, and these people themselves had probably seen someone else just happen to get sick right after eating a plum. Such was the kind of baseless information he had been given, and had himself believed in all the time. His mother also taught him not to mix hot food with cold, because this combination would upset his stomach, give him a bellyache, and cause diarrhea. This, too, he had swallowed whole. If truth be told, however, they themselves followed each hot meal with some cold fruit; wasn't that mixing hot food with cold? Besides, someone had once told him that in America people always ate ice cream after their main meals. How then do you explain that? And his parents were the ones who instilled in him the fear of automobiles. To this day he kept his distance from them, dodging cars from miles and miles away. To this day he also avoided getting his head wet with rain at all costs because his mama had told him he would catch a cold from it. His papa was the one who taught him how to cure mosquito bites by pinching the top half of the swelling with his fingernail. And his father was fond of saying, and thus he, too, liked to say, "His mother's whatchamacallit . . . " What a filthy, despicable thing to say! And his father was the image of the wrathful deity, furor itself, when it came to chewing out an inferior or some young kid, and, alas, even in this he himself, much to his horror and shame, was the spitting image of his papa. There was no question about it, the resemblance he bore to his parents, and particularly to his *father,* was undeniable. Ever since he entered the university, not a few people remarked on it: "Like father, like son." Such remarks tore through him like the lashes of a whip. But it was true. In his hours of quiet self-examination he could no more deny it than not be pained by it, for like his father he was cowardly and weak, and in certain situations he was indeed like his father, lacking in ambition and combativeness. But having established the cause of his own defects, he could not vent his frustrations upon his father without first directing the hatred at himself.

It hit him all of a sudden – and the revelation came with a jolt – he no longer cared, one way or the other, whether his parents lived or died. He had lost that terrorizing anxiety that was like the shadow of a huge mountain cast over his childhood. He had gradually come to understand this fear that, as he now realized, had little to do with the apprehension of emotional trauma but was, for the most part, due to his ignorance regarding funeral rites, and his dread of the crowds that he associated with funerals. The shadow drew back as he grew up and became, in time, less and less of a threat to him.

Such were the many and sundry mistakes his father had made, but yet the most inexcusable of all his unforgivable wrongs was the way such a papa wronged his own family by his irresponsible conduct; a responsible father would never have allowed his family to sink into the depths of poverty in which they now found themselves. And even toward his own father, Fan Yeh's grandfather, he was just as irresponsible. Not once had he ever heard this father of his say anything about sending money or anything back to his own father. Nor was this father of his in any way close to the half-brothers and half-sisters, who, after all, had the same father as he. Granted, they had been separated for most of their adult lives, since the others were stuck on the mainland, but even so you'd think that Father would at least have tried to stay in touch with them somehow, or you'd think he would talk about them sometimes. But there were no letters, no recollections, let alone any nostalgia. And surely Father must be held responsible in some way for his sister's death! Just look at the way he treated his mother when she got sick. Was it not irresponsible of him, for example, to give her whatever leftover medicine there was, stuff that had been lying around for years, no matter the disease or what the medicine had been intended to cure in the first place, tricking her, making her believe it would cure her? Indeed, how could he conclude from this kind of behavior that his father even loved his mother? How were they, this father and his mama, brought together in marriage in the first place? More likely than not, their marriage had been arranged by others, and they themselves were merely commodities in the transaction. And what about his eldest brother, what made him leave home? And how was it that his second brother had to be taken out of school halfway through? Even he himself, his schooling, too, was very nearly cut short. Invariably, when he arrived at this thought, irrepressible tears rose like steam into his eyes.

It was true. Father had failed at every duty ever entrusted to him. But then again he couldn't help suspecting that there was something else, that it was not just the fact that he didn't earn enough money to support them, but rather that he had used up his money elsewhere. This suspicion naturally led him to the following conjecture: Why should it *not* be in the realm of possibility that Papa was spending his money on somebody outside the family? Of course he was keeping a mistress! Surely he wasn't expecting his father to be trustworthy? Almost everyone else's father was fooling around. How could his father be the exception to the rule? And his mother, could she too – true to the norm – be unfaithful, unchaste? She was only human, after all! Who then might this other person be? Could it maybe be Mr. Chang next door? He was always hanging around in the courtyard in his pajamas at all hours of the day. No, no, it couldn't be him! It had to be someone from the outside, not likely to be someone from the neighborhood. Could it, perhaps, be the man who used to come pretty often, the one who was supposedly from their village back in China, that blacksmith? Could he even be *sure* that they, his mama and papa, were really his parents? A lot of people would say that he didn't look a bit like them. He ran off to look at himself in the mirror. He needed to see if there was any resemblance. All of a sudden he felt utterly exhausted; at the same time he was overcome by a deep sense of shame.

127

Fan Yeh met an old man at the entrance to their alley. His regard for this old man almost surpassed that which he felt for his own father. At the time his father had no idea what was going on. It happened one day on his way to school. Fan Yeh had dropped a book on his way out of the alley without noticing; the old man came running after him with the book. They struck up a conversation, and that was how their friendship began. This old man had a round face that exuded both warmth and refinement; his crew cut made his hair look a brilliant white; his cheeks were flushed with the colors of good health. He had two sons, both studying in America, leaving their parents behind here at home. Home for the old man was also in the neighborhood, near the corner of the alley, at the upper end. The dormitory he and his wife had been assigned was one of those buildings vacated by the Japanese after the occupation; it had a wide-open room that was like a conference room, and the wood on the outside was painted a sea-green shade. He was a retired member of the Central Bureau of Intelligence. He had attended Peking University and majored in politics, which was why he had an almost encyclopedic grasp of global history and East-West relations. Fan Yeh was especially drawn to his high oratory whenever he expounded on the noble views he held. Fan Yeh could be found hanging around the old couple's house five out of seven evenings a week. One time his papa spotted him attentively helping the old man cross the street. His papa was waiting for them on the other side, watching them, but Fan Yeh merely nodded to him, his own father, and went on his way. To his father's questions afterward, when he returned home, as to who that old man was, he simply replied that the man was a professor at his school. This friendship between him and the old couple lasted a little under a year, when the elderly gentleman and his wife left for America to join their children.

L

SEARCH
For Father

Dear Father,
You have been gone for nearly three months. Please come home. Everything will be resolved according to your wishes.

Your son,
Yeh

Fan Yeh was merely passing through this town when he came upon a large crowd gathered by the side of the road. He went over to see what was going on. In the middle of the empty space created by the crowd of onlookers was a man on his knees. The man had on a torn, white outfit of some kind; he was bare chested, so you could see that he was emaciated, a mere bag of bones. The man was waving those skinny tubes that were his arms. His face looked as if it belonged to a very old person; it was sunken, parched black, withered, aged. A madman. He was attempting to direct traffic. Fan Yeh backed himself out of the crowd. He had to continue on his way toward that shelter for the elderly that was situated in the outskirts of town. No sooner had he resumed his course, however, than he was seized by a burning sensation that the man kneeling in the street could well have been, might well be, his own lost father. Fan Yeh thus turned abruptly and returned to see whether the madman was indeed his father. In the calmness he achieved after a second look, he was able to tell himself that he should have known better, that he knew all along that the man was not his papa.

128

His mother gave his father a ten-dollar bill and asked him to go to the corner store for a bottle of soy sauce. She was in the kitchen at the time. Since it was a drizzly afternoon, his father left the kitchen to fetch his black, folded umbrella before going out. By the time he came back, however, the ten-dollar bill he was sure he left lying on the greasy, round dinner table was gone who knows where. He looked everywhere, searching over and under the dinner table, but he came up with nothing. The only two people who had come anywhere near this table were Father himself and Fan Yeh, who was reading in his own bedroom. This led his father to the depraved notion that he, Fan Yeh, was somehow responsible for the money's disappearance. The old man then proceeded to broach the question, advancing toward the bedroom where his son was engrossed in his reading. "I just now left a bill out here on the dinner table, a ten-dollar bill. Did you happen to have seen it out here or what?"

"No, I didn't see it."

"Haven't seen it? How strange. Where could it have gone to all by itself?"

By this time Fan Yeh had sensed the insinuation in his father's tone of voice. He was incensed, angrier even than usual. He shot out of his room to investigate and discovered that other than the two of them there was no one else in the house – his mother was in the kitchen, on the outside. Then he said, "That *is* strange. There are only two people in the entire house. *Who* do you think it went away with?"

"Whoever it was must have lost his mind; how stupid of him to think that stealing a ten-dollar bill is even worth his while, and to think that there are but the two of us here in the house."

"That's just it. How *could* he, and for that measly sum of money. . . ."

His mama's voice rang out from the kitchen at that point. "Which of you left this ten-dollar bill on the kitchen table? Odds are it's that Min-hsien again. It's just like him. Hey, have you forgotten all about my bottle of soy sauce already?"

His father just stood there like an idiot, staring into thin air.

"So you see!" Fan Yeh let out an apoplectic shriek, jumping up and away in one and the same motion, hurtling his body right back into his own room.

129

His parents showed no signs of letting up on those terrible fights that had caused him so much unhappiness during the years of his early youth. His mother was as insanely jealous as ever, lighting into his father at the slightest provocation. One incident occurred as a result of his mother's seeing his father in the company of a woman colleague, a widow who lived in their section of the dormitory complex. Having gotten off the same bus after work, they were walking home together when his mother caught sight of them, and she proceeded to brood about the incident until it looked to her as if his father were having an affair with this woman.

"Well, well, you don't say. I've got you now. Caught you red-handed, the two of you snuggling up to each other, walking side by side. Let me give it to you straight. I've been following the two of you for quite some time now, and many times I've seen you walking together. I was just waiting for all the evidence to come in, to make sure I have an airtight case against you, before I formally confronted you with it, evidence and all!"

"What are you talking about? It was days ago when she and I got off the bus together and walked home. I'd forgotten all about it."

"I saw you, just today it was, the two of you walking together!"

"No. When were we together today?" He foolishly clung to denial.

"What do you mean, no? I saw you, with my own two eyes, you and her walking together. How can you still say no?" Her fury was now fanned into a tower of flame.

"Oh, then it must have been a coincidence. I had no idea she was in front of me or behind me when we got off the bus. I'm sure there must have been other people walking with us. Besides, I didn't talk to her."

"What do you mean you didn't talk to her? I saw you, clear as day, you and her with your heads together walking side by side, and you still say no? You'd better own up. Tell me now, tell me what freakish, twisted things the two of you have been up to, where you did it, and when . . ."

"Oh good! Very good indeed! Go ahead, chase him down, get to the bottom of it!" Fan Yeh unexpectedly interjected, his teeth clenched, his voice taut.

His mother was stunned into momentary silence, and then, riding on the apparent lift he gave her, added, "You see, even Sonny agrees with me!"

"Oh, so *you* think *I'm agreeing* with *you,* huh?"

Mother blanched. "I see. You're taking your father's side, then, is that right? Well, you'd better think again and decide whose side you're on, I tell you, or else you can get out of my way. Scram, I say. *Out, now!*"

"You just try!"

"What – !" she exclaimed.

"*Now, now,* no, Sonny, *no.* Ch'iu-fang, please, don't let's go on screaming like this. Just look here, Ch'iu-fang, just say it was my fault, everything is my fault, my mistake, okay?"

"You coward, you gutless, spineless . . . weakling!" Fan Yeh was firing directly at his father, pointing his finger right at his face.

"This . . . you, you talking to me . . . you mean me?"

"Yes, you!"

"Oh? This, this . . . he's killing me, killing me, look at the way he's talking to his own papa!" His papa now turned on him. "You shut your mouth!"

"You are nothing but . . ."

"Fan Min-hsien, don't you try to change the subject by going after him. I'm not going to fall for your devious tricks. I know how your mind works!"

"Ch'iu-fang, you . . . I'm truly, honestly . . . I'm telling you . . ."

At that moment Fan Yeh suddenly became aware that all around them, outside the windows, outside the bamboo fence, a huge crowd had gathered to watch. They had forgotten to draw the curtains in the hallway that evening, and now all these people were given an unobstructed view of their entire existence, from the hallway into the house. Now they knew what their furniture was like and how they behaved toward each other inside the house. For instance, these people could see that big, round table in the hallway where they ate their meals, and, about ten paces away from this table, at the far end of the hallway, their two washbasins sitting on top of two wood benches, and even that cheap, old lamp shade hanging from the ceiling, with its greasy yellow rings shown up by the dim light of the bulb despite being covered by a thick layer of dust – and of course the three of them, father, mother, and son, their chests thrust out, poised for war, sparring, waving their arms about among the furniture. At the thought of this, Fan Yeh darted into the hallway and yanked that pair of old curtains shut.

The dispute among father, mother, and son continued unabated. Eventually the quarrel between Fan Yeh and his father became the focus of the fight. Before they realized what hit them, his father was halfway into his act (he knew it to be an act from experience). Hands over his eyes, the old man stumbled forward, faltering, tottering, staggering, and in a barely audible wheeze he whimpered, "Oh, my head, I feel faint!" But this time Fan Yeh also brought his hands up and, clutching his chest, gasped and let out a shaky, desperate cry: "Oh, my chest, my heart. Oh, it hurts right here!" His father was spooked, and in an instant forgot that he was supposed to be fainting. His mother, too, scrambled toward him. For his part Fan Yeh kept up with the simpering and moaning, pressing his hand on his chest and rubbing it. This time his father and mother almost fainted away with fear. His father's face was frozen into a sheet of white, and his mother was in hysterics, staring at him, shrieking and sobbing at the same time. Fan Yeh let them help him to his feet and slowly walk him to a chair. Amid loud labor and great moans, he heaved himself into the chair. Having seen to it that he was safely settled into the seat, his papa scurried off to fetch him a cup of hot water as his mama stayed with him, beseeching him, calling his name, begging him to please come round. And Fan Yeh sat, sipping his cup of hot water. Little by little he allowed his eyelashes to flutter, and blinked his eyes, and finally opened them; then, speaking in a voice suppressed to impart weakness, he whispered, "I . . . I'm much better now." Looking at them, he saw the utter misery on their faces, saw how scared and stricken with care they were, and, involuntarily, shame and remorse welled up in him. He waved a hand at them to go away and leave him be.

130

They were caught in the giant whirlpool of a typhoon. Three panes on the window in Fan Yeh's bedroom were shattered. It was a night filled with deep, dark shadows. The house was in shambles; it was an eyesore.

131

Even before he had time to wonder why the courtyard seemed suddenly to be filled with smoke that evening, he heard a woman's desperate cries for help: "My baby! Fire! Fire!" By the time he took a second look, their courtyard was ablaze with scintillating bursts of firelight. The source was behind the large tree across the road. A bright orange pillar of flame discharged bolts of fire up into the sky, and with each outburst great clouds of thick white smoke swirled out. Like meteor showers, swarms of fiery sparks were sent flying through the trees, into the bamboo fence, even landing on the wooden boards in the hallway. He could see it coming; their building was going to be engulfed by this raging fire. Like him, his father and mother were also dashing about, opening windows and doors. Then Fan Yeh began madly throwing together as many of their belongings as he could, dumping bundles and boxes, suitcases and sacks out the nearest opening. All he remembered was the frenzy of trying to move things out with the fire at his back, and at the same time shouting and cursing at his parents for not helping. The fact was that his father, scared out of his wits, was standing in a corner with his mouth hanging slack, doing nothing; his mother, normally unable to lift heavy things anyway, was also standing there dazed. Fan Yeh was thus the only one scrambling to save their possessions, scurrying in and out, so caught up in the panic that he didn't even notice he had no shoes on until, near the end of the uproar, he caught sight of his bare feet. Simultaneously he felt a twinge in his stomach, followed by progressively painful spasms, most likely caused by the terrific scare combined with the cold he had probably caught in the process. The whole time he was vaguely aware of other people busily moving things out of their houses and of the neighbors calling to each other, and he seemed also to have heard a fire engine and its siren go by. Finally, when nearly everything had been moved out and the danger had passed, Fan Yeh stopped to survey the scene, whereupon his eyes fell upon their sundry belongings and the assortment of boxes and ragged suitcases, scattered and displayed all over the roadside, so tattered, torn, rotten, wretched, poor.

132

It was during this same year, in the early fall, that Fan Yeh, like other college graduates, reported for military service and entered the officer training camp at the army base.

133

It happened about three months after he came home from the officer training camp. Unexpectedly he was fortuitously given the occasion to reinvent the image he had of his father. It so happened that, on the afternoon of the event in question, he found himself in the vicinity of that rickety, wooden civil service building where his father worked, and decided he might as well go in to see about those proof of employment forms he needed from his father for his own teaching assistantship application at the university. He headed straight for the cubicle his father shared with the other office workers. After looking around without success, he was told by his father's office mates that his father was no longer there, that he had been moved, temporarily, to the office in the back, the director's office. It turned out that the director had been called away on business and had to be gone for over two months, and that, as chance would have it, the several managers under him were also out of town on assignments, and thus the director solicited his father's assistance and asked if he would be so kind as to take over while he was gone. The moment Fan Yeh stepped into the director's office, which was now occupied solely by his father, he felt a strange sensation come over him, a combination of disbelief, astonishment, and, indeed, delight – there sat his father behind the huge desk at the far end of the office. When Fan Yeh came in, he casually looked up and said, "Come, do come in," sounding and acting not at all like the father he was used to, but rather more like a superior talking to a subordinate. Fan Yeh was in raptures; it was like a benediction; he was profoundly comforted, immensely grateful for this glimpse into the possibility for commanding respect that seemed to have been hiding somewhere in the wings of his father's personality. Unfortunately this lasted for less than two months, and then, just as unexpectedly as it began, his papa's new image fell apart like a bad joke.

It happened like this. Out of nowhere an unnamed person in his father's office reported him. The informer charged his father with falsifying accounts, drawing a whole year's wages in the name of a nonexistent pedicab driver, and keeping the money for himself. And the fact of the matter was, it was all true. It was also true, however, that each and every one of the middle-tier workers at the office was doing exactly the same thing; they used the money to supplement their meager wages. Unfortunately for his father, this person, whoever it was, must have borne a secret grudge against him and somehow decided to get back at him by this stab in the back. And what a vicious blow it was. For not only did the informer tell, but he went right to the top, to the Superintendent's Council, and if the case were to be forwarded to the courts he would surely be sentenced to four or five years in jail.

Naturally, he and his mother were on pins and needles when they heard what happened. Fan Yeh and his mother pleaded with him to do something about it. They remembered that there was a person in the office called Lin Ah-kuang, who was the section chief for general affairs. This Chief Lin was from their own village on the mainland, and he even knew their family slightly. Thus Fan Yeh and his mother urged him to seek out Chief Lin quickly to see if he couldn't do something for him. His father complied. The result was that Mr. Lin advised his father to locate the pedicab driver in question immediately (the very one, that is, that Father had once employed and then dismissed, continuing nevertheless to use his name to draw money from the business to line his own pocket), to give him a little cash, and ask him to come forward the next day (it was that close), when the investigator from the Superintendent's Council was scheduled to come to their office to look into the matter. All this to prove that the cab driver did indeed exist and thus overturn any such charges brought against Father by the accuser. That very evening his father set out to look for this pedicab driver. It was just before 8:00 P.M. when his father left on his search, but he managed to drag it out into the night, and it was not until almost 9:30 before he came home. He had hailed a pedicab to take him there but on the return trip decided to wait for the public bus instead. And to top it all off, the object of the chase, the prize itself, eluded him, for the cab driver he went to look for was not yet home when he arrived, and even though the driver's wife urged him to stay and wait a while for him, this father of his had lost his courage, turned tail, and run home, all without being discouraged by anyone other than himself. After his return home, his papa grew more and more agitated, but when asked what he intended to do next, said, of all things, that he trusted the investigator who was due in the morning. He couldn't possibly want to harm him. He had heard from somewhere that this investigator was a devout Buddhist, a sincere and pious man. He then went on to say with great confidence that, as far as the cab driver was concerned, he was sure he could trust him to show up in the morning at the office. When Fan Yeh pressed his father as to why he felt such confidence, his father replied that the cab driver's wife had assured him that he would show up in the morning. Fan Yeh then asked how much money he had given them to thank them for their trouble, and his father replied, "I left the woman with fifty dollars."

"What? Fifty dollars?" Fan Yeh asked in censorious disbelief.

"What the hell do you mean? How much more should I have given her?"

Fan Yeh knew that if he let things go on in this vein, matters would only get worse; it would be like watching the walls start to collapse and threaten to bury them alive, without trying to stop the process. Consequently Fan Yeh withdrew to his room, took out what money he had saved in the last few months from private tutoring, and bore down on his father to go with him one more time to that cab driver's place. And this father of his, believe it or not, was at first unwilling to go, because it was too embarrassing already and altogether too troublesome. It was only after his son hurled a barrage of threats and abuse at him that he finally agreed to go, and then, amazingly enough, just as they were about to leave, his father managed to discover that he had crumpled up the piece of paper on which he had written down the cab driver's address and tossed it away when he came home.

Fan Yeh's initial response was outrage. He was left with no choice but forcibly to escort his papa out for another visit to that section chief, Mr. Lin, so as to request the address of the cab driver yet again. They hailed a pedicab and sped toward Mr. Lin's house; by then it was nearly ten. They found Mr. Lin, got what they were looking for, got back onto the cab they had come in, and were finally on their way. It was by now past ten, ten forty-five to be exact. The streets were almost entirely emptied of pedestrians. A long time passed. It was eleven, and they were still on the road; their cab driver was not in a hurry to get anywhere. Cooped up in the backseat, Fan Yeh imagined the horror of discovering the cab driver and his family all fast asleep by the time they arrived; he began to believe they were in fact by now all fast asleep. And what was this cyclist doing anyway? He was pedaling with less and less conviction, it seemed; they were almost at a standstill. What if, even if they found him, the driver refused to show up so early in the morning and go to his papa's office to testify on his behalf? At this juncture, they arrived at Sincerity Street, where the driver they had come looking for lived. Their cabby turned around and asked whether he should go left or right. He in turn asked his father, who, having by now completely lost his bearings, was no help at all. The dark didn't help either, and, sitting in the backseat, it was impossible to make out the lot numbers on the street signs. Several times he consulted his father, and every time he asked him whether that was the place, his father said, "That's it!" And each time he was wrong. Until finally, for the last time, he asked him, and his father said, "No, that's not it." It turned out to be the right place. Incredible!

Looking from the street into the alleyway, one could see

that this was a poor neighborhood; the buildings were mostly shacks. He made his father get down off the cab with him at the entrance to the alley instead of riding all the way to the house, so as to avoid this cabby seeing them visit that cabby and giving them funny looks. The first thing that greeted the visitor on entering the cab driver's home was a hazy twenty-watt lightbulb dangling from the ceiling, casting its dim light on an almost unfurnished room, where, scattered about on the sooty dirt floor were two spindly wooden chairs and a few cane stools. The cab driver's three or four children were playing on the dirt floor, banging on some biscuit tins. Surveying the scene, Fan Yeh took in the fact that these people were far worse off than even he himself was, that this was a very poor household indeed. In the middle of the room, standing right under the dim lightbulb, was the pedicab driver. He was young, healthy, and tanned, very young and very tanned. He had a broad smile and thick, full lips, and his teeth were neat, white, and sparkling. Fan Yeh approached him to explain the situation. Fan Yeh was extremely embarrassed, turning red as he spoke, for this was the cabby his papa had once fired, and here they were coming to him for help. Far beyond his expectations, the driver proved to be remarkably kindhearted and reassured him in a gentle voice, saying, "Yes, of course I remember. Indeed, Mr. Fan, old Mr. Fan, he was very good to me, your father. Yes, Master Fan, of course I will come; even if you had not personally come to seek me out, if I had heard about this matter, I would have gone on my own to sort things out and do what I could to help old Mr. Fan. I can't read or write, but I know enough to know that a man must show his gratitude to people who have treated him well."

His speech caused Fan Yeh even greater shame and embarrassment, sending a numbing sensation down his spine. This driver was truly a good man; not having borne any ill will toward his father for dismissing him in the past, he never even thought of vengeance. Fan Yeh was greatly moved. He pulled the seven hundred and fifty dollars out of his pocket and presented it to the driver as payment in appreciation for his willingness to help out. Naturally a scuffle ensued in which Fan Yeh tried to press the cab driver to take the money while the driver insisted on giving it back. The whole time he and the pedicab driver were discussing the problem, his father stood by in utter silence, maintaining the icy, bleak, expressionless face of the bureaucrat, as if he were still the cabby's boss, and the latter was simply beneath contempt and certainly not worth talking to. Then, as they were leaving, his father even had the nerve to say to the driver, "When this matter is taken care of, I'll see what I can do to take you back as my driver, okay?"

On the way back home, sitting beside his father in the pedicab, he did not scream or curse. On the contrary, he simply sat side by side with him (this man who was his father) in somber passivity.

With his heart in his throat, Father rushed off to the office early the next morning. When lunchtime rolled round, Fan Yeh was the first one home, waiting for his father's return. By and by, his father finally arrived home. No sooner had he stepped in the door than Fan Yeh pounced on him, asking him how it all went. His father responded, "It's over. The superintendent said there is no need for any further investigation into the matter." Nevertheless, his father looked funereal, like one defeated.

"That cabby *did* show up this morning, didn't he?"

"Yes, he came . . . yes."

But something still nagged at Fan Yeh, so he kept on at his father, asking him this and that, and his father kept saying that everything had been taken care of. Finally Fan Yeh decided that the only way he could get any satisfaction was to go pay a visit to Mr. Lin and find out exactly what had happened. Accordingly, soon after dinner that night, he slipped out of the house, got on his bike, and headed for Mr. Lin's.

Mr. Lin was a middle-aged man. A smooth and shiny

bald spot graced the top of his crown, and a thin, half circle of wispy hair grew around the back of his head; an enormous, fleshy, garlic-shaped nose stuck out in the middle of his face, and he spoke in a dry, husky voice with a heavy, provincial accent. Having served his visitor a glass of boiled water, Mr. Lin proceeded to relate the following story: "Aiya, quite true. The matter has, one might indeed say, been resolved. But your father managed to handle the matter in an extremely, extraordinarily disastrous manner. At 9:30 sharp the investigator from the Superintendent's Court arrived at our office. He asked for your father and summoned him to the room next door to Section 3 for a private meeting. Since the walls are paper thin and one could hear everything on the other side, we all went into Section 3 to listen through the wall. The interrogating officer began by feigning knowledge of the entire event, telling your father that he already had in his possession all the details pertaining to this case and that your father needn't bother denying the veracity of the charges, that to conceal the truth would only be a waste of time and effort, and that it would be best for him simply to own up to wrongdoing to avoid further and heavier penalties hereafter. Believe it or not, that little speech was all it took for your father to give himself up right then and there and tell all. The investigator then proceeded to question him about others in the office, whether they too were making false claims, and your father answered that, yes, they were, and even went on to list each and every one who had made false claims. After that, the investigator asked him a string of questions pertaining to the tiniest details of his case, and when he got to questioning him about the exact period of time for which he had truly hired that pedicab driver, your father said to him, 'That cab driver's outside right now. Would you like me to bring him in so you can ask him yourself and see if I've told you the truth?' Whereupon the investigator said, 'Yes, indeed, why don't you go bring him in?'

"Can you imagine the panic I felt when I heard that? Your father scared me to death! So I ran downstairs to get hold of that cabby and chase him out of there. You see, your father. . . . How can he be so stupid sometimes? What if that cabby had dashed in there and told that story we prepared for him, wouldn't that just be putting a horse's mouth on a donkey's head? What a mess. We'd have shown our cards before the game was over. And on top of that, what sort of trouble would we have gotten that driver into? He wouldn't be able to explain himself! After dismissing the cabby, I immediately told your father to go back upstairs and tell the investigator that the cab driver was nowhere to be found, and that perhaps the man just decided to leave without telling anybody. Your father seemed quite perturbed by my suggestion, but he had no choice but to go back in and do as I told him. He was not in there for long. Probably, because that investigator saw that your father was already getting on in years – and, besides, the sum he embezzled was really nothing to speak of – he chose merely to upbraid him a little and, without further review of the issue, let him go. However, this investigator immediately summoned our Director Hsu into the office and gave him a hard time about the whole business of falsifying claims and told him that if any government servant in this office were caught making any such claims in the future there would be hell to pay. That means that from now on our office will be on notice, and that group of people who have been supplementing their incomes with this practice will not be able to continue doing it. It is no wonder then that all these people, your father's colleagues, call him traitor." Mr. Lin paused at this point in the narrative, and Fan Yeh lowered his eyes to the floor. Catching his breath, Mr. Lin continued, "And I really can't say I approve of the way your father habitually treats other people at the office either. He's always bad-mouthing this one and criticizing that one. Such a mean mouth he has on him, and he's so petty. At the same time your papa is such a clown, going around teasing people in the most disgraceful manner, like a half-grown kid, often going up to someone, for example, for no apparent reason, and stroking him on the cheek, and saying, 'Well done, my son!'"

Fan Yeh's cheeks were burning like hot iron.

"And one time your papa even started a big fight and ended up tearing a whole piece of cloth off that person's clothes."

"What? A real fight? With whom?"

"With Huang Chuan-ou. It got so out of hand that even the military police from the local station were called to come stop the fight."

"What were they fighting about?"

"Who knows? I don't remember how it started now . . . over some petty thing or other, I'll bet."

"Yes. Huang Chuan-ou!" Fan Yeh thought. Huang Chuan-ou was the man who lived on the second floor of their boardinghouse. He used to run into them in the streets and had been very friendly toward them. No wonder this Huang Chuan-ou had suddenly turned cold recently; he wouldn't say hello or even look at them anymore. His mama had remarked on it and said something about how she couldn't understand why he should suddenly act like a snob toward her, and what did he have to be so uppity about anyway? Everything became clear in an instant. "By the look of things, do you think, from where you sit, do you see . . . eh . . . if there's . . ."

"Oh, no, no, it probably won't come to that. The matter has been resolved. Your father has already apologized and everything." Mr. Lin then added, "Of course, it's not entirely your father's fault. He's not alone to blame. The others do tend to bully him from time to time. They like to gang up on him, I know. He's kind of *short* and slight, you see, and he's got this limp. One time I remember seeing four or five of them tormenting him by pouncing on him en masse and carrying him off to one of the office desks, where they proceeded to scribble all over his body with lipstick. . . ."

Fan Yeh buried his face in his hands. "Mr. Lin, sir, I'm much obliged," Fan Yeh said. He couldn't take much more of this. "I'm totally ignorant of his . . . well, I knew of course. . . . But I had no idea he was quite like that."

On leaving Mr. Lin's house, Fan Yeh wandered aimlessly in the streets, going wherever his bike took him. The truth of the matter was, he dreaded going home; he was avoiding what would greet him there. He stayed out till almost midnight. By then his leg muscles were aching from the long ride. Only then did he turn homeward.

The next morning his father asked his mother for two dollar bills. This was because he wanted to avoid taking the office bus, where he would have to sit and face his colleagues. Like a thief, he went to work and came home on the public bus, in stealth and alone. He continued riding the public bus for a period of four, maybe five days.

134

According to regulations, his father was due to retire that year; the paperwork for his retirement was to have been completed by October. This was an impending economic disaster for Fan Yeh and his family. The pension was a pittance and simply insufficient to keep them going. If they were to leave it in a savings account and draw interest from it, they would get six hundred dollars a month. On the other hand, if they were to take it out in one lump sum, it would barely be enough for them to live on for a year. If Father were to retire, Fan Yeh alone would have to take on the unavoidable duty of feeding and supporting the entire household. Fan Yeh would *not* assent to this burden; he thus prevailed on his father to refuse retirement, simply to squat in his present position (to go ask the director to find a way). After all, there was an entire contingent of pensioner-aged workers who were holding onto their jobs in just this manner. Nonetheless, his father managed somehow to botch it, and when the time came, had no choice but to retire. Fan Yeh hit the ceiling. He was indignant and sore, but most of all he was seething with contempt for this man who was so stupid and incompetent that he could not even ensure his own survival, that he could never do anything right, never deliver. By this time Fan Yeh had started work as a teaching assistant in the History Department at C University. Now that he had to worry about supporting the entire family, however, he had to go out and find additional work, such as translation and other writing assignments, to supplement his income.

135

Since his father's retirement, the odds of running into him at home were increased many times over. This also meant that he saw more and more of his father's many quirky mannerisms and turns of speech that vexed, irked, appalled, mortified, exasperated him. Morning, noon, and night his father managed to cast a shroud of gloom and misery all about him, and this mournful atmosphere he created in the home affected everyone around him, bearing down like a dark cloud over the family. That barely audible sigh of his was like a puff of venomous gas; in one breath his father could pollute, corrupt, poison everything and everyone in the house. Inevitably, then, the two of them, he and his papa, were in continuous conflict. Hardly a day went by without these two blowing up at each other, eruptions that ended in murderous shouting matches.

136

His father had an extremely strange hobby; he liked to go about collecting all sorts of worthless odds and ends. Fan

Yeh discovered this quite by accident when he opened one of his father's desk drawers by mistake and saw, neatly arranged, row upon row of small bottles, small paper boxes, used see-through plastic bags, and old brown paper bags. These were his father's treasures; he regarded them as part of his personal holdings, his accumulated wealth. His father was thrifty to the point of niggardliness, niggardly to the point of absurdity. He would, for instance, go buy a box of matches, split the contents, and put them into two boxes, thinking that using half a box at a time would make the matches last longer. Then there was the electric fan they had just acquired (it was a joint venture, the cost split fifty-fifty between father and son). His father was loath to let them take it out and use it; he kept the thing tightly wrapped in a plastic bag. Normally, Fan Yeh, delirious with heat, would have to holler at him, "After all the trouble and expense we go to to buy an electric fan so we *have* it to use when it gets hot, now that it is hot we're not using it. Why then did we buy it in the first place? What do we have it for?" Only then did his father take it out. However, when Fan Yeh was not home, no matter how hot it got, his father obdurately forbade his mother to touch the thing. His father, it appeared, was unable to tell whether the day was hot or cold. For example, on a raw, brisk morning after a cold front had arrived, his father would sit around with no more than a cotton shirt on his back, his teeth chattering, as he shivered and wheezed in the freezing cold. It would be up to his mother to make sure he had enough thick layers of woollen clothes on to keep him warm. And then, once he put them on, they would stay on for the rest of the day, no matter how hot it got in the afternoon; he would stay wrapped up in his wool scarf and sweaters, sweating in the heat. But what got to him the most was the sight of his papa suddenly falling apart in the evenings, when, after dinner, he looked completely spent, as if the touch of a fingertip would send him reeling into oblivion. On such evenings Fan Yeh often found his father, dust cloth in hand, splayed out across his bed (his father and mother had begun sleeping on a wooden bed), dead to the world, snoring like a drunkard – and it wouldn't even be much later than eight in the evening. And there was that time when the son was stopped in his tracks, startled to come upon his father curled up like a snail in its shell, fast asleep on the wood floor out in the front hallway. The father seemed to have lost even the minimum degree of self-respect that any human being ought to have.

137

And his father was always the one from whom the miscellaneous noises and voices came to invade his peace during his private reading time.

138

And this father often wore the hand-me-down, old trousers his son no longer wanted. And, because they were much too long for him, he wore them pulled all the way up round his chest, with the waist folded over several times, and the cuffs also rolled up many times. Dressed like that, his father would go out in the streets. Not only that, but his father could often be seen hanging about their alleyway in his favorite attire – a pair of undershorts, worn so thin that the threads were coming loose and dangling in shreds – strolling up and down, looking left and right, like a watchman on duty.

139

His father's pair of wooden clogs were worn so thin that they were by now scuffed down to half their original size, whittled away till they looked like two thin razor blades, giving them the appearance of a small child's play shoes.

140

From time to time his father liked to draw water from outside their dormitory grounds. He brought it in in a huge washbasin filled to the brim, sloshing and splashing, leaving a deluge behind him on the way back; it never occurred to him to fill it a little less. More often, however, his father could be seen coming down their long hallway with a bucket full of wash water that he had just drawn from the public hydrant. Having heaved and hauled this heavy load all the way from one end of the hallway to the other, where the two washbasins, both empty, stood, he would attempt to fill them. It took great effort on his part to do so, lifting the bucket all the way up to his chest and then gingerly, tremulously tipping the water in. Without fail the water would come gushing out, spilling everywhere, flooding everything. And just as predictably his father, his face scarlet and swollen with the exertion, would stamp his feet and exclaim in grief and indignation, "What punishment! It's a dead loss, a dead loss!" And, getting on all fours, he proceeded to mop up the mess he had made.

141

Father was also glad to lie about the most ordinary things. For example, now that they owned an electric rice cooker, his father was given the task of putting the rice on for the evening meal. On this particular evening Fan Yeh had promised to substitute teach a class for a friend and had to be at a certain middle school by seven o'clock. He had told his father way ahead of time and reminded him that dinner needed to be served earlier than usual that night; but when the time came, the rice needed another fifteen minutes' cooking time.

Nevertheless, his father calmly proclaimed, "Dinner's ready; the rice is cooked."

"This stuff is hard as bullets!" he yelled, jumping to his feet. "You call this rice cooked?"

"Oh, it's just about done, almost done. It's just the teeniest bit on the hard side, that's all."

"Just the teeniest bit hard, eh? When did you turn on the cooker?"

It usually took thirty minutes for their electric cooker to cook the rice.

"I pushed the button on that cooker and had it going more than half an hour ago."

"Nonsense! The truth is right here before us. This rice is clearly not cooked."

"I did plug it in a whole half hour ago and started it going."

"It won't be ready till six o'clock," Fan Yeh's mother quickly interjected.

"It is six o'clock already."

"It *is* six o'clock *already?*"

Fan Yeh pulled out his wristwatch and shoved it in his face; it was more than ten minutes before the hour.

"It's just about, almost six. . . . I'd call it six, wouldn't you?"

142

His mother and father went grocery shopping daily. On these trips to the market his father always stopped off by himself to buy candies, the very cheap peanut brittle that children bought. One time Fan Yeh spotted them as they were heading home from the open marketplace. He saw his father taking a rest by the side of the road, the market basket full of groceries on the ground beside him. And then he saw him, right there in the middle of the street, opening up a packet of that peanut brittle and, tilting his head backward, greedily emptying the pieces into his mouth.

143

And this father was also afflicted by that infuriating old man's disease: forgetfulness. In the course of a single day his father would walk by the wall calendar and tear off sheet after sheet, each time forgetting that he had just done it, so that he often managed single-handedly to transform a working Wednesday into a happy Sunday.

144

But it must be admitted that probably the *worst* of all the observable and provocative weaknesses displayed by his father, was the way he loved to playact in his daily life. He was nothing if not dramatic, melodramatic even! Say someone were to break a plate in the kitchen and the noise of the clatter reached his father's ear: he would give a start, look up and around, stretching his neck out as far as it would go, roll his eyes in an expression of great alarm, swivel his head in all directions, and ask, in a tremulous voice, "Hey! What was that? Ha? What's going on?" The expression, the tone, the alarm itself, were more than half put on, but he was not even aware that he had cast himself in some role in an imaginary play.

And he possessed what seemed like an inexhaustible reserve of self-pity just lying in wait for expression. Say a door should accidentally be shut on his finger: he would jump at the chance to howl and wail and scream. And then, tightening his mouth to form a whistle, bending his head close to his hand, and taking his hand up close to his lips, he would blow on it, caress it. All this was a natural part of his repertoire of exaggerated emotional displays.

145

His father was also liable to get up early in the morning and gulp down a great big bowl of leftover, odd-smelling soupy rice gone sour and, when he had finished, say, "Oh? I couldn't tell. Was there anything wrong with it?"

146

During lunchtime it was his papa who got everything ready, setting the table, putting out the bowls and the chopsticks, and serving Fan Yeh's portion of the meat and vegetables on a separate plate and filling his bowl with rice so that, by the time he sat down, he could start in immediately. All this just so he might have a few extra minutes before having to rush back to teach the afternoon classes again. For all this Fan Yeh did indeed feel more than a twinge of guilt. Nevertheless, when, upon sitting down before his bowl of rice, he saw how once again his father had packed it in, pressing the rice into a stubborn, solid ball, as if he would have to go hungry if he didn't get enough the first time around, as if he were afraid there wouldn't be a chance for a refill, the sight of the hard bowl of rice would again arouse in him that irrepressible rage.

147

Ever since his father's retirement, Fan Yeh took charge of the family's finances; he was tight, and he was harsh. For example, his mother had to come to him daily for the grocery money. The son would then tell her exactly what she could and could not spend so that she would stay within the strictest limits of the budget, down to the cent. In addition, at the end of the day she must account for each expenditure without fail, filling in a ledger and showing it to him. Should it happen that his father had to come to him for money, for the measliest little sum, such as the few dollars it took to buy a cheap, white summer shirt, at such times he would strike the most unwilling of attitudes, grudgingly cough up the money, and, more often than not, accompany the attitude with a string of execrations and wild abuse.

148

Each night, as his father puttered about, getting ready for bed, he would be newly struck by the sudden – so it seemed – transformation that had turned his father into this hideous-looking creature he saw before him. At the back of his skull his father wore an enormous hair net, and on the front, because he had taken out his false teeth for the night, his mouth was pulled up into the tip of his nose. The result was that his whole face became one single incoherent, crinkly blob looking more like a walnut than a face.

Old age was, for his father, indeed that slow dying of the light, and if during this time news of the death of someone his own age, someone he had once known, should reach him, or if he were to receive a death notice in the form of a white envelope in the mail, he would be struck dumb for several days at a time.

149

"What are you grumbling about? You see if I don't go for the cleaver and hack you in half and have you for supper! You dog, you!" his father blasted back at him, cursing and snarling.

They were locked in combat, each trying to force the other into submission. They wrestled thus for an interminably long time until, without warning, his father abruptly broke away and, leaping backward to a spot beyond his reach and pointing a finger at him, denounced him in a thunderous voice: "Desecrator!" He lunged forward and jabbed his fist into his father's chest. All through this desperate struggle his mother was standing to one side, begging them to stop: "No, don't. Don't be like this. Please don't do this." But before he knew where he was, his father, backpedaling three steps and sidestepping two, pulled out from nowhere a razor-sharp, gleaming switchblade and flashed it at him. Chaos ensued. In rapid succession his father hurled a wine bottle at him, smashing it in his face, and picked up a chair and slammed it against him, pinning him down, pressing him hard onto the wooden floor. Lying there on the floor, Fan Yeh knew he might as well be counted among the dead; he could feel the knife wound in his side, feel the thick warmth of fresh blood oozing, pulsing, trickling out like a burbling hot spring from his side. He looked up at his father, only to be met by the menacing grin plastered across his face. He was shaking his fist at him, saying, "I gave you life, I fed you, I have the right to do away with you. I can hit you, destroy you, grind you to powder if I so choose." And on and on. Then his father went back to his drinking, sitting by the desk outside his bedroom, drinking that mellow old rice wine until he was ready to pass out. He had rarely ever seen his father drink before this; certainly he had never seen him this far gone. An insistent rapping broke the silence. Someone was pounding at the door, wanting to get in. His father forced himself out of his drunken stupor and got to his feet. A tall and imposing police officer stood outside the door. Even though he was outside, this policeman somehow knew that a murder was taking place inside the house and had come to investigate the matter. On seeing the officer, Father kowtowed obsequiously, almost doubling over in ceremony, playing the fool. He said he had no idea what the policeman was talking about, that no such thing as a murder could have taken place in his house. Looking the officer straight in the eye he said, "You go right ahead and see if you can find a corpse in here. If you should find it, then we'll call it your lucky day; I'll even come willingly with you and admit to the crime."

The police officer looked into every corner of the house, but strangely enough he couldn't find him. Even when his eyes clearly landed on Fan Yeh's body he missed him, glancing over him as if he looked and couldn't see, saw and couldn't register. Meanwhile Fan Yeh kept gesturing to him, waving and calling, but to no avail. The officer was to make no discovery. Could it be that I am truly dead and gone? Most likely. As he was thinking this, his papa bent down and laughed in his face, gloating, derisive, hooting with abandon. The police officer was long gone. This was also when Fan Yeh reached out and grabbed that sharp blade his father had left lying on the dirt floor. The blade sparkled as he lifted it and swung it back, thrusting it deep into his father's bosom. Dripping with blood, his father made a mad dash for the door. Simultaneously, he pulled himself off the floor and chased after him; he aimed the knife at his father, plunged it hard into his back, stabbing him once, twice . . . and the universe turned topsy-turvy. He felt the heavens swoon and change places with the earth. Fan Yeh woke up with a start. Yes, the earth was quaking; it was an exceedingly violent earthquake. He heard the two old people talking to each other on the other side of the wall. "It's an earthquake. Oh, quick, Min-hsien!" "Yes, yes, Ch'iu-fang." By degrees the earth stopped trembling and steadied itself. The two old folks sank once again into unbroken slumber. He – pupils distended – stared into the lacquered darkness, gazing fixedly before him, until the distant horizon glazed over with a sheen of light.

150

Even though the quarrels between Fan Yeh and his father continued unabated, the son's relationship with his mother was surprisingly quite harmonious. At least this had been the case in recent years. This was because his mother deliberately bent her own will to please him and did as he said, which was in definite contrast to his father, who opposed him and held out against him.

151

It took roughly six months after his father's retirement before Fan Yeh was able to have all the inside walls of their house repaired and refurbished with a fresh coat of paint. It was during this time, too, that he had the two Japanese-style paper sliding doors removed from his and his parents' rooms and replaced with wooden doors, the kind that pushed open and pulled to.

M

SEARCH
For Father

Dear Father,
You have been gone for nearly three months. Please come home. Everything will be resolved according to your wishes.

Your son,
Yeh

Under cover of a pair of oval-shaped, wide-framed sunglasses, he surveyed the pedestrians passing by as they came and went. There were a large number of middle-aged males, and among them must surely be a large number who were fathers. And had he not just read in the paper about how a bottom-rung civil servant had embezzled public funds to the tune of three hundred thousand dollars, and how in his statement to reporters after his case was brought to trial, this civil servant had disclosed the fact that he had stolen the money in order to feed and clothe his three small children? Well, such a man, too, was a type of father figure. Another news item in the paper caught his eye. A crowd of people who were selling their own blood on the black market somehow got into a fistfight outside one of Taipei's public hospitals; not a few among these black-market blood-sellers, too, were fathers. And these fathers belonged to the category of down-and-out, long-suffering middle-aged men who had to sell their own blood in order to provide for their sons and daughters. Just then Fan Yeh turned down a narrow street that had been transformed into a temporary marketplace. A group of laborers was laying tarmac on the road; they, too, were mostly hard-working middle-aged men who lived by the sweat of their brows. On the roadside were the street vendors; some were selling vegetables, others were cloth merchants, still others were trying to interest passersby in the paper windmills they sold. All these people were at least middle-aged, if not older, and among them too must certainly be a great number of men who could claim the title of father. And here they all were, in this open marketplace, among the vegetables and miscellaneous goods, selling whatever they had to sell, expending every ounce of energy, exercising every bit of wit, selling their very life's breath.

152

"Pull out the bolt, and let me go, or I'll break down the walls that have penned me in! Let me go!"

One night, after another hellish fight with his father, he had written in his journal in broad strokes to match his fury.

"Family! What is family? Family is probably one of the most unreasonable institutions in the world! It is absolutely pitiless, the most cruel, most inhumane, immoral social organization! The members of a family are bound by blood in the network of genealogy, yet these people in the same family are in the main so different from each other that their personalities are bound to clash. As fire cannot mix with water, how can we expect these people to coexist in the same environment? To force a family of three people to live under the same roof is like throwing three different species of wild beast together – a ferocious lion, a vicious tiger, and a virulent leopard – throwing them together and locking them up in the prison of one small cage. As a rule human beings tend to find the condition of insult/shame insufferable. But that is not all. So long as one is human one will also find stupidity/obtuseness intolerable. My own parents, unfortunately, had to fall into this latter category, and in my father's case the description is particularly apt. From their point of view, it might look as if I am the one who is mistreating them. After all, I'm always losing my temper. But, in reality, it ought to be acknowledged that they are the ones who are mistreating me. Family life, daily living in this family, is unendurable. Doing time here is worse than having to live the collectivistic life of the army during compulsory military service. After all, there is an end to conscription; it can't last much longer than three years, five years at most. But there is no end to family life, no break in its continuous chain, which goes on and on.

"Why is it necessary to have a family system at all? Who invented it in the first place? Perhaps it was out of necessity that primitive men invented the family, out of the need to band together in order to defend themselves against external attacks. But in this day and age we should surely be free of onslaughts from the outside. Who could have thought we would end up going for each others' throats inside the family instead? Such being the case, is there, at the present time, any need or desire for the continued existence of such a family system, as we have it? If only we would open our eyes and take a good look at other peoples and other countries, look at the different races of Western civilization, take a look at other highly developed cultures, we would see that this thing we call filial piety is not at all important to them and that in all their history they have not seen the necessity to emphasize any such thing in their value systems.

"That protagonist, Fabrizio, in the novel I'm reading right now, Stendhal's *The Charterhouse of Parma,* treats his father the same way he would a mere acquaintance, as if he hardly knew him. Yet this Fabrizio is justly regarded in the novel as a young man of integrity and virtue. Obviously Stendhal is not of the opinion that Fabrizio's 'impiety' toward his father was a weakness or failing of any kind. This is what a truly open-minded author, a wholesome and robust intellectual, ought to think. The nineteenth century is the truly enlightened and freethinking century. As for today, we only have to look to the United States to find a similar situation. Over there fathers treat their sons in exactly the same way as they would their friends; in America father and son are first friends, then parent and child. But in Chinese society, no fear, you can forget you ever thought such a thing possible, not here! And why not? Because of the influence of Confucian thought. No matter that Mr. Wu Ching-hsiung has told us that Confucius' obsession with filial piety had everything to do with his having lost his own father as a young child. Having no father, he, therefore, longed for him. That was it, that was the origin, the sole source, the foundation on which our legacy of filial piety is built!

"Everything can be explained by the two words: *economic necessity.* The aged of today loudly proclaim the virtues of filial piety for one reason and one reason only – necessity, the need to 'store grain for the lean times, rear sons for old age.' This is the sole, selfish reason behind each and every one of their calculations; these old people are thinking only of themselves. But let's say we proceed from some such premise as this. If that were all that were required of the young, if all that the children need do is give their parents money and take care of their expenses, why is it necessary for them to be cooped up all together under the same roof? Cannot these old folks in our Chinese society understand as much? At the root of it all, what they want (these old people) can be summed up in a word: *cash!*

"From what I have observed there are at least two reasons why family members cannot thrive and live peaceably with each other in today's Taiwanese society. All other problems stem from these two reasons.

"1. Houses here are too small. Living under the same roof, everyone is getting into everyone else's way. To reach the state of out of sight, out of mind, one must first get out of the way. It's all very well for the aristocracy of the past to pursue filial piety, abide by Confucius' doctrines down to the most minute detail; their houses were more like mansions with rooms galore. With conditions such as theirs, of course it was easy for them to be particular about filial piety; let them come and live in the narrow confines of our Japanese-style paper houses and see what they have to say then.

"2. A great number of problems in today's families arise from the fact that people like us, those of the younger generation, have no real way of taking our parents to task, no way to punish them properly, since we can't very well string them up and give them a good thrashing. If children misbehave or cause trouble, you feel free to yell at them, beat them up even, and then, afterward, your anger and frustration are dispelled and the problems that have brought on the bad feelings too are also dissipated. But toward one's own father, one's own mother, this means of expression is out of the question. Bad blood accrues in this stagnant pool of resentment where anger increases hatred and hatred multiplies upon itself!

"I really can't stand living like this anymore! How much longer, how many more months and years must I live under these conditions? What if they both live till they're eighty, ninety even? . . . Father is made of steel. He's many times stronger than me; he's sure to last many times longer as well.

"In my future, I swear, here and now that there will be no marriage in my future. And even if, for whatever reason, I have to break this vow, I definitely, absolutely refuse to bring any children, male or female, into this world. I am determined to discontinue this line of descent bearing the name of Fan."

153

It was a still and somber night. Amid the extraordinary calm and quiet all he could hear was the rhythmic and continuous heave and snore of his parents on the other side of the bedroom wall. The pangs of remorse he felt took him by surprise; his contrition was directed at his father. They always turned up in the still of the night, these painful mortifications, coming at him from the darkest recesses of his heart. A knotty proposition in the daytime may suddenly be easily resolved at night, for the mind sees the same problem from an entirely different angle then. Hence this matter for which he did not feel in the least apologetic in the heat of day became clearly disgraceful to him in the calm of darkness.

During these times he felt with all his heart that he had done his father wrong. He was undeniably violent, brutal even, in the way he treated his father. This man, his father, was really a very good man, loving and kind to him, and a good husband to his mother. He was sure his papa had never been unfaithful to his mother, had done nothing he need be sorry about. Indeed, his father was a man of character; he had never engaged in any illegal activities, never embezzled money or taken bribes. (As for that incident with the pedicab driver, well, that was not a true crime; it was the generally accepted practice, the sort of thing that was tantamount to seeking supplementary income or overtime pay.) Neither had his father ever willfully caused another person harm.

As for the occasional slow-witted or ill-considered behavior Father might exhibit, well, that too was pretty natural, considering what a hard time he had, weathering one shock after another in a life of continuous adversity. For instance, his mother died when he was very young, and later his first wife died as well; not long after that his eldest son left home and went far away, and only recently even his second son suddenly up and left and cut him out of his life altogether. His father was a person for whom one should feel compassion, a person toward whom pity and sympathy ought to be directed.

"As of tomorrow morning, I will begin, I am determined this minute to begin . . . I am definitely going to root out my inhumane attitude toward him. I will be different; I will be very good to him; I will be calm and gentle."

However, this kind of soul-searching midnight remorse had occurred on numerous other occasions, and every time his resolve had failed him. He could keep up his respect for one day, two at the most, but then could sustain it no longer. Consequently he despised himself, detested his own inability to follow through.

Do I really not love my own father? No, in actual fact, I do. Deep in my heart I love him. If he were to become critically ill, I would, without hesitation, use all my resources, sink every cent I have into making him well again, even if it meant getting myself into serious debt. So thinking, he felt the burden lift and fall away into insignificance. And thus calmed, he drifted serenely into the land of sweet and peaceful dreams.

154

During this interval he and Tan Chi-ch'iu, whom he had known for over half a year, broke up. He was hit so hard that even his heart was affected. For a long time afterward he experienced fibrillations.

155

Of late his father liked to feel him, Fan Yeh, to run his hand across his arm or to lay it on his shoulder. Perhaps this was because his father's voice was losing its resonance and, in order to be heard, he needed to reach out and touch him with his hand instead of using his voice.

N

SEARCH
For Father

Dear Father,
You have been gone for nearly three months. Please come home. Everything will be resolved according to your wishes.

> Your son,
> Yeh

"I look out for this notice in the papers every day," Erh-ko said, pointing to the newspaper in his hand, "although I seem to have missed it for a while. I was under the impression that you had found him. I guess I was wrong." His *erh-ko* spoke with solemnity, but he did not detect any sort of grief or great sorrow from the stern expression on his face. Sitting squarely, holding his body straight, framed by the crisscross pattern of the rattan arm-chair, his brother was the image of reason and propriety. His *erh-ko* seemed to have gotten fatter since he last saw him two years ago; his face had filled out some, making him look heavier, more solid. His brother and his father had kept their distance ever since the former left home; neither one had tried to improve their relationship, although his father did, in fact, one year after his brother left, write him a letter (sent to his place of work). Since he was the first to write, this was his father's signal of a willingness to take the first step toward reconciliation. Unfortunately his *erh-ko* took his time to write him back, and this became the pattern of their sparse correspondence. Nor did his *erh-ko* come home very often to visit them; he came round maybe once a year, if that. The last time he came home was well over two years ago. He had come to tell them about his transfer to Hsin-chu, to a new job, and that he was about to move to a new address. In fact Fan Yeh had no idea what his new address was when he came looking for him this time. All he knew was his *erh-ko*'s office address. Fan Yeh had intended to look him up at his office when he arrived, but since it was a Sunday, this proved impossible. Consequently, Fan Yeh had to call up the office and ask the person on duty for his *erh-ko*'s home address.

"Ah, Auntie, how . . . how is she, at home. She's keeping well, I expect?"

"Yes, so so."

His *erh-ko* had just leaned over and turned the TV volume way down so that they were now sitting opposite a soundless comedy show on the small TV screen; currently airing was a skit involving several ugly dwarfs at a baseball game.

"After you called me that first time I did ask an old friend of mine in the Kaohsiung area to keep an eye out, you know, but since I have not heard back from him all this time, I didn't write you either. I was just thinking I ought to find a way to take a few days off from work sometime soon and come up to Taipei to see how you're doing."

Fan Yeh kept his eyes glued to the flickering, small glass

stage in front of him. An extraordinarily small person, short even for a dwarf, was just then running from one base to another, his little legs working excruciatingly fast as he made his way across the TV screen.

"Well, it's the distance really, now that we're so far away. It's not as convenient as it used to be, that's why I haven't been back for a while. . . . Maybe I really should have gone, should have gone home once. But . . . how did it happen anyway?"

Fan Yeh, his head bent down, was busy examining his fingernails.

At this opportune moment, a round, womanly figure appeared from behind the lifted curtain that served as a permanent partition between this room and the next and called out,

"Lun-yuan! Come help me give this boy his bath, will you?"

"In a minute."

"I guess I should be going!"

"No, no, sit, stay a while longer, and let's talk some more. . . . You've just this minute sat down."

Having said what she came in to say, the woman who was asking his brother to help her give their baby boy a bath, his brother's wife, disappeared once again behind the curtain. His sister-in-law had indeed come out to greet him when he first arrived but soon thereafter had made her exit, slipping behind the curtain into the back room. Other than the two adults there were two children in the family. The older of the two was probably out playing somewhere (from where he sat he could see a schoolbag hanging on a hook on the white wall in the small living room at the front); the younger one was in that room from which his brother's wife had just now emerged and into which she had disappeared again.

"There's no need to panic really. The way I see it, most likely he's gone to stay with some friends, that's all. Don't you worry yourself." He sounded as if he were trying to console Fan Yeh, as if the person were his – Fan Yeh's – papa, and not his own.

Just then drama exploded on the TV screen. One of the dwarfs was knocked down in mid-flight between two bases by an infielder on the opposing team who saw an opportunity to go for the kill. The victim was lying flat on his back, while the victor was waving his arms about, celebrating his kill, dancing around the prize.

"You're doing all right for yourself, I assume? Where are you now?"

"At C University!" he almost bellowed at him. How could he not know already?

"And your children, Erh-ko, they're doing okay?" When it came to his turn to ask after his brother's family, he had to admit that the situation was not entirely his brother's fault; he didn't even know what his nephews' names were.

"They're fine," his *erh-ko* replied, his voice betraying a trace of displeasure.

The TV screen suddenly went blank, a gray, bald, flickering square of nothing, jumping at them.

"I really must go now."

"No . . . uh, no. . . . Why not stay for dinner?"

"No, don't bother. I told mother in my last letter home that I would definitely be back before seven o'clock tonight."

"In that case I won't make you stay, but in the future feel free to visit, and come often, come for dinner sometime. And when you get back to Taipei, if you hear of some really good news, don't forget to write me immediately and let me know. Okay, Sonny?"

"Yes, of course, Erh-ko. You don't have to see me out."

"I'll walk with you to the front gate. You tell Auntie not to torment herself with grief. In my opinion it won't be long before . . . before long. . . . He can't be gone too much longer. I'll do my part around here and continue to comb the area and see."

"Very good. Please go in now, Erh-ko."

Outside, as he turned to leave, he wondered why he had come here at all. At first he had come with the fantastic notion that his father might, for all he knew, be staying with his *erh-ko* and that, if not, at least he would derive some kind of moral support from his brother. Now he knew he needn't have come in the first place.

156

In the normal course of a day his father was to him no more than an eyesore. He avoided looking at him and simply ignored his existence. He was especially irritated by that nasally, nagging voice of his; at the first sound of it, his brows would involuntarily contract into a knot. The tones of voice and kinds of phrases he himself routinely used when he spoke to his father may be described mostly as imperative, usually underscored by loud and vituperative curses. Since his retirement his mother had also got into the habit of ordering his father around, telling him to do this and that, such as preparing the coal and lighting the stove, cleaning the kitchen and getting down on all fours to scrub the tatami floor mats. Sometimes mother and son could be seen laughing and talking, having a tête-à-tête as if they had forgotten, for the moment, the father's very existence. At such times his father would display his jealousy and resentment, usually at dinnertime, by putting on a miserable expression and shouting irritably at his mother, "What's taking you so long? Time to clear the table and do the dishes now." After which his father would sit in a corner and sulk, a dark cloud cast over his face. It was during this period that Fan Yeh began to permit himself the admission that his father's presence at the dinner table was more than he could endure. Thus it was that he decided to eat alone. Accordingly he announced a new arrangement. The table was to be set for one; his parents would eat a little later, setting the table for themselves after his dinner was cleared away. His excuse was that this schedule gave him more study time. Also during this period his father developed a peculiar behavioral abnormality: he often lost his grasp and seemed unable to hold onto the smallest of objects; he was particularly good at letting glass tumblers fall out of his hand and smash on the floor. His father also liked to dilute milk with boiled water, transforming a small glass of milk into a huge glass of milk water, thinking that the greater the volume of liquid, the greater the volume of milk. He truly believed that the water did the trick. And then there was that incident that, had it not been for its touch of the macabre, would have been comical in its absurdity: the morning when he came home and claimed to have bumped into Su Han-hsien, and how they had had a long chat right there by the roadside. His mother, eyes wide with terror, said in a quiet, tremulous voice, "Min-hsien, what a fool you are! Su Han-hsien has been dead for over a year!" "Oh? Really? Then . . . then who could that have been?" Nobody knew.

Since his father's agency did not provide any allowance for electricity for its retirees, his parents stinted as much as they could in their daily use of electrical appliances. Of course Fan Yeh was now the one who paid the electric bills, and for this reason his parents tried, as best they could within their limited sphere of activities, to conserve. Their room was dark enough as it was, even in the daytime, but these days, in order to save electricity, they never turned on the light in the daytime. Even after nightfall their room was barely lit by a ten-watt bulb. Life after retirement for his father and mother was lived out in this burrow of a room, surrounded by barely visible objects such as their tattered clothing and threadbare bedding, blankets, and such things as they had accumulated through the years. On top of everything, because both front and back doors to this room were kept closed most of the time, miscellaneous odors remained to stagnate inside the confines of this room, and intensely foul smells oozed from it to attack one's senses whenever one came near it. During this period his father and mother could often be seen tottering about, engaged in some trivial activity in that dimly lit, poorly ventilated, meager space they shared with each other. Watching them move about in the gloomy chiaroscuro of that bedroom gave one the impression that these two small figures would soon be taken back by the darkness.

After that the family came together to eat at the same table only on festival days or on birthdays. One such day was his father's sixty-sixth birthday. His twenty-six-year-old son sat opposite him at the table, facing him. At the moment it was just the two of them, face to face, sitting there at the round, wooden dinner table. His mother was in the kitchen, stir-frying some meat and vegetables. (She was bringing the dishes out one at a time so that they could have each dish while it was nice and hot.) He felt extremely awkward sitting there, facing his father. Besides, he was harboring a deep animosity toward his father, one that had been brewing for some time now. The old man's chomping and slurping gnawed at him; he sounded like a rat at his meal.

"And what is that?" his father asked as his mother brought out another steaming hot platter and laid it on the table.

"You don't even recognize that? Look again. This is something that is eaten by all people all over China – any child can tell you what that is. It's pork, of course!" he spat out in contemptuous rage. So he can't even tell that it's pork. But then again, why should this surprise him? This sort of thing had happened like clockwork at every meal when they used to eat together. If they were having pomfret, a fish he must have had hundreds of times during his more than sixty years of living, he'd still have to ask what fish it was. Even if they were having spinach, he'd still have to ask what vegetable that was. Even tofu appeared before him like a foreign object, and he'd have to ask what it was.

Having served up the last course, his mother sat down at the table and began eating with them. This last bowl she brought out was a clear soup, prized for its purity both in appearance and in aroma; it was a clear oyster soup that was double boiled to preserve its full flavor. His father, nonetheless, asked Mother to fetch him the little bottle of MSG. For Fan Yeh this was déjà vu; he opened his eyes wide and glared at his father, who, oblivious to his scrutiny, took the bottle of MSG and emptied a good half of it into his own tiny soup bowl, which he had previously filled with soup from the main bowl. At this Fan Yeh slammed his palm down on the table and cursed at him, demanding to know if he realized what sort of soup this was. How dare he abuse heaven's bounty like that! He then proceeded to forbid his father to taste the soup, not even the soup that was already in his bowl. And thus his father kept his hands off the little bowl of oyster soup. All was well until his father, having polished off all the rice in his rice bowl, attempted to serve himself a little oyster soup from the main bowl. Fan Yeh caught sight of this and immediately pounced on him, snapping, "Oh no, you don't! *This* is not for you. Put down that spoon; you're not to have any of this soup, not even a sip." His mother then intervened, pleading with him, "Please, let him be. . . . Sonny, it's his birthday, after all. . . . "

"So what if it is his *birthday?* Does one suddenly become king on one's birthday? He's the one who made out as if it wasn't good enough for him. Fine, he doesn't have to eat this soup! Eat, everybody, get on with it and stop fussing. Just get on with your dinner!"

Everyone thus picked up chopsticks and continued with the meal as if nothing had happened.

Father let mama take his bowl and fill it with more rice. Even before the fresh bowl was set down before him, however, he was already reaching for the meat and vegetables dish in front of him, and started tipping the saucer, pouring the ink-dark vegetable sauce onto his pearly white mound of white rice.

"Now what do you think you're doing?" Fan Yeh yelled, throwing his chopsticks down with an ear-splitting crack. "How could you mess up a pure, snowy white bowl of clean rice with that dirty black sauce? All right, that does it. I don't see why you should eat this rice at all! One way or another you're bent on fouling heaven's gifts. Okay then, you leave the table right now. You've had enough. That's it for you. You're not to eat any more. Don't you touch that food again. You get out of my sight now!"

"He's not had his fill yet," his mother interceded, appealing for leniency.

"What does it matter whether he's had his fill? He can eat again tomorrow. Out, out of my sight, you hear me, right now. Away with you. Go!"

The father did as he was told and left the table, sighing and shaking his head.

His mother sat motionless, stunned into cataleptic abstraction.

"Eat, eat, finish your dinner, go on!" Fan Yeh hollered at her.

Obediently she managed to go through the motions of finishing up dinner with him, after which he heard her fill another bowl with rice and some meat and vegetables and carry this into her own room for his father, knowing he was still hungry. He also heard his father's deep sigh and caught the words, "Oh, what's the point? I might as well go to a monastery and be a monk." His mother quickly shushed him, fearing Fan Yeh might overhear him and become incensed again.

After this episode his father was repeatedly denied meals in his own home as punishment for one thing or another. At times Fan Yeh chose to turn a blind eye to the fact that his mother was going behind his back to feed his father, but there were also times when he adamantly refused to allow it. Then something happened that left him no choice but to seriously step up the chastisement he dealt his father – it was virtually scandalous, what his father did. It was like this. Fan Yeh had a distant aunt who had emigrated to the United States a long time ago and had lost touch with their family for twenty or thirty years. One day one of their meddling relatives visited and, for lack of something better to do, left this American aunt's address behind. Now, not only did his father keep the address, but he surreptitiously wrote to this aunt, asking her for money, explaining to her how badly off they were, and how their family had fallen on hard times, and so on and so forth. As a result, and to his father's own surprise, this aunt responded and even sent them a sum of money. The day her letter arrived his father came rushing in with the news, bursting with the story of his windfall. This same event, the occasion for such rapture for his father, also occasioned the blazing inferno of Fan Yeh's rage. This time he had to really come up with a way to punish him once and for all, in such a manner and to such a degree that he would not be likely ever again to repeat the same offense. Acting at once as judge, jury, and executioner, he came to the rapid decision that his father was to be kept under lock and key, sentenced to three days and three nights of solitary confinement; that meant that he was to limit his activities to the narrow enclosure of his bedroom and not be allowed out of it at any time for whatever purpose. In addition he was to miss that evening's dinner entirely and not to have breakfast the next morning either. He had no choice. Harsh as it was, this was the only way to leave an indelible impression on his father's mind, to help him remember in the future not to commit this crime again. When his father was finally let out of his room, it appeared that his limp had grown worse, that he was hobbling even more than before. His hair, too, had turned entirely white, almost within the last few days. It occurred to Fan Yeh that this could not be possible, that a whole head of hair was not likely to turn white within three or four days, that this should be a gradual process over a long period of time. What he saw, he concluded, was merely the end result of a long process.

From then on his father was even more circumspect in his speech and ponderous in his activities around the house. This latest development, this slowing down of everything that he did, inevitably served to further aggravate Fan Yeh – especially when his father came in to clean his room while he tried to concentrate on his reading, because now these sessions of dusting and wiping, sweeping and mopping, took longer and longer.

And later on something else occurred that might even be deemed supernatural, or at the least incomprehensible. Fan Yeh couldn't fathom why it was that from that time on his father often called him by someone else's name; he called him Lao-erh, which was what he used to call his second brother. Whenever he was thus mistaken, Fan Yeh felt angry, confused, and, at the same time, not a little hurt and diminished by it.

157

Father fell ill. He caught a cold. It was obvious too how he had caught it. The day before he had gotten up early in the morning and, even though there was a chill in the air, had neglected to put on another layer of clothing. Hence the red eyes and runny nose, the series of ear-splitting sneezes. His mother scolded him mercilessly. Fan Yeh similarly flared up at him in a thunderous, frenzied eruption of curses and rebukes. The illness kept him in bed for a week, one long week of mortification. He slept the whole time, all day, every day, lying there, emaciated, weak, soft, and docile, like a tiny newborn kitten curled up in his bed. By and by he came out of it and was able to sit around the house, quietly convalescing, taking it easy, whiling away the time for several days thereafter. And then, as he grew strong enough eventually to recover his freedom of movement and walk once again, not two days after that, this father, most mysteriously, without letting anyone in on his motives, went out the door and disappeared.

O

Time passed. It was almost two years to the day. The father had still not returned. For Fan Yeh, however, life at home, living with his mother, simply, from day to day, just the two of them, was much happier, much easier than it had ever been before. As for the plans and other such arrangements that he should be making to go out once again in search of his father, this son, it would seem, had almost put them out of his mind. During this period of calm Fan Yeh enjoyed a physical well-being, a degree of good health, that he had never, in any other period of his life, enjoyed. Consequently, he became rosy cheeked and robust and was already prematurely acquiring the fullness of figure of a middle-aged man. As for his mother, her hair, it must be admitted, had more white in it than before, but it was a shiny, healthy white, and it had a brilliance about it that exuded vigor. Judging from this, she could easily, as a matter of course, live for another twenty years or more.

Not long ago, Dr. Susan Wan Dolling wrote to say that her translation of *Chia-pien* (Family catastrophe) would be published soon, and she asked if I would write an afterword for the occasion. Words cannot express my thanks for the time and energy she spent on this novel. *Chia-pien,* it is true, took me seven years to write, but it took Dr. Wan Dolling no less than five years to translate it and win acceptance for publication. I regret not having been able to contribute more to this process, but because of the distance — she lives in the United States, while I am in Taiwan — I was not able to be of much assistance to her, and now that the English translation of *Chia-pien* is about to greet the world, I cannot help but feel like one who is guilty of "reaping the harvest of someone else's labor."

Here I do not want to talk about my own novel. As far as *Chia-pien* is concerned, all I have to say ought to have been said in the book; any amendment is therefore extraneous. I would rather talk about what, to me, is the ideal novel.

That novel would make the kind of music the cello makes; I am speaking of style. This comparison I borrow from Flaubert, who said that the style of the novel ought to be like the music of the cello, deep toned and mature. Was it by chance that in my youth, on encountering the novel, I chose Maupassant as my model? Maupassant was, of course, Flaubert's student; his style was obviously influenced by the author of *A Simple Heart* and *Madame Bovary.* I vowed then not to read any novel other than those written in this style. The following selection itself may be questionable, but in my youth I had already made the final judgment, and those who made it into heaven were Saint-Exupery, Gide, Tolstoi,

Conrad, Hemingway, Virginia Woolf, Katherine Anne Porter, Lu Hsün, Shen Fu, and Tu Fu. I must single out Tu Fu, who to me is the greatest poet who ever lived. But even in Tu Fu's case, if we were to take that deeply resonant and vigorous style from his poetry, nothing would be left. Thus it is that to this day my passion for the "cello style" of writing remains unchanged. Maybe I am biased, but I'm afraid there's nothing I can do about it.

The story line of my ideal novel must be mythic. Perhaps it is because *Oedipus Rex* left too deep an impression on my youthful mind; in terms of story line no play or novel I have ever read can come close to this play. By *mythic* I don't mean the thunder-and-lightning, ghost-and-goblin genre. I mean the kind of story that possesses the spirit of the myth. Essentially, this type of writing must concentrate on the fundamental emotions of humankind and must, at the same time, be a record of some life-and-death struggle. Out of this kind of story comes the mythic character, one who is larger than life; his speech and actions may seem no different than ours, but they are of greater import than yours or mine. This is because the protagonist carries symbolic significance. He may embody centuries of an emotion shared by all who are human, or he may represent an entire era. He is Captain Ahab, Julien Sorel, Joseph K., Yevgeny Barzarov; she is Natasha, Anna Karenina, Emma Bovary, Becky Sharp, Daisy Miller.

The third thing about my ideal novel is that technique does not matter at all; only its manifestations of life's experiences matter. There is no doubt that a highly crafted Henry James novel gives immense pleasure, but it cannot be denied that D. H. Lawrence's *Sons and Lovers* can arouse in us an even more passionate response. When we read *Dream of the Red Chamber* or *The Water Margin,* we are fully sated; yet these works are unwieldy in structure and loosely told. Technique is not that important; the quickening of the pulse, the immediate experience of life, these are more important to these long novels. Chinese critics consider *Journey to the West* not a novel, but rather "a book of truth." The ideal novel ought indeed to be a book of truth.

The novel I have written does not come close to the ideals that I have just described. Once again, allow me to express my heartfelt appreciation to Dr. Wan Dolling for choosing to favor it with this English translation.

Chia-pien is Wang Wen-hsing's first full-length novel and was published in Taiwan in 1972. Initial response to the novel was not promising. Critics were outraged and indignant either because of its challenge to the deeply ingrained Confucian value of filial piety or because of its seemingly irrational stylistic inventions and linguistic difficulties. Despite its controversial reception from the outset, however, and despite the violent attacks launched against its author by the influential advocates of "homeland literature" *(hsiang-t'u wen-hsüeh)* in the 1970s, who called it elitist, corrupt and corrupting, self-indulgent and socially irresponsible, this novel has managed to become a best-seller in Taiwan and has indeed survived to become an acknowledged masterpiece of modern Chinese fiction. In 1976, the prominent critic Joseph S. M. Lau, who too had rejected the novel on a first reading but was open-minded enough to give it a second chance, proclaimed it "the most provocative, thrilling/shocking/moving novel to come out of Taiwan in the last twenty years and truly a breakthrough in novelistic accomplishment."

The story of how I came to translate *Chia-pien* must begin with the late James Liu, whom I had met at Stanford at an NEH seminar in the summer of 1985. He liked my work and recommended it to his student, Yvonne Sung-Sheng Chang, who then introduced me to the work of her other teacher, Wang Wen-hsing, with the intention of persuading me to translate his novel, *Chia-pien,* into English. Eventually, it was Yvonne who took my sample translations to Taiwan with her to show Wang Wen-hsing and came back with his permission and, indeed, the exclusive right for me to translate *Chia-pien.* That was in 1988.

After three years of work on the novel, in 1991 I was fortunate enough to receive a substantial grant from the Council for Cultural Planning and Development in Taiwan and was able to devote an entire year to this project. The translation was completed just in time, as it turned out, to be one of the books to come out of the University of Hawai'i Press' new series, Fiction from Modern China. For the honor of inclusion I must thank my editor, Sharon Yamamoto, and Howard Goldblatt, the general editor of the series.

As a translator I have before worked only with ghosts. I was not sure how a live author would take to having his work torn apart, reconstructed, and given a new face in another language, especially an author who had said, "Without its words *Chia-pien* would no longer be *Chia-pien* . . . because its words, its language, are its everything" (from his 1978 preface). Nevertheless, he was not inconsistent when he granted me permission to translate: "This book is as it is and cannot have another manifestation in the Chinese language," he wrote, "yet . . . there are all sorts of possibilities for its manifestation in English."

Thus I thank Wang Wen-hsing for his book, of course, and, beyond that, for his attitude toward literary translations. As writers we are in agreement that *how* something is said means everything to *what* is being said. I am thus doubly grateful to him for the latitude, indeed, the autonomy, he has given me to make my own choices as well as my own mistakes with his *Chia-pien.*

Finally, I wish to thank all my friends, old and new, who have urged me on in one way or another to see this project through to its logical conclusion – Carolyn See, Peggy Fox, John Espey, Joseph Lau, Chung So, Nadia Benabid, John Rumrich – and my families – the Wans and the Dollings – and especially my partner in the family proposition, David Dolling.

For fifty years, from 1895 (the end of the Sino-Japanese War) to 1945 (the end of World War II), Taiwan was a Japanese colony, which explains the leftover Japanese-style houses found in the story. When, in 1949, the Chinese Nationalist government lost the civil war to the Communists, they left the mainland and retreated to Taiwan, where the Republic of China was set up. Many Chinese, whether they were actively involved in the war or merely caught up in it, also left the Mainland. In this novel the Fans were one such family. The population in Taiwan thus came to consist of "native Taiwanese" (the original islanders of Malayo-Polynesian descent), early Chinese settlers (who are usually referred to as "Taiwanese"), and the new immigrants from China, sometimes called "Mainlanders." Mandarin Chinese became the official language in Taiwan, replacing Japanese and the Taiwanese dialect. Nevertheless, not even the "Mainlanders" all spoke Mandarin, especially those who did not have any formal education. In the early years depicted here Fan Yeh's mother, for example, speaks a provincial dialect. Further, the "Mainlanders" often looked down on the "Taiwanese," and thus Fan Yeh's father objects to his stepbrother's marriage. A few explanatory details follow:

"Search" ads are quite common in Chinese newspapers and are almost always for "lost" family members.

Lao-erh is literally "old number two," a familiar address in the family for the second son. *Erh-ko* is "older brother number two."

A "Republic-style suit" is a button-down tunic, sometimes referred to as a Mao suit by Westerners.

A "savings club" is a practice common in many Chinese communities, especially among the less well to do. A group of people agrees to put a fixed amount of money into a pool every month, and each person bids for that month's pool. The winning bidder then repays the club through the rest of the year.

At the time the story takes place one U.S. dollar is worth approximately forty Taiwan dollars. The dollars mentioned in the novel are all Taiwan dollars.

FAN YEH

Chia-pien, beyond the Fan family experience, is a metaphor for modern China's loss of, for worse *and* for better, the Confucian father figure and his moral values; it is a provocative document mirroring the contemporary Chinese psyche. The title of the Chinese novel is *Chia* (family) *Pien* (change), where *Chia* signifies family as well as the extended family of the homeland. Indeed, given the reality of the Chinese diaspora, one might even extend this reading to include all who identify themselves as culturally Chinese. In other words, all Chinese people in this century have undergone the metaphoric change of the family in *Chia-pien.*

To support this reading one might cite the fact that the protagonist is given the name *Fan Yeh.* Attention is focused on this name early in the novel at the end of B in Part One, where our protagonist goes to the police station to report his father's disappearance. The officer on duty, like the average man on the street, is not familiar with the word, and our protagonist has to explain that it is written thus: "Sun radical by the side of the character for *China.*" Now, the character for *China* is pronounced "hua," not "yeh." Thus, in the Chinese text, the reader is actually reminded both in sound and in sense that this name is meaningful, at least in two ways, beyond the fact that our protagonist's father has given his son a rather genteel and antiquated name.

First, this name might be interpreted to mean "the sunshine or splendor of China." We name our children for promise. Given the context, this promise is especially poignant. Moreover, the family name, *Fan*, it so happens, shares the same sound as the character for "to transgress, cross, or to commit a crime." Thus, even though the father could not have meant it, embedded in his son's name is its own opposite.

Second, in the early episodes the young Fan Yeh often uses sunshine and its properties – such as brilliance, warmth, strength, height, and the power to sustain and nurture – to describe his father. *Hua,* the character for *China,* also reads "flower." These facts, together with the many references to songs and poems in Part One, must recall to the Chinese reader's mind the well-known poem that every schoolchild knows by the T'ang dynasty poet Meng Chiao, called "The Wanderer's Song," although, in the novel, the mother's place in the poem is taken by Fan Yeh's father:

> Mother's gentle hands have sewn
> these clothes I wear, far from home.
> Stitch into stitch on the eve of my leaving:
> hope against hope I'll soon come home.
> Can the inch-tall grass ever return
> the favor of sunshine in the heart of spring?

For me, one of the most wonderful things about this novel is how the father's tender feelings for his son remain vivid to us (and indeed to his abusive son) despite all the nasty, petty, despicable things we discover about him. If our parents, or our parent culture, are the stuff that we are made of, must escape from, and, in escaping, recreate, then this novel is about parenting, and parenting is culture.

Having said that, I must point out that the author may or may not agree with my reading. Having made as much as I have about the name he gave his protagonist, I must confess that, when I first began translating this novel, I had made the plebeian mistake of pronouncing *yeh* as "hua" and that, when I wrote him to apologize for the mistake and make the correction, Wang wrote back to say, "As for Fan Yeh's name, if you have already translated it as *Fan Hua,* there is no need to alter it back to *Fan Yeh;* it doesn't matter anyway in an English translation."

About the Author

Wang Wen-hsing was born in Fujian in 1939 and grew up in Taiwan. He received his B.A. from the National Taiwan University and an M.F.A. from the University of Iowa; he is currently a professor in the National Taiwan University Foreign Languages and Literature Department. By the time *Chia-pien* was published in 1972, Wang was already an important voice in Taiwan both as a critic and as a writer. His short story collections include *Lung-t'ien lou* (Dragon tower) and *Wan-chü shou-ch'iang* (The toy gun and fifteen short stories). Since 1972, Wang has published one other novel, *Pei-hai ti jen* (Backed against the sea), translated by Edward Gunn in 1993.

ABOUT THE TRANSLATOR

Susan Wan Dolling is a Chinese American writer who was born and raised in Hong Kong. She has studied in Japan and the United States, received her doctorate in comparative literature from Princeton University in 1982, and was an English professor until 1991.

Production Notes

Composition and paging were done in
FrameMaker software on an AccuSet
Postscript Imagesetter by the design
and production staff of University
of Hawai'i Press.

The text and display typeface is Garamond 3.

Offset presswork and binding were done by
The Maple-Vail Book Manufacturing Group.
Text paper is Glatfelter Smooth Antique,
basis 50.